D0277065

Husband,
Missing

By Polly Williams

The Rise And Fall Of A Yummy Mummy
A Bad Bride's Tale
A Good Girl Comes Undone
How To Be Married
It Happened One Summer
The Angel At No. 33
Husband, Missing

Husband,
Missing

POLLY
WILLIAMS

headline
review

Copyright © 2013 Polly Williams

The right of Polly Williams to be identified as the Author of
the Work has been asserted by her in accordance with the
Copyright, Designs and Patents Act 1988.

First published in 2013 by HEADLINE REVIEW
An imprint of HEADLINE PUBLISHING GROUP

1

Apart from any use permitted under UK copyright law, this publication
may only be reproduced, stored, or transmitted, in any form, or by any
means, with prior permission in writing of the publishers or, in the case
of reprographic production, in accordance with the terms of licences
issued by the Copyright Licensing Agency.

All characters in this publication are fictitious and any resemblance
to real persons, living or dead, is purely coincidental.

Cataloguing in Publication Data is available from the British Library

ISBN 978 0 7553 9239 1

Typeset in Sabon by Avon DataSet Ltd,
Bidford-on-Avon, Warwickshire

Printed and bound by CPI Group (UK) Ltd, Croydon, CR0 4YY

Headline's policy is to use papers that are natural, renewable and
recyclable products and made from wood grown in sustainable forests.
The logging and manufacturing processes are expected to conform to the
environmental regulations of the country of origin.

HEADLINE PUBLISHING GROUP
An Hachette UK Company
338 Euston Road
London NW1 3BH

www.headline.co.uk
www.hachette.co.uk

In memory of my grandparents,
Muriel and Frederick Sutton

Acknowledgements

A big thank you to Imogen Taylor, Lizzy Kremer, Jane Morpeth, Laura West, Frankie Gray, Vicky Palmer and Caitlin Raynor. Katina, Andrea, Mum, Shanna, Mandy – I would never have written 'The End' without you. Thank you also to Lucy for the photo. Rob for the movies. Tammy for reading. Ben, Oscar, Jago and Alice, for the love. Finally, I owe a huge debt to my wonderful grandparents – the greatest of readers – who married weeks after meeting and died shortly after one another seventy years later – while I wrote this novel – not wanting to be separated at the end of their own long story.

Prologue

It was a Sunday and I had plans to be miserable. I would lie in bed, hungover, eating granola out of the packet, watching Grace Kelly in *To Catch A Thief* and wallowing in the contrast between the glamorous 1950s Riviera and my life in recession-hit Hornsey.

Ten minutes into the movie, Lucy screeched up outside the flat in her banana yellow Beetle. Muttering something about not letting a man ruin my life and backside – did I know how many calories there were in granola? – she pushed me into her deathtrap of a car and accelerated wildly in the direction of Hampstead's ladies' pond, belting out black smoke and ignoring the slamming horns of other drivers.

Four hours later, having politely refused Lucy's offer of a lift home, I found myself alone on the Heath, trying to navigate my way to Gospel Oak Tube and not look lost, which I was. The sandals I'd bought a week before in the sales were rubbing up a blister the size of a ten piece coin on my big toe. My sarong slipped around my waist as I walked, exposing a legacy of cheap white wine and take-out eaten with flatmates late at night, consumed to fill the hole that couldn't be filled. My long red hair – he'd called me 'Ginge', the bastard – fell in damp fuzzy ropes around my shoulders.

As the first hot sunny day of spring is always my cue for dispatching sunglasses – this time by sitting on them by the ladies' pond – I took the shaded path beneath the rustling plane trees. This led me past a wooden bench where a short, dark-haired man in minimal neon-yellow running Lycra was stretching out his calves and mouthing along to his iPod, which was strapped to a hi-tech contraption on his arm.

The man was you. (I wouldn't find out you were listening to Aerosmith until a couple of weeks later, just as well.) Your olive skin was lacquered with a thin sheen of perspiration. Handsome, too. Probably gay, I decided.

The path twisted away through a shady copse of trees. A white butterfly spiralled up from the gravel path. That butterfly was the very last thing I noticed before someone shoved me hard, really hard, on my upper back. I stumbled forward, arms outstretched. When I looked up someone was sprinting off with my handbag. 'Hey!' I shouted weakly, hands on my knees, marvelling that I'd actually been mugged. So this is what it felt like.

And that's when you appeared, the man in the neon. I'd never see anyone run so fast. 'Oi,' you shouted, speeding after the mugger in a flash of trainer soles.

'Don't!' I tried to call after you. Even I didn't want someone stabbed over a handbag.

You caught up with the mugger within seconds, yanked the bag out of his grip with one hard tug. He gave you an astonished stare – he could not believe either your speed or audacity – and hammered off down a grassy slope without attempting to grab the bag back.

'Twat!' you shouted after him, turning to run back to me. 'You alright?'

I can remember just feeling embarrassed at that point. Embarrassed for causing a commotion. Embarrassed for making someone rescue my crappy handbag. 'I'm fine, thank you, thank you.'

'You better sit down.'

'Really, I'm OK.' But you wouldn't let me walk off. And the way you said, 'No, sit down,' made me do it. Like I owed you that.

Sitting down, a bit shaky, I looked up and met your eyes properly for the first time. That look, our first proper look, bolted me to the bench. Your eyes were ink-black with dilated pupils, flashing with adrenaline and something else that made me blush volcanically.

'I'm afraid the bushes of Hampstead Heath attract men with a penchant for ladies' handbags,' you remarked dryly, confirming your own lack of gayness. I blushed again.

You asked my name. Gina. You told me yours. Rex. Rex? Like T-Rex, you said. I laughed, forgetting to be embarrassed. You sat down beside me, stretched out your legs. The black hairs were dusted with a fine layer of pollen-like dust from the path. The sun dappled us, dying my hair red again. Locks like a woman from a Rossetti, you observed. (Big improvement on the 'Collar and cuffs, love?' leer I was used to.) As we sat there chatting, easy in each other's company, the Heath seemed saturated with colour and light, sunnier than I'd ever seen it. I noticed things then: the sinews of your thighs; the way your smile started in your eyes before it twitched the corners of your mouth; the lack of a wedding ring on your finger. It was getting later and later, the sun pinking and sinking behind Parliament Hill. I realised I couldn't sit on that bench much longer without it looking weird, although I didn't want to leave. My mobile rang. You eyed it combatively, challenging whoever was competing for my attention. I sent my sister to voice mail, thanked you again, got up to go. Not missing a beat, you asked for my number. I gave it to you with a silly girlish giggle, having no idea that you'd phone me twenty minutes later and ask me out to dinner that evening. 'If you're sure you're OK,' you said gently, resting your pulsing hand on the bare flesh of my shoulder. It released a charge right down my arm. I caught my breath. You grinned.

We both knew.

One

'That's Rex's bed.' Jake nods to the narrow bed beneath the window, looks away quickly. Fear smashes across his face like glass.

The bed is unmade, white sheet yanked back, its sky-blue blanket rumpled. The pillow still has the imprint of your small, round head, a scattering of short, dark hairs. A book, a well-thumbed travel book on North Africa, is on the floor by the bed's metal legs, next to a half drunk bottle of mineral water. You look like you've just popped out for a couple of hours. You've gone for a jaunt inland perhaps, or for a run. Not unlike last Easter when you decided to run ten miles of South West coastal path on a whim. Yes, that's it. In a few hours' time we will emerge on the other side of this, laugh about it. One day we will bore our grandchildren to death with the anecdote: 'We'd only been married six months and guess what? Granddaddy Rex gave us a right old fright. He was on holiday with the boys, took his windsurf out early one morning and didn't come back for *hours* . . . Oops, sorry kids, I've told you this story already, haven't I?'

'I'm afraid poky doesn't do it justice.' Your brother smiles uncertainly; there is a polite stiltedness between us that is at odds with the urgency of the situation.

I smile back dumbly. The beach cabin is certainly tiny, panelled in varnished marmalade pine with two small gauze-covered windows. A pendant light with a cheap plastic white shade dangles low – even you must have had to duck as you walked beneath it. There are four narrow beds, a small kitchenette area with a minute humming fridge and a navy blue sofa, shiny on the arms. If it weren't for the thump of heat and tick of insects we could be in a cheap surf shack in Cornwall rather than the southern coast of Spain. Not that you would have been happier in a luxury hotel, double-glazed and air-conditioned. I know this. Your money has bought you the greatest luxury of all, freedom, a chance to slam yourself hard against mother nature. Well, I guess you must be doing that somewhere now for real.

'Don't worry, I've sorted you another cabin.' Jake pushes his glasses up his sweating nose with his thumb. They sit askew on his face. 'It's not far.'

'I'd rather sleep on his bed. If you don't mind?'

'Not at all.' Jake looks bemused. 'But I have to warn you that it's like sleeping on a plank. Tim talks in his sleep about football. And Raf has the loudest snore known to man.'

'I'm not bothered, really.' I stare down at the incongruous neon pink nail varnish on my toes, my eyes filling with tears. I don't say that I cannot face being alone. That it's far harder to keep it together than I imagined. That a repressed scream sits like a lump in my throat, a large pill swallowed without water.

6

Taking off from Gatwick, I'd felt optimistic: our paths were two red dots converging on the electronic map on the back of the plane seat. I was cutting through the sky towards you, getting closer and closer. But now that I am actually here – and you are not – it all feels much more desperate. You are meant to be in Tarifa, too.

'You must be thirsty, Gina. Water?' Jake walks to the mini fridge – stacked with beer, cheese and not much else, I see – and picks out a beaten-up metal water bottle. I wish I knew him better, not just as your younger half-brother whom we rarely saw. I might be able to gauge more about the severity of the situation then. 'Cold at least,' he adds apologetically.

The water soothes my throat, which is hoarse from trying to cry noiselessly on the plane. (It didn't work. A handbag-skinned lady wearing leopard print offered me a tissue and said kindly, 'He's probably not worth it, you know.' I didn't try to explain that my husband had gone missing, it sounded far too implausible. And yes, you're totally worth it.) Jake watches me drink, eyes shattered by red veins behind boxy tortoiseshell glasses. I'm hit by the injustice that it is you, not him who has disappeared. Apart from the fact that Jake looks so much more like a man who'd get in trouble on a windsurf – or in any water sports, frankly – I know you, the big brother, would be able to find him more easily than he will be able to find you. While you are compact, taut and purposeful, built like a hammer, Jake carries his height with a worryingly relaxed lollop and seems vaguely surprised by the length of his own limbs. You always used to say he is one of those men whose intelligence clouds his common sense.

'Um, hungry?' he asks, putting the water bottle back in the fridge.

'No, no thanks. I can't stomach anything.' The silence stretches between us, swelling with fear and disbelief. What are we doing here? Where are you? My body begins to feel leaden-heavy, like when you pull the plug in the bath but remain in it as the water level drops. I sag to your bed. It is then that I begin to hear the bass of waves beneath the tinny buzz of insects. 'Is the sea close, Jake?'

'Five minutes.' He looks at me, slightly baffled. Like there's been some mistake and I've pitched up on the wrong holiday. 'Would you like to see the beach?'

'I . . . I don't know.' The word beach. Sandcastles. Ice creams. Sand between brown toes. You snapping open a beer, congratulating yourself on a windsurf that buffeted you around the crispy edge of Spain for the ride of your life. Yes, that is it. You'll soon be grovelling to all the people who've been up all night looking for you, apologising for the upset you've caused. 'Is it the beach Rex . . .' I trail off, unable to complete the awful sentence.

'Yes.'

'We don't need to crack on with the . . . the search?'

'We're meeting the police in an hour for a quick briefing. There's not much point in doing more until then.' Jake's voice changes to something more officious, more in control, and I wonder if it's his journalist voice, the one he uses in the newspaper office. 'The missing person's report is filed . . .' He stops, weary of the bureaucracy. 'Sorry, Gina, the short answer is that we've got time to see the beach, if you'd like to, that is.'

I look at him doubtfully. How can we possibly have time? The first forty-eight hours are critical, I remember reading that in a newspaper once. It's nudging thirty-four hours now. No one's found any sign of you, your windsurf, beach bag or phone. You've vanished.

It was six am this morning, already a lifetime ago, when Jake's phone call woke me in our Marylebone flat. His voice had sounded strangulated, faint, like he was speaking at a distance from the mouthpiece. He told me that the reason I hadn't been able to get through to you wasn't because the signal had dropped or because you'd lost your phone – '*The number you are calling is currently unavailable. Please try again later*' over and over – it was because you'd taken your windsurf out alone yesterday morning at dawn, while the rest of them were sleeping, and not returned. He was so sorry, he had stuttered. They'd all assumed you'd turn up. They didn't want to worry me unnecessarily.

'Are you saying Rex has *disappeared*?' I'd asked with a wary laugh. If this was some stupid blokey stunt I wasn't going to fall for it. 'Jake, what the hell's going on out there?'

I'd heard muffled voices in the background then, someone saying, 'Jake, come on.' 'Look, Gina, I've got to go.' The voices became more urgent. 'Wait,' he said firmly to some-one who wasn't me. 'Just keep your voices down, will you? I'm speaking to Rex's wife here.' I knew then that it was no joke.

'I do think we should go to the beach. It'll help you get your bearings.' Jake studies me with a worried expression. 'If you're sure you're up to it? You look kind of pale.'

'I'm always this colour.'

He flickers a tiny smile, pushes his mop of dirty-blond hair off his face. I notice how it tufts from his head like a schoolboy's at the back but swings across his glasses at the front, as if he is sporting two different hair types from his crown. 'Come on then.'

Shoving my hastily packed bag towards the bed, I step out of the cabin into a whip-crack of early evening heat. Outside the cabin door is a pile of bloke's holiday paraphernalia – surfboards, a crate full of empty beer bottles, ropey old trainers. The sight of it makes my stomach lurch, like when you're in a plane and it suddenly loses height. It was only ever meant to be a bloke's holiday. I follow Jake through the small estate of wooden beach cabins, grubby outdoor showers and sun-yellowed patches of grass. By the gated exit to the site is a small shop selling water, ice cream and loo roll. A guy wearing a red bandana smiles hopefully at Jake. 'News, bro?'

Jake shakes his head, puts a hand on my back to steer me quickly past, not wanting us to get sucked into a conversation. We take a scrubby path across the sand made from planks of wood tied together with wire. Grass spikes up between the boards. I slip off my flip-flops and wonder how many times you've walked along here too, my bare feet on the same warm planks as yours. Oh, how I wish I could pause you at that exact moment, as your size eight sole hit the wood, press rewind and make everything go backwards five days in superfast speed until the moment we kissed goodbye on the doorstep outside our flat. When things were normal.

'OK?' Jake is sweating profusely beneath his mop of hair.

I nod. My mouth tastes of copper coins. Fear is clawing at

my belly. I'm scared of seeing the sea. But I know that I must be brave. If *I* went missing, you'd be able to find me in minutes from the other side of the world. I must help find you.

'Not far now.'

The path's incline is steep. The sun's rays pierce through the light seersucker cotton of my blouse to my skin beneath. Even at this hour, I feel like I'm burning up. At the top of the dune is a sweeping panorama of sea and sand, buffeted by a salty wind, seagulls screaming as they pitch its thermals. The beach is bleached and sculpted like the bottom of the seabed. The sea meets its gentle slopes with fury. I'm shocked by the way it broils, the waters of the Atlantic and the Med smashing together to create huge swells and towering walls of waves that crash and foam towards the shore, tossing surfers around like matchstick men. 'Bloody hell. Is it always this rough?'

'This isn't rough,' replies Jake.

'Oh.' I pinch and roll my lips with my fingers anxiously, staring out at the kite surfers. Their brightly coloured kites tug the riders high into the air then smack them back down punishingly on the water. And beyond the kites? Windsurfers, rising and falling on the swell, catching the light, cutting up the water like knives. I examine one then the other. Any one of those guys could be you.

To my left I notice a row of small yachts and windsurfs pulled up on the beach. Their sails and ropes snap in the wind like out-of-tune guitar strings. 'No one saw him go out? I can't believe it, Jake.'

Jake taps his thumbnail against his teeth. 'They must have done. But no witnesses have come forward to say they saw him. Not yet anyway.'

11

'Someone must have seen him. A fisherman.' I nod towards the boats on the beach. 'Another surfer.'

'You'd have thought so.'

I point to a dark smudge on the horizon. 'That's not Africa, is it?'

He nods. 'Morocco.'

'Shit! It's so close! It looks like you could practically swim to it.'

He rubs his blond stubble, making a rasping sound. 'Fourteen miles, across the Strait of Gibraltar.' He points to the right. 'Tangiers, just up there.'

'Jake . . .' His jaw is set, as if steeling himself for the inevitable question. 'Oh my God, could he?'

For a moment I don't think he's going to answer me. 'It's been done before,' he admits eventually.

I remember the dog-eared book about North Africa beside your cabin bed and the sea gets bluer, the snapping sail ropes louder, as my head starts to buzz with possibilities. 'Hang on a minute. So he could have windsurfed to Morocco?'

Jake swaps his glasses for Raybans, reminding me of one of those yachty blokes you get in expensive bits of Devon, the 'lightweight weekenders' in branded gear whom you looked down upon. 'In theory.'

There is a whoop of laughter as a dreadlocked man chases a bikini-clad woman across the beach, leaving a necklace of footprints on the sand. There is something wrong about this. And there is also something wrong about Jake in his floral shorts and sunglasses, me in my billowing sail-white blouse, pink shorts and neon nail varnish, a terrible pastiche of a couple on holiday. What are you meant to wear when someone disappears? Black? No, I won't wear black. There is no reason to wear black. 'He's not drowned. I know he's not drowned, Jake.'

Jake removes his sunglasses, flicks them against his brown thigh with his hand. I notice the blueness of his eyes – the jaunty blue of a deckchair stripe – so unlike yours, the colour of caves.

'I'd feel it if he was. I know I would. Anyway, he's a bloody brilliant swimmer.'

Rex Jerome Adler. Marathon runner. Mountain climber. Hi-tech consultant swinging dick superstar. T-Rex.

In Latin Rex means king.

'We have to consider the possibility that he got into trouble in the water.' Jake starts to breathe faster, his red T-shirt rippling as his ribcage bellows in and out beneath the sun-bleached cloth.

No, I won't consider this possibility. I must remember that Jake is a journalist who reviews films for a newspaper, a man who has spent too many hours in darkened screening rooms detached from reality. That's what you always said, a bit of a flakey dreamer. Maybe he's acting out stuff he's watched. That's why he's not more positive. 'What do the police think?' I dare to ask, swallowing the rock of fear in my throat.

Jake doesn't meet my eye. 'Drowning seems to be their main line of enquiry. But it's difficult to know what they're thinking. All of us speak crap Spanish and they speak crap English. There are three different police forces . . . shit, it's really fucking complicated.' His voice breaks. He rubs his eye with his knuckle. 'The whole thing is turning into an unbelievable fucking nightmare. Sorry if I'm not making much sense. I haven't slept.'

'There is no body, Jake. I can't believe I'm saying the word "body". It's ridiculous. This whole thing is ridiculous. Rex must be here somewhere. He must be.'

Jake emits a small groan, covers his face with his hands.

'If there's something you're not telling me . . . Please, Jake.'

'I've told you everything.'

'Sharks?' my voice quavers. There is an oily curdling in my belly. 'Are there sharks here?'

'Yes, but they wouldn't eat a board, or a whole surfer. They might take a bite if he were hugely unlucky, that's all.'

I sit down heavily on the hot sugary sand, cover my mouth with my hand, panic gripping my stomach tight in its fist. 'Oh God.'

Jake squats down beside me, slips on his sunglasses again. 'Let's not go there, OK?'

I nod, wiping away my tears. I must be brave. I must be brave.

'One day at a time. Everything can change in an instant.'

'I know that now.' I glance up at him. My stricken face is reflected in his sunglasses. Already it does not look like me.

'We're doing everything we can, Gina,' Jake says softly.

'I know, I'm sorry. None of this is your fault.' As I speak, doubt shudders through me in hot sick waves. I clutch my throat and vomit violently on to the sand.

Two

'I envy you both your decisiveness actually,' Jake had said, digging his hands into his frayed jean pockets.

It was only last autumn, the first time I'd been to your mother's house, the second time I'd met Jake. I was doing my best to charm your brother and win his approval. It had been such a whirlwind. Eyebrows were raised at how fast everything had gone: living together two months after meeting, married after six. I had loved saying, 'When you know, you know,' to all the doubters, but I still desperately wanted your impressive family to accept me.

'Never quite managed it myself,' Jake added wryly.

I laughed, unsure if he was being serious or not – he seemed more playful, less intense than you – and tried to work out the status of his girlfriend, Fran – some star in the firmament of mobile phone marketing apparently – who I was due to meet later that evening. Through the trees I could hear the boom of your voice, then a small pause before your mother's delicate laughter as you both made your way up the garden path towards her house. I'd hesitated to follow you immediately because I wanted to give you time to talk to your mother alone. Despite your assurances that she'd love me, every time I spoke Clarice still looked haughtily surprised, as if I had popped up uninvited from beneath her French mahogany dining table. 'So you're not going to try and talk us out of it like everyone else then, Jake?'

Jake looked amused. 'No, in my experience people are more likely to talk themselves out of things than into them anyway.'

I warmed to him then, this charmingly boffinish brother of yours, who had only met me briefly once before and was now being asked to embrace me as a sister-in-law. It could have been so much worse. Besides, you had my sister Dawn to deal with. 'I'll take that as a blessing of sorts.' I kicked my feet out and leaned back on the swing, sensuously aware of the thick ropes cooling in my hands as the evening descended, my long, red hair falling around me, silly and girlish with love.

Jake watched me intensely, nudging fallen leaves with his scuffed brogues. 'I imagine it's your parents you need to convince anyway, not me.'

'Well, yes, there is that,' I shrugged, although the selfish truth was I was so exhilarated by our love affair that I hadn't spent too long worrying about it. Dawn had already decided you were a bit 'uptight' (pots and kettles) and had pointed out that 'He's so not your type,' meaning you hadn't yet displayed any psychopathic tendencies or tried to split a restaurant bill. Mum worried the thirteen-year age gap would be the problem – 'He'll be sixty-three when you're only fifty. Men go downhill rapidly at sixty, love. Take it from me' – and couldn't hide her disappointment that I'd gone for another London man (admittedly, the precedents hadn't been great) rather than returned to the short-vowelled fold up north.

Dad wasn't impressed either. Your suits with their gum pink linings made him worry his beard with his chlorophyll-stained gardener's fingers. He didn't understand what you did at KPHI – me neither, sorry – but was nonetheless convinced it must have had something to do with the shrinking of his life's savings and the imminent collapse of Western society. He didn't trust your lapsed Catholic status either, coming from a long line of lapsed Protestants himself. And ultimately, although he didn't say it outright, I don't think he understood why someone like you would want to be with someone like me. Only the week before he'd cornered me in the kitchen: 'Too much, too soon, Gina. You need to be more cautious, not just throw yourself into these things like a teenager. In case you've forgotten, you're not a teenager. You're thirty in a couple of months. When I was thirty I had two kids, a wife and a shed.'

You will never want a shed. 'They'll get used to it,' I smiled, gazing up at Jake through the blaze of my red lashes.

'That's good.' He looked amused.

I stopped on the swing, digging my toes into the earth. 'Do you think your mum will?'

Jake raised an eyebrow at the candidness of my question, hesitated. 'Rex is a bit of the golden boy, first born and all that. No one would be quite good enough.' He looked away into the darkening trees. 'Don't worry, he can talk her into anything.'

'Oh.' I felt deflated at the confirmation that Clarice – cool, glamorous French matriarch, Clarice – would have to be talked into me, even though I'd suspected it.

'For what it's worth, I've never seen Rex like this with anyone before,' he added shyly.

'Really?' I felt a fizz of happiness again.

'But the thing about Rex . . .' There was a change in the tone of his voice. Like a drop in temperature.

I crossed my arms, pulling my blue cardigan tight around me. 'Oh?' I asked, almost daring him to get involved. It was our love affair. Our bubble. No one could penetrate it. I didn't want anyone to try.

Jake scuffed harder at the fallen leaves with his foot. 'Oh forget it, it's nothing.' He pushed his hair off his face with the back of a hand covered in biro. 'Come on, let's go inside. I don't want the others to think I've kidnapped you.'

I smiled, relieved that it was nothing important, that he hadn't rained on our parade by bringing up the old sibling rivalries you'd occasionally muttered about. I remembered something then about Jake inheriting his London house off an aunt on his father's side. Jake getting an easy ride. You'd muttered that he could afford to go off and be an arty journalist, unlike you. That he didn't need to grow balls.

Our mood a little more sombre, we made our way through the trees to the Victorian conservatory at the back of your mother's house, which was gloomy with the plants that pushed up against the glass as if trying to escape. Through the broad, waxy leaves, I could see your mother waiting, purse-lipped, perfectly coiffed, clutching the bottle of vintage Dom Perignon that I'd spotted you stealthily pack away in the car boot before we left London. Later, you sweetly fibbed that your mum had bought it especially for the occasion.

Three

The sea search is over, my love. Raf has told me that the coastguard is waiting for a body to wash up on the beach. We're not, don't you worry. I can still feel the dark, salty Rexness of you, pulsating around me. I know you are alive. When I do manage to sleep on your bed – bloody uncomfortable, Jake wasn't exaggerating – I dream about you and you are so real that when I wake up it takes a few moments to compute that you are not lying next to me. Not yet anyway.

But you can hear me, can't you? I know you can. We've always been oddly telepathic. Do you remember how I always used to know it was you calling even before I picked up the phone? The way everything seemed to converge that sticky spring day to make us come together, two random people in a bustling city of seven million.

It can't be long now.

Raf – now bearded, bearing an uncanny resemblance to Richard Branson – is re-checking the hospitals and psychiatric institutions, although he seems to do rather a lot of his searching at José's Bar, too. Tim sits up at night picking his nose, combing the Net with chorizo-stained fingertips, as if you might pop up on Twitter sometime soon with a witty aside. Your brother looks increasingly shell-shocked as the hours pass, and the morning begins with another possibility that you may not be back before dusk. It's reassuring: I don't see how anyone could fake that face. He's been liaising with the British authorities and Interpol and doing his best to calm your poor mother, who is apparently climbing the wisteria-clad walls back in Kent. The police? The case is still very much open but it's difficult to have a huge amount of confidence in them. We all fear they're going through the motions, not keen to advertise the loss of a tourist in the area. Even the man in the site shop says it'll be a hush-up. No one wants the beaches to be thought of as dangerous.

I keep telling the police that I'm sure you're still out there, alive. As Raf points out, dead men aren't very good at burying themselves. That's what I told the newspapers back home, too. You were page five.

And right now? It's midday, so hot it hurts to be out-side. I've been up since dawn with Jake, searching Tarifa's winding alleys and dusty backstreets. Nothing. We've combed everywhere. We're flagging. We need to consider other explanations. And I'm back at the cabin for a rest. Only I can't rest. I feel rotten and it's stuffier than ever in here, a locker smell lifting from the beds like old cheese when you open the fridge door. And my brain is whirring at a hundred miles an hour.

Jake's shadow falls long behind the door. 'Can I come in?'

'One sec.' I rummage for the make-up bag that I've stashed

beside the bed and pull out my hand mirror to repair the damage from crying and vomiting – I don't want to look like a liability. I'm shocked by my reflection. Even though I've only been here two days, my hair has matted into dull dreadlocky curls. I have a triangular patch of sunburn on my nose despite sun block. My eyes are ruined, the green irises making the whites look redder than ever, the area around them baggy with worry and frustration. I put in some eye drops in the vain hope it makes me look more together. 'Come in.'

'Tea.' Jake steps into the cabin, hands me a steaming cardboard cup and sits on the side of the bed, his long legs tan against the white sheets. 'You look shattered, Gina. Did you manage to get a bit of sleep?'

'No. I keep going over and over that last morning in London, wishing I'd not let him go this time. He's been away such a lot recently. I should have been more assertive. If—'

'You wouldn't have been able to stop him.' Jake sits forward, slumps exhaustedly with his chin on his hand. 'You know what he's like. He had this holiday all planned out, down to the last detail.' He smiles ruefully. 'Rex needs to get away.'

He's right, of course. Despite your groom's speech – 'Gina's the only woman who made me want to settle down' – it quickly became obvious to me that your version of settling down was a tad different to mine. While I am happy to mooch around the city, mostly eating, you need to escape your job and the grey skies of London on a regular basis. You are at your happiest in London when packing to leave it, rolling things neatly into colour-coded compression sacks: micro-light trainers ('a hundred grams off the foot, a kilo off the back'), state-of-the-art dry kits, wetsuits, Leatherman knives and, at your most enthusiastic, dehydrated food packets. You prepare less for a holiday than a terrorist siege. We are opposites like that. You might get your kicks from inching up a vertical rock face, air wheeling beneath your feet; my kicks come from bringing you coffee and croissants on a tray in bed. It's embarrassing how much I love being your wife sometimes.

'I was the one who should have told him going out in that surf was a fucking stupid idea. I just assumed he knew what he was doing.' Jake closes his eyes and shakes his head regretfully.

I sip the tea. It is unexpectedly sweet. 'I'm not convinced he went into the water at all.'

Jake screws his face up, wrestling with something. He doesn't speak for a while. 'Has he been under a lot of strain recently?'

'Strain? Well, I guess his work has been mental. But that's not particularly unusual.' I think of all the times you have stumbled in from the office at ten pm, still in your suit, the shadows under your eyes so deep they look like bruises. You slept under your desk last month. 'He was about to be made a partner. That was why he was putting in those hours. But he thrives on it, I think. Rex has this superhuman energy. I don't know how he does it.'

Jake taps his teeth with his fingernail. 'Yeah, he mentioned something about becoming a partner.'

'Can you tell me a little more about the holiday before he

23

disappeared?' I ask, reinvigorated by the sweet tea. 'This has all happened so quickly, I haven't been able to put all the pieces together.'

For a moment Jake looks dumbfounded, as if he can't square the blokes' surf holiday before you left with what has happened since. 'We'd been having a good time.' He swallows hard. 'The cabin's cramped. Raf's been a pain in the arse. But we've had a laugh. It's just been a blokey holiday, Gina, a week of surfing, boozing, that's all.' He bites down hard on his lower lip, visibly upset.

'Had he been drinking the night before?'

'No. He was the only one of us who abstained that night. Said he had a headache.'

That sounds more like you. You don't like being drunk, out of control. You're happiest stone cold sober in a wetsuit. 'But he relaxed?' I ask hopefully.

'Using the term loosely. This is Rex we're talking about.'

You could never wholly switch off. I always thought that your restless electric energy had something to do with you trying to please the imagined ambitions of your late father. Jake, whose father is alive, clearly has less to prove. Cod psychology, you'd call it. 'You either make excuses in life or you get on,' you used to say. 'If you keep looking backwards you don't move forwards,' that was another one. I always loved you for that: you refused to allow the loss of your father so young to overshadow the rest of your life. 'Was he in a good mood?'

Jake begins to look troubled. '*Maybe*, in hindsight, he did seem a little agitated, preoccupied. But it's hard not to let this colour everything.' He sighs, runs his hand through his hair.

24

'I just don't know, Gina. I don't fucking know.'

'You didn't row, did you?' I probe further, needing to clear the niggles about Jake from my mind.

He gives me a sidelong glance, as if sensing my doubts. 'Occasional bicker about washing up, Raf stinking out the toilet every morning and using up all the hot water in the shower, that sort of thing.' He stares down at the floor, rumpling the skin of his cheek with the drag of his fingers. 'Nothing major.'

Feeling queasy again, I watch Jake, and wonder. Should I trust him? Why did you keep Jake at a distance? We hardly ever saw him in London. You always made excuses to avoid family get-togethers if Jake and Fran were going to be there. And when we did all meet up, you seemed on edge. The nicer Jake was to you, the tenser you became. There were clearly unspoken issues between you, things you never spelled out to me. I let them lie, sensing that the trick with you was not to ask too many questions, that the answers would eventually bubble to the surface of their own accord. Hopefully they will do here, too.

'This holiday felt like a bit of a fresh start for me and Rex to be honest, Gina,' Jake says quietly, his eyes glistening. 'I didn't expect to be invited. And I got the feeling, from the fact that Rex asked me to come in the first place, and some of the evenings we spent together, that he wanted to build bridges . . .' He looks away wistfully. 'We had some good chats, you know. It felt like stuff was behind us.'

'What stuff?' I ask, maybe a little too quickly.

He hesitates and I wonder if he's deciding what to tell me.

'Oh, I used to give him a hard time for not visiting Mum.

25

She worships him and he can be . . . reckless with her feelings, that's all.'

'Reckless? He whisked her off to Venice for her birthday last year. At Christmas he sent her boar salami from the woods near her grandmother's house in the Loire. Jake, my Mum gets a box of smellies from John Lewis.'

He smiles. 'He is good at the grand gestures, I'll give him that.' Jake's foot starts to tap on the floor. 'Look, there was other stuff, too. But it was small stuff in the great scheme of things. Not relevant now,' he adds quickly.

For some reason I don't feel satisfied by his answer. 'You must have had a lot of this from the police?'

His face clouds. 'A fair bit, yes.'

'They've got to count out foul play, I guess.'

Jake gets up quickly, swigs from a water bottle, his back turned, weight on one hip. 'There's a direct flight this evening. Raf and Tim are taking it.'

I spill a scald of tea on my leg. 'But we haven't found Rex yet! And I've only been here two days.' I've already run out of knickers. I packed too hastily. 'Why are they going already?'

'We were meant to be home by now. Raf's got kids waiting for him. Tim's got work. They can't stay here indefinitely, Gina.' I wonder if what he's actually saying is that he can't stay longer either. He has a girlfriend waiting for him at home, a job at a newspaper he must return to. How long can anyone stay? No, I can't go there. The idea that we could go home and carry on normal lives, as if nothing has happened, makes me want to drop to my knees and howl.

'I think you should take that flight home too, Gina. You're clearly not very well. And you're not going to get better here. Look, I'll phone you the moment we know anything, OK?'

I don't like the word 'anything'. I want him to say, 'as soon as we find you'.

'I've got to focus on looking for Rex. I can't look after you too.'

Something explodes then. All the frustration and worry blasts out of me. 'You don't need to look after me! I can bloody well look after myself! I've picked up some stupid, no big deal tummy bug. Are you trying to get rid of me, Jake?'

He looks really shocked. I feel bad. 'No, no. Sorry, I don't mean it like that. I really don't. But I feel a sense of responsibility to you. You're Rex's wife. I'm his brother,' he says with a simple kindness that makes me feel even worse for doubting him. 'I think it's for the best, that's all.'

I'm about to say OK, but then I am back in Newquay, last Easter, you and me, a cold blustery beach in crystalline sunshine. I'm waving at you from the rocks, wearing your navy fleece, newspaper-wrapped chips hot and heavy in my hands. You are wading out of the sea, James Bond-sleek in your wetsuit. You kiss me and the coldness of your skin makes me giggle and jump. The kiss tastes of salt and vinegar. It is a kiss that reminds me that sometimes life gives you exactly what you need at the very moment you need it. You just have to hold your nerve. 'I'm not going, Jake. I'd feel so horribly helpless waiting around in London. I've got to help find him.'

'Listen, my dad is coming out tomorrow.' I notice the way he says, 'my dad', not 'Dad'. You always refer to Jake's dad as Michael, even though he prefers to be called Mike. 'We're going to Tangiers to raise awareness of him over there. Given half a chance, we can bang this search up a pace.'

'Tangiers?' I leap to my feet. A column of tiny midges spiral upwards. 'So you *do* think he could have—'

'The flight leaves at eleven fifteen this evening,' he interrupts, refusing to be drawn further. 'I've booked you a seat.'

'A seat?' Jake is less passive than he at first appears. Well, he's not going to order me around. He may have me down as your silly, young wife, but I won't be dismissed so easily. 'I can't go home not knowing. I can't go home without him, Jake.'

There is a knock on the open door. Tim is standing there, looking freaked out, his darting green eyes pressed into his doughy sunburned face like peas. 'Sorry to interrupt, guys.' He glances from Jake to me uneasily. 'Look, this is a bit of a weird one . . .' He takes a deep breath. 'The police have just discovered that Rex took out a thousand Euros the day before he disappeared.'

'I know it looks bad but it doesn't mean he's run away, Gina.'

'Something has to mean something, Jake.' I can't hold the sobs back now. They snort out of me in ugly seismic shudders.

'Wouldn't it be a mistake to make facts fit theories? Look, do you want to take a minute? I can come back later.'

'No, no. Don't go, please.' I sniff the tears back down my throat, try to regain some composure. 'Sorry, Jake, it's just

28

that I can't intellectualise it like you.' I drop my head to my hands. It is all too much. 'I can't take it in, none of it.' My voice breaks. 'I just want him to walk through that door and for everything to be normal again.'

Jake touches me lightly, awkwardly. We still don't know how to be with one another. 'So do I. More than anything.'

I take a deep breath. 'I'm so tired, so fried. I really need to clear my head. It's going to explode otherwise.' I stand up from the chair, smooth down my shorts. 'Can we go for a swim or something?'

'A swim? No, I've got to . . .' He stops, shakes his head. 'Oh damn it, let's go for a swim.'

Jake won't let us swim at the local beach, too rough today, he says, so we judder along bumpy, dusty roads in his green hire car to a bay further along the coast, leaving a message for Tim and Raf with site reception. The bay is curved and custard-yellow, fringed by long grasses waving in the wind. The water shocks me with its coldness, a sharp contrast to the heat billowing in from Africa. I tread water, not going too far out of my depth, while Jake backstrokes along the shoreline, watching me, never far away. I try to ignore him, pretend I'm alone, as it makes it easier to commune with you.

Time drifts. A group of windsurfers appears, the sails of their boards catching the sun as they switch angles. One man in particular, a beginner perhaps, falls off every few seconds and then clambers back on to his board. You were not a beginner. And even if you were it looks easy enough to clamber back on. How could the sea have swallowed you? It does not make sense. But then again, nor does the money.

Why on earth would you leave me? Our lovely life.

I crane my neck back so that the cold water creeps up my hairline, cradling my head. I let my head sink slowly beneath the waves, close over my ears, my crown, until I am suspended, rising and falling just beneath the surface of the water and the events of the last few days: the night before you left, you are tapping intently at your laptop late into the night; you crawl into bed after two am, and even though I'm half asleep I feel you silently watching me; you get up at least three times in the night but I'm too tired to interact with you or open my eyes or ask you what the matter is, why you're so restless. How I wish I had.

'Gina!' Someone is pulling me beneath my armpits to the surface in a confusion of bubbles and mouth-spluttered water.

'Gina,' Jake shouts again, his eyes wild and blue without his glasses. 'Don't do that! Fucking hell, I thought something had happened.'

'Sorry.' I wipe the water from my eyes. 'Miles away.'

'We need to move closer to the beach. The tide is turning. It happens really quickly out here. We've been out too long.'

There is shouting from the beach, a voice caught by the wind, cut short by it. 'Jake! Jake!' Above the bobbing waves we see someone waving their arms madly.

'Who's that?' He squints, treading water. 'I need my damn glasses.'

'I think it's Raf.' A hairy middle-aged man in pink shorts? 'Yeah, it's definitely Raf.'

'Come on, quick. Swim, Gina. Swim. They might have found him.'

It's a struggle to keep up with Jake's strong stroke. Waves break into my eyes. The water ropes around my legs and tugs me backwards. It really does feel like that bottomless blue sea is trying to hold me back from you. This only makes me swim harder.

Four

Mandy

Mandy was wrapping the page of newspaper around the roast chicken carcass when a small news story smudged by grease from the chicken's wing grabbed her attention. She stood there staring at it, frozen to the spot, inhaling the smell of on-the-turn chicken bones. Page five. She nudged the chicken aside with a fork and reread the story once, twice, three times. 'British tourist missing in Spain'. It couldn't be . . . The newsprint seemed to expand and shrink in front of her eyes as she strained to digest it. How many Rex Adlers were there in the world? How many Rex Adlers 'originally from Wareham'. It was too much of a coincidence.

'Mum, can I have my pocket money?'

She didn't hear him. Rex Adler. Rex Adler. It couldn't be.

'Mum,' Ryan dribbled a football into the kitchen, wearing a Viking helmet. 'It's pocket money day.'

Not querying whether it was pocket money day or not – it

wasn't, of course – she reached into her purse and pulled out a handful of coins. 'Here, love.'

Ryan grinned. She'd given him double what she usually did. 'Can I go to the corner shop on my own?'

'No.' She could never imagine an age when she would let Ryan out of her sight. He'd be fifteen and she'd make him hold her hand crossing the road like a toddler. 'No, of course you can't.'

'But I'm four!'

'Exactly, little Viking.'

'Aw. Will you take me then?'

Not really listening, she pushed her blonde hair out of her eyes with the back of her hand and looked down at the newspaper again to check she had read it right.

'Why are you looking at the chicken funny, Mummy?'

'Ryan, just give me a minute, OK?'

Ryan seized his opportunity to grab a Penguin bar unnoticed and ran off to eat his unexpected booty in the sitting room.

There at the very end of the article was the clincher. 'We need anyone with any information to come forward immediately,' said Adler's thirty-one-year-old brother, Jake Wilkinson. Bloody hell. There was no doubt.

'Take that! And that!'

She glanced up. OK, that was probably Ryan plunging his plastic sword into the cushions on the settee. Normally she'd try to protect the pretty new cushions she couldn't afford to replace. Not today. Nothing else seemed important. The implications of this newspaper article made her head swim. When it came to Rex she'd gone through every possible scenario in her head a million times. But not this one. How could she ever have imagined this happening?

'Mum?' Ryan ran back into the kitchen, chocolate around his mouth, waggling the sword above his head. 'Can we go to the shop now?'

'Oh, Ryan. Come here.' She hugged him, sank her face into his tousled hair, finding comfort in his boyish sweet smell.

If someone dies carrying a secret . . . Shit.

'Give me a kiss.'

He kissed her dutifully on the cheek. 'You smell of chicken, Mummy.'

The front door slammed. A heavy bag thudded to the floor.

'Alright, sweetheart,' Mark bellowed from the hall. He always bellowed after a day on site, attuned to shouting over noisy work tools.

'Hi, love.'

In the kitchen Mark wiped his hands on his workman's trousers before giving her a soft kiss on the mouth. Even covered in paint he was the sexiest man she'd ever met.

'Will you take me to the shop? Please?' Ryan tugged his sleeve. 'Mum's given me my pocket money.'

Mark laughed. 'As long as you give me a bite. You know I'm partial to a Malteser or ten.'

'Yes!' shouted Ryan, fist in the air.

Mark turned to Mandy, concerned. 'Are you OK, Mandy? You don't look too chipper.'

'I'll tell you later,' she said, nodding at Ryan. Mark frowned, wondering what it was all about; if he'd unwittingly done something wrong. Mandy wrapped up the chicken in the newspaper, stuffed it deep into the bin and shut the lid as firmly as possible. But she could still see the newsprint when she closed her eyes.

Five

When did you actually go missing, Rex? Was it the moment you dragged your windsurf down the beach? Or was it the day you left our London flat? It breaks my heart that I still had time to stop it then, if only I'd known what was about to happen. I keep going over and over our last morning in my head, looking for clues. But hindsight has muddled everything, making that last morning together both sweetly banal and horribly significant.

All I do know is that I woke to that warm spring morning with a sleepy smile, delighted to see you again after the separation of sleep. You were already awake, fiddling with your phone, concentration carved on your brow. I leaned over and kissed you on the hard ridge of your jaw – calcified testosterone, I used to joke – wanting the goodbye over with: the sooner you left, the sooner you'd return. I'd got used to goodbyes. I had never wanted a cloying we-must-do-everything-together marriage.

'Well, good morning, Mrs Adler.' You swept my tangle of long red hair off my face, placed your hand on my hipbone and tipped my body expertly towards yours.

Afterwards, panting on our pillows, you traced your finger through the galaxy of freckles on my shoulder blades that you have taught me to love after a lifetime of freckle hating. 'I will miss these.' A smile pressed that dimple into your cheek. 'And your bottom.'

'Hmmm. I suspect that the moment you see the surf you'll forget all about your new wife actually.' Something about the idea of you not missing me made desire flare again. 'I know you,' I whispered, laughing, rolling closer.

'You reckon?' Your mouth twitched playfully.

I gave you a gentle punch on the arm. 'Yes, I do. Hey, what time's your flight?'

'Sooner than Raf realises, that's for sure.' You sat up, the mood shifting abruptly as you reached for your phone and started stabbing out a message to Raf, your work colleague, the functioning alcoholic, notorious for being late for everything. Below our flat the newsagent's security grille rattled up. London was stirring.

'Don't lie here for my sake. You don't want to miss your flight.' I riffed my fingers along the back of your neck, finding tendons tense as ripcords.

'Ah, that's your game, sweetheart. You seem to forget that you have married the Master of Planning. I have exactly twenty-six minutes thirty-two seconds before I need to leave for the airport.' You rolled out of bed with athletic grace, bounced up naked. At forty-three you still have the compact, wiry, body of a twenty-five-year-old rock climber. I admired you as you stood there, noticing the agitated muscle that had started to tick on the left hand side of your jaw. From experience I knew that you would become more distant as

37

you made the mental leap from Marylebone to Heathrow to Spain. Your brain always arrived at a destination before your body.

'Is it the marmalade or me?' I asked over breakfast, a little put out. You'd become particularly distant. I needed reassurance that I was still at the centre of your world, as you were mine.

You looked up from your uneaten toast as if you'd just noticed I was there. 'Sorry. It's just that Raf and Tim are such total morons sometimes. And you know what my brother is like. He'll turn up with a rucksack full of books and forget his passport.' You drained your black coffee in one throat-clenching gulp, like a mafioso in the movies. 'You're pissed off with me, aren't you?'

'No.' You probably knew that I meant yes. A little bit. 'It's just that I don't feel I've seen much of you this week. And now you're going away.'

'You know work's been full on, sweetheart.' Your jaw tensed, as it always did when the subject of KPHI came up.

'Is this really what you have to do to become a partner?'

'You have to work your bollocks off, yes, Gina.'

I couldn't come back at this one, nor could I begrudge your hours when I so enjoyed their fruits, living a life I'd never be able to afford on my own crappy salary. Besides, as you would always remind me, it was a temporary state of affairs. You had a plan: as a partner in that powerful hi-tech consultancy you'd be earning so much money that you'd be able to stash a lot away, retire early, travel and surf, perhaps set up your own green investment consultancy. You always had big plans, big ideals. There was no middle way. Everything or nothing.

'Wish I was going with you, that's all,' I said, feeling bad for giving you a hard time. I'd always promised to myself that I'd never become one of those wives who resent the very qualities in their husbands that once attracted them. (Dawn used to find Gareth's toy classic car collection endearing but now points to it as evidence that he is her third child. 'I should have realised when he showed me the miniature 911, sis.')

'You hate windsurfing.'

'Love beaches!'

You grinned, picked the small yellow pot of Carmex lipsalve off the countertop, dabbed your fingertip in it, slicked your lips, then, slowly and carefully, ran your fingers over mine as if reading their Braille. Something tugged deep inside me again. But there was no time for more sex.

On the twenty-sixth minute we stood at the front door. You hugged me so hard it hurt. 'I'll phone tonight.'

'Every night.'

You kissed me in answer. I can still feel that kiss, the gluey pull between our lips, our hot tongues. 'Love you,' you whispered, taking my hand and pressing it to your mouth so that your warm breath threaded through my fingers. As the cab drove off, I stood on the front step and waved madly, blowing kisses like bubbles, oblivious. If I'd known that was our last kiss I wouldn't have brushed my teeth.

Six

Absence creates a hell of a lot of admin. That's what Dawn said yesterday as she squeezed out of the front door, glancing backwards over her hunk of shoulder at the pile of unopened post on the walnut sideboard. She's right. There are endless bank letters, bills, catalogues, Amazon offers, weirdly inappropriate 'In sympathy' cards all piled up. I haven't been able to face them. But I haven't been able to face Mum and Dawn going through them either, sucking air in through their teeth as they discover that we blow more in delis and cafés in a week than they do at supermarkets in a month. I chuck more unopened post on the pile and walk to the sitting room's long Georgian window, spreading my hands on the cool glass and peering down into the pretty Marylebone street below. I'm surprised to see that it is getting dark already. Last time I was aware of the time it was morning. What on earth have I been doing all day? Where have the hours gone?

This keeps happening.

I'm on compassionate leave now, a kind of black parody of a staycation. There's no structure to my day. It's harder than ever to order my thoughts. My brain revolves around you, one fear chasing another, so that when I'm on my own I forget to do the basics, like washing or eating, not that I can keep anything down for long anyway, and the day either goes past painfully slowly or in a finger click. I try to fill my time usefully – liaising with missing persons' charities, bugging the Spanish authorities, waiting for people to call me back – but empty gaps still open up in the day, like bloody bits of gum after a tooth is smashed out. I miss you so much it hurts. Imagine the worst headache you can, one of those killer headaches you used to get when you were stressed out, the ones that laughed in the face of Aspirin, the ones that made you want to cut your head off and kick it over the rooftops. That's how I miss you.

It's not so bad when Mum, Dad or Dawn are here, which they have been on and off since I got back from Spain – I hung on as long as I could, darling, but eventually got so sick I had to return home – sharing Gina-sitting duties with Lucy. Dawn, who takes up twice your width on the sofa, insists on the constant background banter of daytime chat shows: 'Good to know that there are people out there fatter than me, sis, that's all I'm saying.' Dad sits stroking his beard at the kitchen table, engrossed in numerous outdated books he got out of Matlock library on Spanish law. Mum channels her anxiety into domestic tasks I never knew existed – cleaning the back of the microwave, scrubbing inside the toilet cistern – making food, and doing a lot of ironing. 'Just in case you need to pop down the police station again, love. No harm in looking smart, eh?'

But when they leave it hits me all over again: it's me and

an arthritic cat. You have vanished. This is my new normal, married to someone who is missing, and I am isolated in a nightmare that begins afresh every morning when I open my eyes, and gets steadily worse as the clock ticks on: every minute, hour, day, your absence becomes more irrefutable, so that it is now as big a presence as you ever were. It defines everything.

This said, Rex, I am ready for everything to change in an instant. For the world to realign itself. I have kept your armchair empty, not even Whippet the cat is allowed upon it, ready for you to sit down and crack open one of your little green bottles of boutique Cornish ales that you loved to drink while watching the kind of tense, violent crime dramas that gave me nightmares. I've collected your dry cleaning, hung it in the wardrobe. Your immaculate navy bespoke suits are ready for Monday morning, five forty-five am sharp. I've left the bathroom as it was, too. Your half empty tube of shaving foam is still on the shelf next to your deodorant. Your electric toothbrush is still half charged. Every night I lie at the very edge of our enormous lonely bed, leaving room for you to stumble in late, cursing the time lag between London and San Francisco. I've kept the remains of the coffee that you ground for your last espresso the morning you left for Spain at the bottom of the grinder, perfectly ground of course. You were particular about your coffee. And I've kept that little pot of Carmex lipsalve that we used the morning you left. It still has the square swirled imprint of your fingertip in the gunk.

The doorbell goes, jolting me out of my thoughts. My heart leaps. It could be you.

It is not you.

Femi and Lucy clatter up the stairs in their heels, trailing perfume and cool spring air. Lucy is wearing a circular skirt and shrunken pink cardigan, like a glamorous 1950s house-wife, while Femi is wearing neon-yellow platforms and a khaki playsuit. They are reminders of life outside this flat, a life that has been suspended, a city where shoes and style matter.

'Oh, Gina, *look* at you.' Femi rubs my arms. 'Oh, hon, you poor thing. You look terrible. All skin and bone.'

Lucy hugs me. My face is lost in her cloud of fine blonde hair, just as it was when we slept side by side in my bed like two girls on a sleepover the week after I got back from Spain. 'I'm moving back in,' she declares, staring at me with barely disguised horror. 'I'm definitely moving back in, Gee.'

'You don't need to, Luce, honestly. I'm managing,' I protest, wishing my voice didn't sound so husky and weedy. It's hard to explain that, awful though it is being alone, I also need space, space to be alone to talk to you. That the nicer people are, the more they help, the more helpless it makes me feel. 'Really.'

Lucy does not look convinced. Nor will she let go of my hand.

'You're much missed at Grey Home.' Femi smiles, trying to lighten things. 'Although I'm getting a lot more work done.'

I smile. The peppy pitch of Femi's voice plugs me back in to the person I was before you vanished: the happy, excitable new bride at the water cooler, the chirpy designer of Corgi print cushions. 'What's been going on at Grey?'

Femi rolls her eyes. 'Oh, Hector Grimes is back from

43

Hong Kong, giving everyone the embarrassing pep talk about "pulling together in these tough times", i.e. not asking for pay rises, despite rumours he has just bought a spanking new flat in Holland Park. Andrea and Kit are still pretending to come into work separately in the morning, even though we all know they've just come from another dirty stop out. Martin's still mincing around as if he's head designer at Armani Casa. What else? Fabric prices rising. Big stock returns. The usual.' She shrugs. 'It's a less fun place without our sunny Gee, that's for sure. Oh, and before I forget . . .' She digs into her handbag and pulls out a huge card. 'From the guys at work.' The card is handmade and covered in swatches of fabric, all carefully stuck on the front to look like a patchwork quilt. Everyone has signed it. Even Hector.

'Ah, it's gorgeous. Thank them for me?'

'Course.' Femi smiles that big, soft smile. A mother of two, she's also the studio's reigning matriarch. And she's my mate, the person who gave me my first break after I retrained as a designer after a decade in marketing. I realise how much I've missed her. 'It's weird not working, Femi. I keep forgetting that I'm not coming in tomorrow.'

Femi's eyes round with pity. 'I'm sure if you wanted to come back . . .'

I shake my head. 'No, no, I can't. Not yet. I've got too much to do here.'

Femi and Lucy exchange a fleeting glance.

'We thought we might make you supper?' says Lucy, changing the subject. Lucy, loud at the best of times, speaks to me in an even louder voice now, as if I'm slightly deaf. Lots of people have started doing this.

'Supper?' I repeat blankly. Whippet rubs against my legs, vying for my attention. 'I'm not really hungry.'

'A drink. A cup of tea?' Femi fiddles with her diamond nose stud. 'I don't know about you but I'm going to pass out unless something passes my lips very soon.' I walk towards the kettle. 'No. Don't move, Gee! We'll do it,' cries Lucy.

'I bring wine.' Femi pulls a bottle of white out of a supermarket bag. She winces. 'Or is that unhelpful?' No one is sure of the protocol. What does one do when a husband walks out of a beach cabin one morning and doesn't come back?

'Go ahead. I won't.' Femi looks concerned: I'm not known for turning down a cold glass of white. 'My digestion is shot. That tummy bug I picked up in Spain,' I explain.

'Oh bad luck.' She looks down at the floor, embarrassed by the understatement.

I pick the corkscrew out of the drawer and hand it to her. I want things to be as normal as they can be, and that means my girlfriends having a bottle of wine on a Friday night. 'I'm sure Lucy will join you.'

'Right, I've brought some goodies.' Lucy begins to unload a big brown bag of groceries that I had assumed were hers – cakes, yoghurts, chicken slices, broccoli – into my fridge, which is already stuffed full with uneaten tubs of lasagne Mum made.

'That's so sweet of you, you don't need to shop for me.'

Lucy gives me a stern look. She pulls out a bag of nachos, shakes them. 'Don't tell me I don't know all your weak spots.'

I smile, feeling a burst of love for her. 'Thank you, Luce.'

We sit down at the kitchen table. Normally, we'd be

laughing and gossiping about work, telly and boyfriends. Not today. It's not just you I miss, it's my life before this happened.

'Any news?' asks Femi, looking a little scared of my answer.

'Not yet.' I tear open the nachos bag with my teeth and eat them with greedy urgency, as if I'm going to find you at the bottom of the packet.

'Oh,' she says quietly, dropping her eyes reverently to the table. 'I'm sorry.'

'But you've met up with the caseworker again I hear?' Lucy says brightly.

'Yeah, yesterday.' The caseworker, Emma, is a sweet, earnest woman who is liaising between us and the Spanish investigation. I worry that she is a formality rather than anything else, a person put there to make us feel that the authorities are doing something, when they're not doing much.

'Great. That's great,' smiles Femi, doing her damnedest to be positive despite the absence of even the smallest scrap of good news.

'And the charities have been a big help too, haven't they, Gee?' says Lucy, sipping her wine. She has blue painted fingernails. Again, they remind me of my old life before this hurricane ripped through it.

'A lifeline, eh?' says Femi. 'Someone to talk to?' She glances at Lucy. 'Lucy says you are spending a lot of time in chat rooms and things.'

'Well, the physical search has drawn a blank, but I'm sure that there are clues out there. Somewhere. It's a good place to research, you know, talking to people who've experienced something similar, finding out reasons he might have . . . disappeared.'

'Oh?' The atmosphere tightens – even with dear friends there are pockets of awkwardness whenever I talk about my theories about where you are.

'One is that he banged his head on the windsurfing board, or a rock or a boat, and got amnesia. There are a few cases of that.' Just thinking about it makes something in me lift.

'Yeah, you mentioned that before.' Lucy presses a crumb hard on to the table with the pad of her thumb.

'The other is fugue.'

'Fugue? What's that?' Femi looks doubtful.

I lean forward on my elbows, feeling my heart quicken beneath the dirty old T-shirt that I slept in last night. 'A kind of amnesia. Dissociative amnesia, I think that's the word. It's caused by stress. And it means he could *look* like he's acting normally, with full awareness, but when he recovers he will not be able to remember anything he's been doing. Nothing at all! He's not himself, you see.'

'I see,' frowns Femi, not looking like she sees at all. Lucy is biting her blue nails.

'At some point he'll come back to normal consciousness and remember me, London, everything!' My voice comes out squeaky and out of control. 'Well, that's the theory.' I try to sound more measured, but I think it's too late.

'Gee . . .' Lucy touches my arm lightly to interrupt. The features of her face suddenly don't make sense. I can't place her expression at all. 'Please.'

'It's not as rare as you might think, Lucy, especially in men over forty. A lot of missing people are men over forty, did you know that? But, of course, we don't hear about them. The media aren't interested. We just hear about the beautiful lost children.' I'm on a roll. I've been on my own all day with this stuff whizzing around my head and it needs to come out at a hundred miles an hour. 'But the men, the missing middle-aged men, are the ones most likely to be affected by this kind of stress. This fugue. Mostly, they turn up. They really do!'

'I know Rex worked hard, Gina. But he was, I don't know, alpha. He liked working hard. Why would he suddenly not be able to cope?' asks Lucy quietly. 'Married. Successful. Fit. You'd have known if he was in a really bad place, surely?'

'Maybe we can never know everything about someone's life?' I try not to think about the things I omitted to tell you about mine.

'It was in the paper again last week,' says Femi, cheerfully attempting to change the subject. 'You're doing a sterling job of keeping him in the spotlight, Gee.'

'Oh, that's Jake's handiwork. They only ran that story because he works there. No one else is that interested.' My spirits crash again. I'm like this all day, weirdly optimistic one moment, overcome with doom the next. 'He's become an unresolved statistic.'

'Oh, love.' Femi cups my hand in hers.

'I just wish Rex would talk back and tell me where he is. That's all I want. All he needs to do! I just want him to talk back. Then it would all be OK.'

'Talk back?' repeats Lucy, alarmed.

'I feel like I can talk to Rex. That he hears me . . .' I stop because Lucy and Femi are staring at me as if I've stripped off all my clothes standing on the kitchen table. 'It's just that we had a connection, that's all,' I whisper, wishing I hadn't mentioned it and making a mental note not to do so again. I can't expect other people to understand. 'It doesn't matter.'

'A connection?' Femi says slowly, putting her wine glass down.

'We always seemed to know what the other was thinking, that's all.' Admittedly, it sounds less plausible spoken out loud. 'I still feel that connection. That's how I know he's not dead, you see.'

The silence spreads. Something else spreads, too. A gap. Our experiences have always echoed one another's – bad love affairs, comic dates, muddy festivals, power-crazed bosses, cocktails, hangovers – and now they are canyons apart. I am in new territory. Alone in a place where everyone wants to hear me scream. They want me to end the uncertainty for them. I understand this. The uncertainty is the worst part.

'Do you remember that counsellor I mentioned?' Lucy breaks the silence. 'She's meant to be very good, plus she works round the corner. Off Great Portland Street. I really think she would help.' She rummages in her cavernous red handbag and scraps of paper and sweet wrappers fly out of it, a Lil-Let rolls across the kitchen floor. 'I've got her number on my phone, if I can find the damn thing.'

'Lucy, a counsellor won't make this better. Only Rex coming home will make this better.' I try to smile. 'Thanks, though.'

'But she may help you reframe it? Live with it?' Lucy

begins to look upset, her pretty pixie features scrunching with concern.

'I don't want someone telling me how to live without him.'

More silence.

'Gina, it's never a good time to bring it up.' Lucy glances at Femi for support. Femi does a minute head nod. 'But we were wondering whether you've given some thought to doing something that might give a bit of . . . well, closure.'

'Closure? Why do I want closure? Lucy, I'm not a widow. Why is everyone treating me like a widow?'

Lucy frowns, starts biting off her split ends, something she only does when she's very upset.

'I know everyone means well but he's not even been gone three weeks . . .' I stop. Have you really been gone that long? No, it's not long. Three weeks is merely a holiday. It's not even a menstrual cycle! Not-even-three weeks can still be written off, a blip in the course of a long lifetime.

'Oh, Gina.' Femi reaches across the table to grab my hands. 'Sweetheart, the police found Rex's bag in a sand dune. It does *suggest* . . .'

'Just because a sand dune spat up an empty bag doesn't mean he drowned.' My breath comes harder and faster. I remember swimming towards Raf on the beach as if it happened moments ago. The waves crashing into my face, desperately trying to get to the shore, certain they'd found you. But they'd only found the bag. That yellow North Face day bag that you took everywhere. I picture it, neat, pristinely packed, slung around your strong shoulders. It is so normal and familiar, the thought of it reassures me.

'But it does mean he went windsurfing,' says Lucy. 'That he went into the ocean, Gee.'

'His wallet, passport and asthma inhaler were *not* in the bag.' I cling on to this detail like a drowning woman to a life raft. Wherever you went, you took these. Freedom. Money. Breath. 'Nor was the cash he took out the day before. He used to travel with this waterproof pouch on a string that he wore around his neck to protect his valuables. Jake couldn't find that in his belongings either. The chances are he had all that stuff around his neck.'

'Shouldn't you at least consider the possibility that he's drowned, Gee?' Lucy's blue eyes beg me to see sense. 'I know it's terrible, but I'm not sure that holding out hope like this is much better.'

'He's not dead. Not to me. Not to the police. It's an open case.' I am aware on some level that I'm being a pain in the backside, that my friend is only trying to help, but it doesn't make any difference. I've got to make them both understand that you're alive. I know you're alive. 'There's no body.'

'No body,' repeats Femi gloomily, like this is bad news.

'Have you both decided to come round here tonight to make me accept his death or something? Because if you have you're wasting your time, really you are. I'm sorry.'

Lucy looks close to tears now and I feel bad, one giant downer landing in the middle of other people's happy, busy London lives. 'Why is it so hard to imagine that he might have . . . just walked away?'

'Walked away? Gina, the man *adored* you. Worshipped you! He put you on a pedestal. It made us all want to chuck the way he was over you. He was positively Heathcliffian.'

Lucy flushes as she speaks. 'No man has ever been like that over me.'

'Nor me.' Femi sighs. 'He did raise the bar on the romance stakes, that's for sure.'

My eyes fill with tears, remembering those early days. You eating strawberries off my tummy. The car journeys that I wanted to last forever because we had so much to talk about. The rush of connection. The sex. Dawn says we were both insufferable and it was just as well we didn't get out of bed for weeks because she wouldn't have wanted us to come to Sunday lunch anyway. It would have put her off her food. And that's saying something.

You changed how I saw myself. You made me look at my naked body in the mirror afterwards and smile at it straight on, rather than squint at it, head cocked on one side, as if this could shave off a dress size. You made me want to run across meadows naked. It was like winning the lottery. It wasn't that you were rich, Rex – I would have taken you dirt poor – it's that you scooped me up, a broken hearted podgy thing, fed me ginger and kale smoothies and champagne and showed me how to make a fire with a bit of flint and silver bark on a Cornish beach at dusk on my thirtieth birthday.

'It must hurt so much to think he might have run away,' says Femi quietly. 'Even if he had this fugue thing. I'm not sure I could bear the idea of that.'

'It hurts less than thinking he's dead,' I reply.

Lucy sucks in her breath and we sit very still, the kitchen clock pulsing into the hush.

'What does Jake think?' Femi asks eventually. 'He's been

back and forth constantly since it happened, hasn't he? He must have some idea.'

I feel myself tense. Jake. Could he have had something to do with it? Would that explain my niggle that he is holding something back? That niggle won't go away. I stand up and begin pacing the kitchen, as I always do when I think about Jake. It's been so conflicting, half of me wanting to trust him – he's the closest thing I've got to you after all – and the other half on a state of high alert, terrified of missing some vital clue that could reveal he played a part in your disappearance. 'Jake doesn't know,' I manage to say, leaning against the worktop, closing my eyes, suddenly swimmy. 'He doesn't know.'

'Here, sit down.' Lucy pulls out a chair. 'You've gone white as a sheet, Gee.'

I sit down but the chair seems to sway, as if a high spring tide is foaming at the chair legs, trying to suck me out to sea.

'Gina, are you OK?' Lucy's eyes blink frantically, like a doll's. She's trying not to cry. This keeps happening: people come round here to support me and end up sobbing on my sofa.

'Just keep getting these dizzy spells, that's all.'

'Girl, you need to eat. I'm cooking you supper whether you like it or not.' Femi leaps up and starts busying herself with food.

'Were you sick again this morning?' asks Lucy, as we watch Femi wash potatoes purposefully, humming beneath her breath in the way someone who loves to cook can't help.

I nod, my mouth dry. 'Yeah.'

She reaches across, squeezes my hand. 'Gee, I'm not trying to scare you but have you considered the possibility you might be pregnant?'

It takes a moment for the words to sink in. 'Sorry?'

'Pregnant. You're showing all the signs, Gee.'

My hand instinctively checks in with my belly. 'I can't be. I can't possibly be pregnant.'

Seven

Your finger travelled through my breasts to my belly button, coming to rest on the curve of smooth waxed skin on my pubic bone. 'You know what, Gina?'

It was a month before our wedding. I had shed a stone from sex, sushi and happiness. And I had absolutely no idea what you were about to say next. I never did. That was one of the most wonderful things about being with you, that heady mix of familiarity – I felt like I'd known you forever – and mystery.

'I think I might like to see you barefoot and pregnant one day.'

I started, turned towards the wall of floral green wallpaper in your mother's spare room. As I turned, your hand slipped around my waist like a silk sash. How I wished that I'd told you everything then. That I hadn't left it so bloody late. But our relationship had accelerated so fast, bits of undeclared baggage had slipped off its roof.

'Gina?' You sounded hurt.

I turned to face you. 'We haven't really had a proper baby conversation have we?' I said tentatively. Something of an understatement. Looking back, I think we'd both avoided the subject of babies, not wanting to disturb the idyllic status quo. That seems so naïve now.

'That's because you're young.'

'Twenty-nine?'

'Believe me, that's young. You've got loads of time.' You started to look worried. I didn't want you to worry.

'I don't need anything else, just you,' I whispered, the hard ridge of your jaw thrilling beneath my fingers.

Cradling the back of my head with your hand, you bent down so your face was millimetres from mine. Our eyes locked. 'How come you're the coolest woman in London, Gina?'

'Western hemisphere, please,' I grinned, relieved that the sudden heaviness had just as suddenly lightened. 'But don't speak too soon,' I teased. 'You may yet find me gazing at prams and dreaming of mini-Rexes.'

Your hand tightened on the back of my skull. Then your mother called, 'Breakfast!' from the landing. Your grip loosened. Another heady, giddy day began apace. We parked that conversation – like our pasts – at the bedroom door.

Eight

'Oh, it's lovely when you get a bump, isn't it, Dawn?' Mum is smiling too hard. 'I loved it when I started to show.'

I stare down at my stomach in shocked disbelief. How can I be pregnant without you here? How is this possible? Oh my God.

'I always showed.' Dawn snorts, dunking her custard cream in my tea. 'Within hours of getting up the duff I was the size of a small bungalow.'

'You were carrying twins, Dawn,' Mum laughs, refilling Dawn's cup. She's doing her very best to make this as normal as possible. But it's a tough task. 'Here, eat one of these biscuits, Gina. Eating for two now.'

Dawn winks. 'Or three? Twins run in families, sis.'

'Don't. Just don't, Dawn.' I cannot help but wonder if there is a little part of my big sister that is enjoying this. Dawn, married at twenty-four, mother of twins at twenty-six, a size twenty at thirty, still living within five miles of the sleepy village in Derbyshire where we grew up. There's always been this unspoken assumption that I was the one who escaped and left her behind. Now look at me.

'I just can't believe you didn't realise.' Dawn flicks crumbs off pale blue jeans pulled taut over her thighs. 'Sick? Tired? I mean, hello?'

'I just thought I had a bug.' I put my hand on my denim skirt's waistband. Yes, it's tighter than it was, the only bit of me not to shrink in the last few weeks. 'And my periods were so light as to be negligible anyway.'

'Only you, sis.' Dawn pulls out a hairbrush from her bag and starts to pull it through her frizzy strawberry blonde hair, yanking down on a tangle. She twists around to check on the twins, who are fiddling with the buttons of the DVD player. 'Tom! Danny! Paws off.'

'Well, at least it's not some horrible foreign stomach bug.' Mum sips her tea. 'That'd be all you need, eh?'

I don't know how to answer this.

'Get through the first semester and that wretched queasiness stops. You'll be home and dry.' Dawn ties her shoulder-length hair back with a yellow scrunchie. 'You know, everything will be fine with the baby,' she spells out.

'Oh, right.' I stare off into the middle distance.

'Don't look like that. I know what you're thinking. Miscarriage wouldn't be a happy way out of this.' Dawn's eyes soften in her pretty pudding face. 'It really wouldn't.'

I look away, ashamed that it had occurred to me and surprised that Dawn can read me so easily.

'It'll be OK,' she says reassuringly. 'Really, sis.'

'But what do I know about babies?' Whippet jumps on to my knee and pads around in circles, sniffing my belly, as if curious about the developments inside it.

'You're bloody brilliant with kids. The twins totally adore

you. It's actually quite annoying.'

'I don't want to be a single mum, Dawn.'

'You won't be.' Dawn grabs my hand and plays with my fingers, lifting one up, then the other, just like she used to do as a girl. 'You'll have all of us. Me, Gareth . . .'

I let out a small groan. And it's not just at the idea of Gareth acting as a surrogate father. I need my energy to find *you*. No wonder I've found the last few weeks such a struggle. My body has been working overtime.

Dawn crunches me to her giant bosom. 'Gina, it'll be fine.'

'Stop!' cries Mum with unlikely force.

Dawn and I turn to look at her in surprise.

'If Gina really doesn't want the baby we should support her, Dawn, not talk her into it. Gina, if you wanted to . . .' Mum forces the words out with effort. '. . . take a different route.' She blows her nose loudly into a tissue. 'Well, how can anyone judge you in this situation?'

'Mum, don't say that!' Dawn turns on Mum, eyes blazing. 'For Pete's sake, she's *got* to have this baby! It'll break her heart if she doesn't, I swear it will.' She turns to me earnestly. 'Gina, you'll regret it forever. You really will. You totally know that I'm right. I'm so right. Please.'

Bizarre to think that it was only twenty-four hours ago that I came out of the bathroom holding a test stick and Femi, Lucy and I sat watching the kitchen clock, no one daring to breathe. As soon as the blue line appeared, solid and irrefutable, Lucy said, 'I knew it.' I yelled, 'Fuck!' Femi crooned, 'Honey, this will be the best thing that ever happens to you.' Femi's words have been wheeling around my head ever since. Could she be right? Could I really have both the best and the worst thing ever to happen to me occur in a matter of weeks?

'Sis?' asks Dawn, twisting the gold locket at her neck. 'Tell me you'll keep it.'

'I wouldn't have planned it like this,' I say, my voice quivering, as I finally make my decision, right there, sitting at the kitchen table, staring at a custard cream.

'Of course not,' says Mum tearfully, patting my hand. 'Of course not, love. Here have a tissue. Another biscuit.'

'But just this once, I admit that Dawn is right. I could never live with myself if I didn't have this baby.'

Mum embraces me, her cheeks hot with relief. 'Oh, Gina, a baby is *always* a blessing.'

'Rex has got more reason than ever to come back now, hasn't he?' My voice rises in pitch. This is the exciting bit. 'As soon as he finds out about the baby, it'll jolt something in him and he'll come home! I'm going to ask Jake if he can get the newspaper to run another story, "Missing man's wife pregnant!" or something.'

'If you think that might work, love,' says Mum, looking doubtful.

'You're making the right choice, sis.' Dawn nods approvingly, solemnly taking one of my hands, then Mum's. We sit there in silence for a few moments, hands linked, as if we're having a séance around the plate of biscuits.

There is a loud crash. Dawn jumps up. Whippet scatters. 'Danny, stop it! This is Aunt Gina's flat. Oh, I'm sorry. The boys aren't very good in fancy places. Take your eye off them for one sodding minute . . .'

Danny has somehow managed to bind himself to a chair

leg with a long strip of Sellotape. The chair has tipped backwards. He is on his back.

'Danny, why don't you go play with your little cars? Go and play with Tom. And give me the Sellotape. Yes, me. Now. Thank you.' She grabs it off him, helps him up.

'We'll all go together for the appointments, don't you worry,' Mum says. 'There should be a scan soon, eh, Dawn?'

'Rex could be back for the scan,' I say before I think better of it. 'You know, once he hears the news.'

Dawn sucks in a mouthful of air and holds it in her ballooned cheeks. Mum's pursed lips twitch. Your disappearance has made familiar faces look different somehow, as if they're struggling to translate a new emotion.

'He *may* not be back, love,' Mum points out gently. 'He may not hear the news.'

'Well, if he's not back, I've got to be able to do this on my own, haven't I?' I set my jaw determinedly. 'I have to be able to cope on my own, now more than ever.'

Dawn crosses her arms beneath her chest so that her breasts bulge out of the top of her polka dot blouse. 'You really are daft as a brush sometimes, Gina.'

'Now what about Clarice?' Mum switches to the hushed reverential tone that she reserves for when she's discussing a member of the royal family, a dead person, or your mother. 'I bet she's over the moon.'

'I've not told her yet.'

Dawn sucks in her breath. 'Gordon Bennett, better make sure she's sitting down. You do like to keep a secret don't you, sis?'

61

'Secret?' I say, tensing, as another crash ricochets from the twins' direction. What does she mean by that?

'I knew attempting London with Beavis and Butthead was a bad idea,' despairs Dawn. 'I should head back soon before we end up on first name terms with the local A and E. Why don't you come with us, Gina? There's room in the car – if you can bear the screaming and farting – and we'll be able to pack some things up for you in no time. I promise to remove the lizard tank from the spare room.'

'No,' I say a little too quickly. 'No, thank you. It's just . . .' I hesitate, unsure how to explain. 'If Rex comes home, he'll come back to the flat. What if he comes back and I'm not here?'

There is another intake of breath. I may as well have suggested I'm expecting Elvis Presley to drop round for tea.

'It's a big if after all this time, love.' Mum twists her wedding ring around her finger. 'But I suppose miracles *can* happen. And if there's anything that life has taught me it's that people, well, people do the strangest things. Especially men like Rex. You know, the . . . enigmatic type.'

This is not a compliment. But the things that make my family wary about you make me love you more: your brooding intensity, your inability to suffer fools, drink tea or watch trash TV, even your darker moods, the way you withdraw sometimes – sink back just out of reach – as if conserving something precious inside of you. It is in such dignified contrast to the loud melodramatic emoting I've grown up with, the clumsy abundance of noise, love, fat and food.

'Come back to Derbyshire with me, Gina.' Dawn is

starting to look annoyed by my resistance. 'You need to be looked after. For Pete's sake, I *want* to look after you, sis.'

'Oh, Dawn, I can't. I need to wait for him here . . .' I put my hand on my tummy, remembering that morning at your mother's house, the flock green wallpaper, your hand circling my waist. '. . . barefoot and pregnant.'

Nine

'Pregnant?' Clarice tries to still her hands on the kitchen table, fingers curled inwards like crab claws. '*Mon Dieu.*'

Today my belly just looks swollen. Like it could be a storage tank for my tears, or trapped wind. I still cannot believe a baby is growing inside there. 'Yes.'

'There's no doubt about it?'

'I've done six tests, Clarice.' It hits me that it's the first time Clarice and I have ever met up alone, the only time we've been in a room together without you or Jake there too. And that she still makes me feel like your date, probably one that won't stay the course. 'The doctor thinks I'm eleven weeks pregnant.'

'*Merde*,' she mutters under her breath. 'Well, this is news, isn't it?'

We stare at each other in mutual bewilderment.

'This is a lot to cope with, Gina.'

'I know,' I say, not sure if she's talking about me or her. Clarice looks thinner than ever in a pale pink tweed jacket, one of her Italian jester print silk scarves wound twice around her elegant neck, her hair blow-dried to hide the thin shiny facelift scars behind her ears. But her grooming is at odds with the strain beneath her eyes. She looks ten years older than when I last saw her, with you, which was when we went to Kent for lunch and her dog dumped a bloodied hedgehog on the stone kitchen floor. Unlike my mum, who would have bolted from the room screaming, arms waggling in the air, Clarice coolly raised one eyebrow, looked at the dog and said, 'Serge, is this a cry for attention?'

She smiles tersely. 'Babies never do come at the right time.'

'That's what my mum says.' I cross my arms across my chest. My breasts throb like bruises.

'And you will manage, Gina. You are that type of English girl,' she adds, making me feel like a sturdy Shetland pony. Clarice plays with the string of small gold beads at her throat, stares out of the kitchen window to the street. 'No, we must not see this as bad news. We must not.'

My eyes start to swim with tears and, not wanting to cry in front of your mother, I stand up to hide my face. 'More tea, Clarice?'

'No, thank you. No more tea.'

'A biscuit?'

'A biscuit?' she repeats, managing to sound both offended and confused. 'No, no thank you.'

I put the kettle on anyway and reuse my mint teabag. Our conversation, strained at the best of times, feels like it's dried up altogether.

'Now, there are other things we must talk about,' she says, flicking invisible dust off her sleeve.

'Yes, of course,' I say, thinking she's referring to the baby.

'I went to see . . .' She flushes slightly. 'A medium. A spiritual lady.'

I drop the teabag into the sink. *Clarice visited a medium?*

'We have to try everything now, Gina,' she says, sounding slightly defensive. 'We cannot rely on these useless Spanish police.'

'What . . . what did she say?' I stutter, amazed.

Her eyes dart, full of light. 'That Rex is alive, Gina. He is alive!'

'Oh my God! Have you told Jake? What does—'

Clarice shakes her head. 'Jake, my dear, is a rationalist. He thinks this lady is a charlatan.'

'Well, he would,' I say before I can stop myself. 'What else did she say? Where is he? Where is Rex?'

Clarice's face clouds over. 'Ah, well, she is not sure about that. The signal is weak, she says. But he *is* alive. Somewhere hot.' She flaps her hand in front of her face to emphasise the point.

'A bit vague,' I point out.

'Yes,' she concurs. 'But it has given me fresh hope.' She smiles fraily, exposing neat rows of pearled teeth, receding gums. 'So I've hired a private detective.'

Hope flares inside of me too, just when I need it most. 'You have? Oh, Clarice, thank you!' It's something I suggested a few weeks ago but wasn't able to finance on my own.

'Yes, a man, a man in Spain . . .' Her voice trails off as if she hasn't quite got the energy to finish the sentence. 'We shall see. And we must pray to Saint Anthony, too, of course.'

I want to hug her. But as my body leans towards hers, she bends minutely away and tightens the scarf around her neck.

One of those silences that I always dread with your mother starts to spread between us. And I feel bad because I know she's suffering. I just don't know how to reach out to her, crack that icy surface.

Even though you always said she isn't posh, just French, she *is* posh, Rex, and she's lived in England for thirty-five years so it's no excuse.

'He'll be happy about the baby anyway, won't he?' I say in a pitiful attempt to pull her into cosier granny territory.

She pauses for a little longer than is comfortable. 'Will he, Gina?'

I'm so startled by this I almost spit out my mouthful of mint tea all over the table.

'Yes, yes, of course he will,' she corrects quickly.

'We weren't trying for a baby, Clarice. It was an accident.'

'And you two were getting on before he left?' This is not the first time she's asked this.

'We were very happy, Clarice.' I am scared that she blames me, that I won't be able to convince her.

'So I am to be a *grand-maman*,' she says after an age.

Grand-maman. The word suits her better than granny. 'You are, Clarice.'

She does her best to smile. 'So you will have to see the doctor? And scans. You have lots of scans nowadays, I'm told. I never had anything like that when I was pregnant. Everyone left you alone to get on with it in those days.' She taps the tips of her painted nails on the side of her teacup.

'Was Rex's a . . . a good birth?' I ask, lamely angling for maternal common ground.

'No, it was terrible. Terrible! I hated giving birth, awful

bloody business. It took days. I was certain I was going to die.'

I cross my legs with foreboding.

She raises one waspish eyebrow. 'What do you think, Gina, a boy or a girl?'

'I've got a hunch it's a boy.'

'Oh.' Her features slacken with disappointment. 'A boy. A boy needs a father.'

'So does a girl.' I think about my dad. Always there. Solid. Slightly rusty. Can move fast if he has to. Like the wheelbarrow in his beloved shed.

'After Ronald died it was very difficult for Rex.'

I jolt at the unexpected mention of your late father. Usually it's out of bounds. Every time I'd tried to talk about it with you, you closed slowly, softly, like a clam under running cold water. Clarice has never spoken his name aloud to me. There aren't even any photographs of him on the walls of her house. If it weren't for your existence there wouldn't be any proof of his.

'Being a mother. It's not an easy job, Gina.'

'You did a good job with Rex.'

'I can't claim any credit for his success,' she says dismissively.

I wonder again about your childhood, what it must have been like growing up with a mother who was struggling to cope after the death of your father, a mother whom, you say, only felt happy again after she met Michael and had Jake. You were ten when Jake was born.

'He was spoilt, I fear.' She looks wistful. 'I never said no to Rex.'

Spoilt isn't a word that comes to my mind, but I don't say this.

'It was different with Jake, you see. It took me a child to practise on. By the time I had Jake I was much better at being a mother. Much better.' She shakes her head and an emotion I can't translate flickers in her eyes. 'The first baby is a mystery, Gina. It really is.'

'Maybe it's just that Rex and Jake are such different characters?' I suggest, gently.

'Oh, so different, *c'est vrai, c'est vrai.*' She gazes out of the window. I wait patiently for her to expand. 'Jake. Easy baby. Easy boy. He never got ill. He slept from the start. Just a gorgeous fat thing who was always smiling. He's not that different now, eh?' Her features lighten and she allows herself a small laugh. 'No, Jake never causes me any worries. But Rex . . . Rex . . .' Her forehead scrunches. 'He was a little difficult, Gina.' Without warning, Clarice screeches the chair across the floor, stands up and snatches at her handbag with birdlike hands. 'No, I cannot talk about him like this! I cannot be here now that he's gone!'

'Oh, I'm so sorry, Clarice. I didn't mean to upset you.' I am mortified, wondering what I've said wrong.

'Here, talking about the past. No good comes from talking about the past. It is too much for me. Too much.' She touches her flushed forehead with her hands, like a woman about to swoon. 'I'm sorry, Gina. I must go.'

'We can go to the café?'

'No, I must catch my train. I really must catch my train.' She knots her silk scarf tightly around her elegant neck. After two quick, dry kisses on either cheek, she's gone, leaving behind a small cloud of Chanel No. 5 and a storm of question marks.

Ten

Why isn't there someone I can ring and scream: Stop! My husband has vanished! Stop it all, now! Instead there is a computer somewhere in the Far East spitting out letters offering overdrafts with appalling interest rates and fining me for being late to pay something I didn't know I owed in the first place.

Dawn says I must get my house in order before I get any fatter. Practical things, she says, are only going to get harder. It doesn't help that you dealt with the money side, Rex. That you were so bloody good at it. And now you've gone. Well, I must stay on top of it until you get home. That is how I'll fill the hours of today.

I tear open a letter from the pile of unopened post on the sideboard and try to focus on the jumping columns of numbers. OK, the joint account. Overdrawn. I open another letter. Again, overdrawn. Not good. What are all these direct debits? Standing orders? So many.

I have a vague recollection that somewhere there is a list of our outgoings on a spreadsheet, some kind of breakdown of our hugely complicated finances. That would help a lot.

You've shown it to me before. Where have I seen it? I poke around the living room, picking up magazines, scanning the bookshelves, rummaging in the lower drawer among the Swiss pens, designer clothing receipts and unpaid parking tickets. Then I remember: it's on a laptop.

You have three laptops, I remember, not two: an old one you talked about throwing out but never did, 'steam power' you call it, the one you used for basic household stuff like the Waitrose shop. Retarded of me to forget it. Straight after you'd disappeared, Jake took away your two swanky Macs to look into their Internet search history. But you'd wiped it from both computers. Jake's techie mate at the newspaper promised he could still unearth the cookies, whatever they are, dig up your online trail, but you'd gone too deep even for him, deleting things on the hard drive. I explained to Jake that this was not hugely unusual: you were always anxious about Internet security, hated the thought of companies or search engines secretly building up information on you and using it for profit.

It takes me a while to find steam power. You always were ingenious in your careful storage, outwitting the burglar that never came. I finally discover it at the very bottom of your desk drawer, hidden away in its padded case beneath copies of fitness magazines. I turn it on. After an age it chugs into life.

I'm loathe to touch it at first, scared that I'll open up the chunky black casing and memories will flutter out like butterflies. All those small, quiet domestic moments we have lost: me, flicking through rival catalogues, you shifting columns of numbers on one of your spreadsheets, the smell

72

of freshly ground coffee, the toot of black cabs beneath our window, the rattle of the shop's grille coming down in the evening. Do you remember when we had sex on the office chair? I ended up face down in this laptop, my nose crushing into F, T and G.

Password? The password to steam power – I didn't have the passwords to the others, the techie guy had to unpick them – is written down in my pink notebook, thank goodness. You can't go wrong with paper. I find the notebook, tap in Ronald349* – your father's name, of course – and all your folders flip up immediately. Of course, I cannot resist dropping in on the Find Rex Adler facebook page. In recent days Jake has discouraged me from spending too much time on the Net. In the absence of facts have come theories. There was a suicide theory circulating last week, the week before something involving you faking your own death and moving to Caracas.

There are more messages since I last looked. The last one was sent last night: 'Is this your latest bet, Rex? Shall we hedge on it?' I don't recognise the person – 'ballfastdude' – who posted and consider reprimanding but don't have the nerve. People either loved or hated you, and you felt the same about them. And you weren't good at hiding the fact. It was one of your best and worst traits, that brutal honesty. It was also one of the things that made me feel safe: I knew where I was with you, Rex. And it was the thing that made me feel most guilty: I couldn't ever claim that honesty.

I click on to your personal Facebook page. Your unbearably poignant last posting is as it was the day before you left: 'Off to Tarifa for some serious wave action. So long, desk dwellers!' I scroll down to your other entries. How cocky your online voice is. It doesn't sound like you at all, not the Rex I know, the Rex that washed my knickers in Dorset when we went camping and I discovered I'd forgotten to pack any. The Rex who would paint my toenails before sucking each one to check 'the paintwork'.

Your mail folder is stuffed. Two hundred and fifty-two new messages since you disappeared, messages that Jake tells me he is monitoring carefully. I click on a few of them. Many are spam, messages from fake banks and outdoor gear shops, but there are also messages from your mates and work colleagues, jokey and disbelieving – 'Where the fuck are you?' 'Enough now, adventure boy'– and getting progressively more desperate. Then . . . what's this? Five emails from Jake, sent last week. Last week? I read them, heart starting to skitter.

Dear Rex
Everyone is going out of their fucking minds. Whatever it is that's made you go, we can sort it together. Please just come home. Call me. We miss you so much. Gina needs you.
Love, Jake

Shakily I open up other emails sent by Jake. They're similar, pleading for you to come home, for any kind of contact. Relief shudders through me in waves. Firstly, they prove that he believes that you could have run away. I'm not going bonkers. They also prove that Jake wasn't responsible for your disappearance otherwise he wouldn't have written them. Why would he?

74

A huge weight slips off my shoulders. Not being able to wholly trust Jake has been terrible, I realise. I need to believe in him. I need to believe he can find you. Oh, thank God. Jake is one of the good guys.

Charged now, I start clicking frantically around your screen as if I might be able to find you, crouched behind an icon or a download. I press something and a song by Manic Street Preachers blasts out.

They never did find Richey Edwards, did they?

Pushing the dark thought from my mind, I nose through your music downloads, hypnotised by the songs that are the soundtrack of our short blast of a marriage, the car journeys down the M40, the late night dinners. I close my eyes and lean back in the chair, listening to that Killers song you used to play over and over. And we are driving, window down, to my parents' house last summer, you such an intense, fast, brilliant driver, without a point on your licence. The sun is shining. I am gazing out of the window at other cars filled with arguing couples and whining kids and lonely people picking their noses, and I feel like the luckiest woman in the world, zooming away from that other bleak, cruel car journey that marked the end of my last relationship.

The track ends like a goodbye. I sit there quietly for a moment, lost in memories, missing the song, missing you. I click open a new folder.

It is then that I see it.

Eleven

'We must call the private detective right now!' I grab the frayed sleeve of Jake's blue corduroy jacket. 'What's his number, Jake?'

'I will phone him later today.' Jake unclips his cycling helmet. His hair is spiky with sweat and rain. His takes his misted-up glasses off his nose, wipes them on his sleeve.

'Later? Now! How can you be so bloody laid back about it? The document on the computer is addressed to *me*, Jake. It changes everything! He talks about "the still point in all the madness", for God's sake. What madness? Oh, Jake, this shows that something was—'

'Gina, calm down. One step. Please, one step at a time, OK?' He loosens the collar of his blue shirt. 'I'm not dismissing this, really I'm not, but it can wait.' He holds my arms so I face him directly and he has all of my attention. 'This is the day of your scan, Gina, don't you remember?'

I stare at him blankly. The scan, the scan . . .

'The hospital appointment. The scan of the baby?' he repeats slowly. 'You told me last week it was today. At lunchtime. It's almost lunchtime, Gina. I thought I'd pop round and see if you fancied some company?'

'Why would he leave me a list like that if he didn't have an inkling that something was going to happen? What if he's got enemies or something?'

'Gina, we need to leave.'

'I want you to phone the detective first.' I can feel my eyes stinging and know that floods of tears are seconds away. 'Please, Jake.'

He shakes his head. 'You'll miss your appointment.'

'I don't care. I'm not going unless you call him first.'

'Get a grip, Gina,' he says with surprising force. For a moment he reminds me of you. 'This is more important. Right now, the baby is more important, OK?' He opens the front door, presses his hand on my lower back and steers me through it. 'I know you are determined to go on your own. But you're in no state, Gina. I'm coming with you.'

I compare the bump sizes of the other women in the hospital waiting room. The whole world is represented here, every nationality and colour, shape and size. The pre-natal ward is a Noah's Ark for pregnant mothers. Some bumps are low, watermelons hanging beneath sweaters. Others are hard, high balls. Quite a few of the women are so fat they are enormous spheres of flesh. It's a wonder they can even walk up the stairs. Others don't look pregnant at all from the back. There are women who are pregnant and, confusingly, also have teeny babies. How can this be possible?

I fidget on the hard plastic seat, impatient to get this over with and speak to the detective and the caseworker. I've already given blood, attempted to pee into a teeny plastic pot

– imagine trying to aim into a thimble from a great height – and then had to put it in an undignified basket on the desk, the label wet with urine, in front of everyone. My appointment was meant to happen two hours ago. Everything's running horrendously late, but no one seems to think there is anything unusual about this. The nurses behind the reception desk roll their eyes when anyone asks how much longer they have to wait.

Would I be here if you were here? Probably not. You'd have splashed out on somewhere swanky and private for your firstborn. I'd be in The Portland Hospital, peeing into a crystal jar.

Right now, I'd prefer to be here, I think. I'm no less or more important – or tragic – than anyone else in this room. Anyway, your smarter friends always did make me feel a little nervous, especially the women with their gleaming impenetrable smiles and just-so tailoring. I could never shake the feeling that they thought I was a gold digger, a young floozy whoring her youth for your money. They're the kind of people who go private, I imagine, them and the celebs, people who think that what is good enough for us lot isn't good enough for them.

I glance over at Jake. He studiously ignores me lest I try to bring up the subject of the detective again, taps emails out on his phone. His long legs protrude into the crowded waiting room, his feet comically outsize in their gnarled brown suede brogues, a shoelace undone, red stripy socks. When I pointed out a beautiful pair of brown suede brogues in Church's window, you said that such shoes were only for Italians or gay men.

'Gina Adler?' A nurse scans the waiting room.

I freeze. The terror races back; the baby has gone, vanished like you. I've heard of that before, women who were pregnant and then go to the scan and discover that they are mysteriously no longer pregnant, that the foetus has just disappeared, the body reabsorbing it back into its tissues. As if it had never existed at all.

'Gina Adler?' the nurse repeats, brisker now. I squeeze my plastic water beaker too hard. It crushes and spills water on my skirt.

'Gina, it's your turn.' Jake tugs me up by my forearm as if I were an old person in a wheelchair. 'Are you sure you don't want me to come in with you?'

Women turn to stare at us curiously. Fear tightens my throat. Suddenly I'm not so sure at all.

The nurse, a small, wiry lady in her fifties, beckons us into one of the side rooms. It is strip-lit like a grocer's and has a window framing a view of a metal air conditioning vent on a brick wall opposite. The nurse pulls a long roll of rough blue paper over the bed and tells me to lie on it. Without asking she pulls up my T-shirt to expose my rounded hill of pale belly. Heat rises on my cheeks: I feel exposed like this in front of Jake, displaying all the fleshy consequences of our passionate love making. Jake looks away, sits down on the red plastic chair next to me, focusing his attention on the screen.

'First time?' asks the nurse breezily, squeezing blue gel on a probe-like scanner attached to a machine.

I nod nervously, hoping she won't ask any more questions.

'Bit cold, sorry,' she says, pressing the scanner into my stomach.

I gasp with the unexpected firmness of her push, and stare at the screen. Nothing. More nothing. She twists the scanner painfully. Suddenly there are shapes flickering in its darkness. White lines. Stars in the black screen sky. Is that it? Is *that* . . . ? The nurse frowns and presses harder, making me gasp again. She is clearly looking for something. And whatever she's looking for is not there.

Panicking, I turn to Jake, but he is staring at the screen, clicking his thumbnail against his front teeth. The nurse keeps pushing into me, searching for the lost thing. The baby has vapourised. 'What's wrong?' I ask.

She gives me a harassed smile. 'Sometimes it can be hard to find the heartbeat. Everyone's different.' It's another few agonizing moments before her frown clears. 'Aha. Alright, monkey. There. The heartbeat, see.' She points at something flashing on the screen and starts moving the scanner around more gently. 'Heart, head, rump.'

'That's my baby?' I can hardly believe it. 'It's there? Alive?'

'Baby didn't want us to find it.'

I glance at Jake again but he is still studying the screen intently, looking like he is concentrating on a difficult subtitled film. I wonder how he can be so unmoved. It's his nephew after all.

I turn back to the screen and the image suddenly comes into focus. Our baby! It's got your long legs, Rex. The head. A heart beating. Wow. I could sit here all day in this little white room with its reassuring beeps and screens. It's proof of life.

'He waved! Did you see that?' I wipe away a tear.

'Saying hi to his daddy.' The nurse gives Jake a quick, slightly concerned smile.

Jake doesn't turn round or say anything but I see his jaw stiffen.

'No, it's not . . .' And then I stop, because where the hell do you start?

Something flickers over the nurse's face then, some kind of recognition. I guess she's heard it all before, or thinks she has. 'Due December sixteenth,' she says smartly, writing something in my notes, once she's finished scanning. 'Just in time for Christmas.'

'Jesus.'

She frowns, looks up. 'Something wrong?'

'That sounds quite soon, that's all.'

'They don't take that long to cook.' She starts writing in my notes again. 'Don't worry. By the time you get there you'll feel like you've been pregnant for decades. You'll be happy to meet baby.'

The enormity of it begins to properly sink in. I am going to give birth to another human being in *six* months' time. Oh my God. We've not got long to find you, Rex. Not long at all.

The nurse offers me a small black and white printout of the scan. 'See you at twenty weeks, Gina.'

'That's *it*?'

'For the moment.' She waits for us to leave. 'That's it.'

'I just go away and . . .'

'Be pregnant,' she smiles, as if nothing could be simpler, and opens the door wider.

Outside Jake and I stand by the hospital's black wrought iron gates, ready to go our separate ways. Crowds surge past us. I clutch the scan photo tightly to my chest in case the downwind from a bus whips it out of my hands. 'Thanks,

Jake. It . . . you being there . . .' I falter, feeling an unfamiliar glow of happiness. 'Thank you.'

'No, thank you, Gina.' He smiles shyly, his eyes full of wonder. 'Actually it kind of blew my mind.'

Twelve

If Anything Ever Happens to Me.doc

Dear Gina

If you are reading this I guess I might be dead. (If not, what are you doing snooping round my computer, darling?) I hope you are OK and not suffering too much. What can I say? I love you to bits. You are the woman who restored my faith in women. You have the sexiest bottom, the filthiest laugh and terrible taste in music. I am not nearly good enough for you but I do totally adore you.

You also know I'm a rubbish writer and terrible at emotional stuff so I'm not going to go on. This letter is about boring practical things, I'm afraid. You may remember that I told you that when my dad died intestate Mum was left bewildered so I always thought it sensible to have something written down, just in case. (You have many talents but administrative skills are not one of them.) So to help you on your way, attached are my bank details, insurance, boring details about bonds and ISAs, flat deeds, will, all the stuff that I never bother your pretty head with.

What can I say? I love you, Gina. You are my free-spirited red headed woman, the still point in all the madness. Be strong. Don't mope. We hate mopers, remember? Don't wallow in self-pity. You have your life ahead of you. I know that you will be fine. Dust yourself down. Work hard, spend less and don't drink so much white wine.

Love always, Rex

Thirteen

I am eighteen weeks pregnant. The baby flutters like a butterfly in my tummy. This feels amazing. I also have piles, which does not. And nor does this maternity frock.

'Lots of room for the belly.' Lucy cocks her head on one side, hand on her hip.

'I look like a pie chaser, Lucy.'

'You look gorgeous.'

The changing room smells of sweat and something else that I've never smelled before even though it's coming from me. It's a sweet hormonal smell that feels too intimate to share with a friend in a confined space. I really want to leave. All my life I've been one of those women who loved stepping into that wall of heat and music that separates a shop from the pavement. Now the shop environment feels alien, almost threatening. I'm only here to show Lucy, Dawn and Mum that I am not in denial about the pregnancy. That I'm not just focusing on the search for you and spending all my free time in pyjamas with tea stains down the front, Googling stories about missing people and re-reading that 'If Anything Ever Happens to Me' document.

'Maternity trousers?' Lucy holds up the world's most unflattering trousers.

'Rather die.'

Lucy laughs. 'You can't walk around much longer with the top button of your jeans undone, Gee.'

'Can I have a peek, love?' Mum yanks back the curtains, presses her fleece of curly grey hair through the gap. 'Oh, you *do* look preggers in that, Gina,' she marvels, as if she didn't quite believe in my pregnancy beforehand. 'Look at your bosom!'

I tug up the neckline. Old women have bosoms. Now I have a bosom. 'Shut the curtain. I don't think the whole shop wants to see me.'

Mum shuts the curtain, but with herself the wrong side of it. It's even more cramped in here now. 'She'll be needing a new bra too,' Mum asides to Lucy, while I struggle out of the dress. 'It's such a shame Dawn gave away all her maternity clothes. I told her not to.' She raises an eyebrow. 'Lots of stuff from Next, you know, very smart.' There is a rattle of metal hoops on the rail as she pulls back the curtain again, exposing me to a clutch of startled shoppers. 'Any recommendations for maternity bras, Dawn?' she bellows across the shop floor.

'Debenhams!' Dawn barks back. 'Good for the big cup sizes.'

'I'm not sure I've got the energy left for bra shopping, Mum,' I whimper.

Mum looks disappointed. 'Really? It's been an age since we've all been shopping together. Just us girls. It's so nice.'

Dawn shoves her huge face through the curtain, grinning

like a loon. 'You see. We get our hands on you at last, Gina.'

Dawn always complained that since marrying, I never saw enough of my family. We just hunkered down together in our own little world, didn't we? We thought we had plenty of time to do the family thing.

'Time for a cream tea then,' Mum says brightly, as if a cream tea will solve everything. 'Dawn's booked somewhere dead posh.'

The duck egg blue tearoom on the fourth floor of Fortnum and Mason, Piccadilly. It's busy: tourists, mothers and daughters, groups of old birds with stiffly set hair combatively eyeing petit fours, immaculate waiting staff pouring ropes of tea with unnecessary wrist flourish. On our linen-draped table is a tiered cake stand full of perfectly round scones, pots of stiff white cream and the reddest jam I've ever seen. I'd like to say that I'm missing you so much that I cannot touch a thing, but the pavement pounding and dressing room struggles have brought my appetite back with a vengeance. It's as if every cell in my body is howling for calories and I can't consume fast enough. Mum's eyes shine watching me in the way new mothers do when their toddlers eat a green vegetable. 'Have you shown Dawn the scan pic, love?'

'No! She has not. Naughty. Get it out, sis.' I click open my purse and slide out the thin magic square of shiny paper. The starlit galaxy of my womb.

'So amazing,' sighs Lucy, hand at her throat. She's not really the type to go soppy at a scan picture but I guess we're all in new territory now. 'Is that the head? I cannot work it out!'

'No, that's the foot.'

'That's the hand, right?' says Dawn, frowning, head cocked to one side.

'The knee.'

'Oh yes!'

'It's so . . . so formed, isn't it? I thought it would be like a blob alien this early,' Lucy says with a grin.

Dawn wrinkles her nose. I think she'd rather she liked Lucy less. She's exactly the kind of skinny blonde London girl that Dawn distrusts. But Lucy charms everyone eventually.

'The baby is such a blessing, Gina,' Mum sighs, as if it's the first time she's said this today rather than the fifth.

'More importantly, it's got long legs,' notes Dawn, glancing down at mine, which are notably stumpy. 'I wonder if it'll get your red barnet.'

'And a button nose! Isn't that a nose?' says Mum. A woman on the adjacent table glances over, recognises what we're looking at and smiles. Mum does a proud bottom-shuffle in her chair, delighted that the woman has noticed. 'It *is* the nose.'

Part of me catches their joy, but the other half of me feels as if this happy tableau – a scene played out all over the world: mothers, sisters and friends poring over the first baby scan – is so perilously delicate it could collapse at any moment, like that hopeless chocolate sponge I made for your last birthday, the one with an enormous air bubble in the middle of it. The fragility of it all scares me.

This keeps happening. It's as if my life is taking place on either side of a screen. At the front, in public, I manage to maintain some normality and react in the way a pregnant

88

woman might to all the milestones. In my brain's backroom I'm thinking about you, the same thoughts looping over and over, trying and failing to make sense of it all.

'Have you shown Clarice, love?' Mum asks.

'Sorry?' I pull myself out of my thoughts.

'Have you shown Clarice the scan?'

'No, I don't think she's really the type to be into scan pictures.' I fold the photo up and slide it back into my purse, remembering the bizarre way she'd fled from the flat the last time I'd seen her.

'Nonsense! It's her grandchild. It'll be a real comfort. Poor woman.' Mum shakes her head. 'To lose a son,' she mutters under her breath. 'Goodness.'

To lose a son.

It hits then. The white-noise fuzz behind my forehead. The thudding panic. It's all wrong, wrong, wrong: the plates, the jam, the cream, the tablecloth, the conversation, the *jokes*. What the hell am I doing eating scones when you're missing? I have to hold on to the edge of the table to stop myself running out of the tearoom and searching for you, somewhere, anywhere, or sprinting to the airport and jumping on the next flight to Spain.

'You OK, Gee?' whispers Lucy, concerned.

I try to smile to stem the scream. It fools no one. A solemnity breaks over the table where a few moments ago there was joy. This keeps happening too, the jolt from everyday benignity to horror.

'What does Jake think about those notes on the computer?' Dawn asks, her blue eyes beadily watchful over the top of her teacup. 'The ones you keep talking about.'

I take a deep breath, begin to reign in my panic. 'Jake thinks that there's a . . . a danger we read too much into it,' I falter.

'I'm beginning to think that man's the voice of reason,' says Mum, dabbing at the corner of her mouth with a napkin. 'Back in Spain again, is he, love?'

'Meeting the private detective,' Lucy says, helping me out. The words 'private detective' sound absurd and Scooby Dooish when spoken out loud in Fortnum's. 'And he's doing a fresh trawl of local hospitals, homeless hostels, that sort of thing, isn't he, Gina?'

Mum crushes her hand to her mouth at the word hospital. 'Oh, oh dear.'

To my relief, I begin to ground again, my heart slows a little. Hopefully I am not going to be the first person to have a scone-fuelled panic attack.

'Well, if a journalist and a private detective can't find him, I don't know who can!' snorts Dawn, spraying a fine mist of scone crumbs over the table.

I roll my eyes. 'He's a film reviewer, Dawn. He sits in darkened rooms in Soho.'

'Well, you never know,' says Mum doubtfully, exchanging a quick glance with Dawn. They both clearly think that they do know. That you've been digested by a great white. She grabs my hand. 'We're all still praying for Rex, love. Nana, Aunt Jools, Dad.'

'Dad's about as religious as my teacup.'

Dawn sniffs disapprovingly. She has started going to church to get the twins into an acclaimed Church of England primary school, and has found religion to her liking.

'Have another scone, love,' says Mum, offering the plate. 'You must eat. Eat and sleep and pray. You really do need to put your feet up too. For the baby's sake. Oh, I wish you weren't going back to work, I really do.'

'I'm going to work until the due date.'

'What?' she yelps, as if I'm suggesting touring Bhutan on a Harley. 'Work at the catalogue until the due date? You can't possibly!'

'I will go nuts just hanging out in the flat, Mum. I've tried it. I need to get back to Grey Home.'

'I don't know about that,' Mum says, still looking appalled. 'I really don't.'

'Apart from anything else, I need the money.'

'You need money? Oh, bloody hell, sis.' Dawn reaches for her bag. 'How much do you need? All you had to do was ask, honestly. You are so bloody clandestine sometimes. I'm your sister, for Pete's sake.'

I blush. 'No, no, I wasn't asking for money, Dawn.'

'You're sure?'

'Absolutely.'

'Well, I'll pay for this spread. No arguments.'

Mum is staring at me intensely as if something has just dawned. 'Gina, they haven't stopped Rex's salary, have they?'

I stare down at my bitten nails. I've been stupidly applying Gina's philosophy of finance to our growing debt: don't think about it too much, it goes away. Only it hasn't.

'Gina?'

'They will pay me a quarter of Rex's salary until the end of the month on compassionate grounds.'

'Oh my God. What then, sis?' Dawn is frozen, a lump of scone protruding from her cheek. Lucy is biting off her split ends.

I take a deep breath. 'It is . . . suspended.'

'Flaming Nora,' cries Mum, crushing her napkin to her mouth. 'All we need.'

Fourteen

Mandy

Mandy tried not to think about spiders as she groped into the darkness. Her fingertips walked the walls, searching for the light switch. Only once she'd found it did she dare heave herself up through the hatch door and slam-dunk on the grimy attic floor. She looked around her. The small, gloomy space was crammed with boxes. 'Sorting the loft' was one of those chores that sat permanently at the bottom of a never-ending to-do list. There were stacks of cardboard boxes – Ryan's outgrown clothes, toys, photos, spare china – some labelled but most not.

There was only one box here that really mattered. Where the hell was it?

Wanting to get out of the spider zone as quickly as possible, Mandy searched furiously, ripping open taped boxes with the sharp edge of her long fingernails, breaking one in the process. She got more frantic as the minutes ticked past: she hadn't much time. She needed to pick up Ryan from nursery in forty-five minutes and had a terror of being late.

Ever since her parents had died, that was her recurring nightmare: something happening to her. No one being able to contact Mark. Ryan waiting at school for someone to pick him up who never came. There was no safety net in her life, none at all.

Oh where was it? She hadn't touched the box since she'd sealed it, knowing it needed to be buried until the time came. And now was the time. It was like a demented itch: she needed to see it. Where the hell would she have stashed it? Somewhere no one would easily find it, that's where. Somewhere no one would accidentally stumble across it and ask awkward questions. One of those easily forgotten 'safe' places. Damn it.

Every time she closed her eyes she saw Rex. When she awoke, random unconnected memories that she'd long forgotten would shimmer in front of her, their shards as clear and sharp as the wine glass she'd dropped that morning: Rex wiping the contents from her phone when he'd got jealous in the pub that time; Rex raising his hand to her when she called him a 'fucked up little rich kid', and that awful pause before he slammed it into the kitchen wall when she thought he might actually hit her; Rex eating strawberries off her tummy that flowery summer's day in Cornwall, making her feel like a goddess; Rex saying that he couldn't give her everything. She knew the deal. He couldn't do, could never do, what she asked. She always demanded too much, pushed things too far, misread the rules. Who did she think she was?

Damn him.

Was that it? Her eyes alighted on a box pushed right against the eaves, not an old cardboard box like the others, but a blue metal box bought expressly for its purpose. Spotting a patch of rusted metal on the lid, she yanked it out, desperately hoping that the contents hadn't been spoiled. She carried it down the stepladder, balancing it on her head. She crouched to her knees on the landing, lifting the lid with shaking hands. The hinges squeaked, as if reluctant to release its contents to close scrutiny.

As the lid fell back, she exhaled a low moan of recognition.

Fifteen

You and the baby's lives exist in parallel. It's just that every week that passes I get closer to meeting the baby and further away from the last time I saw you. Sadness and happiness yank me in opposite directions. I'm super aware of this at the moment as Femi has subscribed me to a pregnancy calendar that emails me every week with exciting updates of the baby's developments in the womb. In this, its twenty-first week, it can hear things outside the womb. Can you believe that, Rex? It can hear!

I'm not exactly productive now; I spend so much time thinking about you, reading those baby emails and, last but not least, going to the toilet. I never stop peeing! It's a miracle that this morning I finally managed to finish designing the children's curtains – boats, a turtle motif. That set me off, of course. It was the turtle, you, seen from under the water as you paddled on a surfboard. Sometimes it's the little things.

My phone rings, startling me.

'Hello, Grey Home design team.' Out of the corner of my eye I catch Hector sauntering out of Martin's office dressed in his trademark unstructured navy suit, startling black eyebrows and tousle of wavy silvering hair. He is tanned from Hong Kong, jet lagged puffy, but otherwise exactly the same as he ever was. I quickly click shut the pregnancy calendar email on my screen, sink down in my seat to avoid attracting attention to myself. Please don't let him come and chat to me. 'Hello?' I repeat, when the person on the other end doesn't answer. Hector has disappeared into a production room now. Stress over. 'Grey Home design team.'

Silence. Only the sound of someone with a heavy cold breathing down the phone. My heart starts to scatter, all thoughts of Hector forgotten. This is how it would start. With a silence. Like in the films. 'Is that you? Rex? Rex, is that you?'

Femi looks up, wide-eyed, a blue zip dangling from her teeth like a tongue.

'Gina? Gina Adler?' a man says. It's not you. It's not your voice. To make things worse, Hector has emerged from the production office and is heading this way.

'My name's Dom, an old friend of Rex's.' The man's voice is warm, cockney, a bit gruff. The voice of a smoker. I don't recognise it. I cup the phone close to my mouth so it looks like I'm taking such an important call that not even Hector should disturb me.

'I heard about Rex. I'm sorry,' the man says.

'Thanks.' I wait for him to expand. Damn. I've caught Hector's gas-ring blue eye now. He strides effortlessly towards my desk, running his fingers through his hair. As he approaches, heads dip and faces scrunch into expressions of exaggerated concentration. Just as Hector likes it. King of the studio. He's back.

'I don't think we've met.' Dom cracks some phlegm down

the line. 'But Rex and I go back a fair bit.'

'Everything alright, Gina?' Hector mouths silently. He is standing too close in a force field of aftershave.

I smile politely, mouth 'yes', then furrow my brow in an attempt to look like I'm fielding a critical call from a supplier. Looking faintly irritated by my non-availability, he turns on his Italian leather sole. My shoulders drop. I apply myself to the caller. 'Sorry?'

'I wanted to know if there was any news. Any new leads?' He sounds concerned. But I begin to feel uneasy. I wonder if he's a member of the press. I've been asked for quite a few quotes since the news of my pregnancy came out, the reporters always trying to feed me lines to make me sound as tragic and desperate as possible.

'The situation hasn't changed.'

'I'm sorry to hear that, Gina, really I am. You're up the duff, I heard?'

Femi looks up from her desk and raises an eyebrow. I shake my head. She looks puzzled.

'Look, I'm at work, can I—'

'I'll cut to the chase, Gina. I'm phoning about money.' Something about his voice makes me think that if I put down the receiver he'll phone right back. It's hardened.

'Money?'

'Rex owes me a bit of money.' He pauses, one of those deliberate too-long power pauses that hold a threat. 'I need to get it back, Gina.'

'Sorry, but I'm at work. I can't speak now.' Who is Dom? Why have you never mentioned him before? How does he know where I work?

98

Shit, Hector again. I need to get off the phone quick. The last thing I want is Hector thinking I'm bringing my dramas to the studio. It's been hard enough convincing Martin that I'm up to being back at work at all. I need this job. I need to work to stay sane.

'If you give me your phone number I'll phone you back later.'

He reads it out gruffly and I scrawl it down in a madwoman's loopy handwriting. 'When?' There is an unmistakable edge to his voice now. 'When will you phone me back, Gina?'

'Later,' I manage, my heart starting to thud. 'Later this evening.'

'I can't write this off, OK? Are you getting what I'm saying, love?'

'I've got to go.' I crash the telephone back on its stand. Hector excuses himself from Andrea and swivels towards me as if he's had me in the corner of his eye all the time.

'Bearing up?' One black eyebrow arches like a crow's wing.

'Yes, thanks,' I stutter, aware that we're the focus of Femi's curious gaze.

'No news?' That quiet toffee voice. Hector is one of those bosses who whispers rather than shouts when he wants to assert himself. He likes to appear minimal, quietly powerful, perfectly cut. Like his suit.

'No news.' I bite hard on my lip, terrified that I will cry in front of him. I can't imagine anything worse than crying in front of Hector right now.

'We should have a chat sometime,' he says with a twitch of a smile. 'A catch up would be good.'

'Sure.' My heart sinks.

'Next week, OK?' He walks away through a studio full of quickly lowered heads.

I'm not sure if it's the phone call or the thought of a 'chat' with Hector but I feel shaky, a little sick. I close my eyes for a moment, sink my head to my hand.

'Ciggy?' Femi's message pings.

We stand outside the building on the pavement, Femi smoking her Marlborough hard and fast, me dodging the smoke. I tell Femi about the phone call and her face puckers beneath her sweep of fringe. 'And Rex never mentioned anything to you about this?'

I nibble off a strip of loose skin on the inside of my cheek, taste blood. 'No.'

'Didn't say how much?'

'I guess this guy wouldn't be chasing a tenner, would he?'

'Seems unlikely.'

'Fuck.' I flap my maternity blouse to get air on my body. It's stifling hot today, summer arriving with a slash of heat this morning, another reminder of the growing expanse of time you've been gone.

'I don't like the sound of this, Gee,' says Femi. 'What if he's some con artist? I've heard of this happening. There are some terrible people who prey on the vulnerable left behind after a tragedy.'

'It's not a tragedy, Femi,' I say quickly, reaching for my phone to call the only person I trust to sort this out.

Sixteen

The less I respected myself, the more desirable Hector became. That was the problem, Rex. The dynamic seems so obvious now. It was right here, in the damp leafy expanses of Regent's Park, that I would wait for him that long, cold winter before I met you. I'd sneak through the black iron gates in my lunch hour, hood pulled up in disguise, never totally sure if he'd turn up, my self-respect draining out of me with every minute he kept me waiting. That relationship stripped me of all my values. That's why I never told you it was him. Partly.

People say you can only find true love if you love yourself, don't they? That was not true for me. I was hollow: you filled me back up. You didn't see my failings. I'm still not entirely sure what you did see to be honest – I was just a pudgy ginger northerner with a weakness for movies, food and crap men – but it was heavenly just the same. I guess the point is, we were the right fit for each other. A love story in a city of love stories.

'Hey, you look well,' says a voice behind me, yanking me back from the past.

I turn to see Jake and something inside me lifts. As the weeks go past he seems to get taller and more confident, less like the diffident bookish flake you made him out to be. Or maybe it's just that he's had to step into your shoes a bit.

'And you're bigger.'

I touch my belly proudly. As Dawn says, I no longer just look like a porker. I look properly pregnant now.

'Lunch?' I take his arm. We're so much easier together since I found his emails to you – I can trust him now – and since he accompanied me to the scan. That experience gave us a short cut into each other, not just into the contents of my womb. For all my determination to stay strong – more essential than ever now I'm pregnant – I cannot help but take comfort in his brotherly protectiveness of me and the baby. We start to walk, falling into the same rhythm as he slows down to match my waddling pace. 'Did you manage to speak to Dom?'

'I did.' He suddenly starts walking faster and I get puffed trying to keep up. No one told me that being pregnant gives you the lungs of a twenty-a-day smoker. 'He claims Rex borrowed a fair bit of dosh off him a couple of months ago.'

'Oh no.' A frown tightens my face. 'How much is a fair bit?'

He hesitates, rubs the side of his nose. 'Two thousand.'

'Two thousand!' I stop in the middle of the path. 'That must be bullshit, Jake. Who the hell is he?'

'An old mate of Rex's apparently, although with friends like that . . .' He shakes his head and we start walking again.

'I've never heard his name before.'

He glances at me warily. 'This guy was from Rex's gambling days.'

'Gambling? Rex doesn't gamble.'

Jake doesn't say anything. His silence is damning.

'Jake? He didn't gamble, did he?'

'He did used to like the *odd* flutter, Gina.'

'Just the odd bit?' Something clenches in my stomach. Why didn't I know this?

'It got him into pretty bad debt in his twenties. Mum had to bail him out.' His face falls into shadow. 'I presumed you knew.'

My cheeks heat up, as if I've been caught out not knowing you properly. 'Maybe, yes, maybe he did mention it, in passing. I know that Rex likes horses, that he has a soft spot for horse racing.' God, my dad would kill you if he knew about this, Rex. If there's one thing he hates it's a gambler. Great-uncle Corin was a gambler. As Dad always tells us, he marred the lives of all around him and died a broken man one afternoon in his chicken coop.

'Any idea what he might have spent the money on?'

I think back but can't remember anything particularly expensive that you've purchased recently. It is tricky though, as so many of the things you think of as normal seem lavish to me: the sports car, that five-star holiday in Mykonos last year, the bespoke mountain bike . . . this ring. It's a deep blue stone set on rose gold, absolutely beautiful but not, I'd assumed, hugely precious. I look at it again on my swollen finger and wonder. 'I don't know.' That old fear starts to claw. 'Oh, Jake, what if more people come out of the woodwork?'

'I'll deal with it,' he says quickly. 'And if I have to pay Dom off I will.'

'No, you can't possibly!'

'You need all your money right now, Gina.'

'But . . .'

His mobile rings. He pats down his pockets, trying to find it. 'One sec, sorry.' He pulls the phone out, sticks it to his ear. 'Hi.' His voice cools. 'You're here? In the park? Oh, right. No, no, of course it's fine. We were just walking to the café, you know the one . . . yeah, five minutes.' He pushes his hair out of his eyes. 'Fran. She's joining us for lunch.'

I try not to look disappointed. But I was looking forward to catching up on the search news with Jake. Besides, Fran makes me feel about as interesting and attractive as a beige fabric swatch.

We see Fran before she sees us, sitting on the café terrace at a small, round wrought iron table, bare leg extended, dangling her red sandal from her heel. Her looks take me aback, as they always do. Her face is the kind of face I dreamed of having when I was thirteen: apple cheekbones, a long, balletic throat, skin as smooth as an egg. I remember how you used to jokingly call her and Jake, 'the beauty and the book beast'. The most likable thing about her is the fact she's with a man like Jake.

'Gina!' Fran jumps up, circles me in her long, slim arms, releasing a scent of something delicate and floral. 'How *are* you?'

I never know what to say when people ask this. Should I answer truthfully? Pregnant! Husband disappeared! Having a ball. But there is only one polite answer. 'I'm fine, thanks, Fran.'

'Jake's been keeping me up to date with all the developments but I feel terrible that I haven't dropped round or anything yet. Work's been *completely* insane. Every week I mean to. I'm sorry to be so utterly, utterly crap.'

'Please, don't worry.'

'Now, you look . . .' She searches for the word, gazing down at my bump. '. . . *miniscule*, Gina. I thought you'd be out here.' She makes a domed tummy shape with her hands. 'How *is* the pregnancy? Are you managing to enjoy it?'

I stare at her blankly, wondering how to answer this one.

'Of course you're not. Of course you're not!' She flaps her hands manically in front of her beautiful face. 'God, I'm so sorry. You don't need to explain to me. Holy crap, no woman would choose what you're going through.'

'Better order,' Jake interrupts from behind a menu. He already seems different with Fran here, tenser, less like the man I've got to know over the last few weeks. I have come to see Jake as existing solely in this Rex-has-disappeared bubble with me, not as a man with other responsibilities, as someone who has a life outside the search for you. Fran is a reminder that this is very much not the case. That he has someone to snuggle up to in bed at night. Someone to make tea for in the morning. No wonder he has become more important to me than I have to him.

'Jake, this shirt, honestly.' She wipes something invisible off his chaotically rolled up sleeve. 'I buy new shirts and he digs out the old ones, Gina. Like a five-year-old boy who won't change out of a Spiderman costume.'

105

'What's wrong with my shirt?' asks Jake, bewildered.

'It's missing buttons, darling! Thread! Shape! Oh, forget the shirt. Bigger things to think about, haven't we, Gina?' She stretches her arms behind her so that her high, small breasts are outlined in her blouse. I think how much I like the lived-in look of Jake's blue cotton shirt, much prefer it in fact to the ironed sheen of her silk shell-pink blouse. 'I'm so sorry, about everything. It must be torment, absolute torment. Jake tells me you're being bonkers brave. Here, eat something from the breadbasket immediately. If ever there was a time to eat bread, eh? Fill your boots. What a total head fuck this money business is.'

I freeze. So she knows about the debts. I feel a shot of betrayal that Jake should have told her about it, and have to remind myself that she is his significant other half. He probably tells her everything.

'Fran. Let's not . . .' interrupts Jake. There is something in his voice that brings her up short. She looks annoyed and stabs a cherry tomato too hard with a fork so that the guts of seeds and juice spurt out on to the table.

'I don't mind talking about it, really.' I smile apologetically at Fran, reminding myself of all the hours that Jake has spent searching for Rex. It must have impacted their relationship, too.

'Don't worry. It's congenital. I had a friend who was exactly the same. Some people are totally rubbish at repaying debts, Gina. They see other people's money as Monopoly money.' Fran puts a hand on Jake's arm. 'I mean, he still hasn't repaid you either, has he, sweetheart?'

My dropped fork clatters to the table. 'Repaid *you*?'

Fran winces exaggeratedly. 'Sorry, I thought you knew, Gina.'

Shooting Fran a dark look, Jake leans forward on fisted hands. 'I lent him a bit of money last year, Gina. I wasn't going to say anything. It's not a big deal.'

'He never told me,' I say, disbelieving. I'm certain your pride would have stopped you borrowing money off Jake. It's unimaginable.

'It was just to tide him over, while he was waiting for his bonus, which he'd—'

'—already spent,' interrupts Fran with unexpected acidity.

'Last year's bonus was, er, less than he expected, I know that,' I say, stumbling to your defence. 'He said they'd over-invested in . . . um, Asian, or was it South American tech shares or something? Sorry, I don't know exactly. I kind of zoned out the rare times Rex talked about that stuff. KPHI seemed such a cliquey, impenetrable business, everyone with those long-winded incomprehensible titles . . .' Something about Fran's incredulous expression brings me to an abrupt halt.

Yes, I should have taken more interest in your work and in our finances, Rex. But you were always so in control. And I knew that your performance-related salary was eye-watering. You told me so many times that we'd never have to worry about money, that you'd invested in all sorts of exciting start-ups. It was just a matter of waiting for them to ripen, wasn't it? I look down at my plate. 'I don't really understand, but I'm terribly sorry if he did borrow from you and not pay you back, Jake. I'm sure he meant to.'

'Don't apologise, Gina.' Jake shrugs. 'We're brothers.'

'Half-brothers,' Fran corrects.

'Er, I've been going through all the admin stuff, Gina, as you asked,' says Jake, as the atmosphere tenses. 'All the post, tallying it up with the lists Rex left you on the computer.'

'Oh.' No more surprises please. 'Great, thanks.'

'Haven't seen him for days,' Fran mutters.

'Gina, it's the mortgage repayments.' His eyes are quizzical, not leaving mine. 'I've been going over and over them and while I am no financial whizz—'

'You can say that again,' quips Fran, pushing lumps of feta cheese to the side of her plate. I wish she'd stop putting Jake down. It makes me uncomfortable.

'—it's clear even to me that you're behind on the payments.'

'Behind? No, really?'

'So you don't know?'

'Rex used to deal with that side of things, I'm afraid. He is so good with money. I'm not.' Fran fixes me with narrowed amused eyes, like she'd always imagined I was the disappointing kind of woman who'd leave all her financial planning to a man. 'Are we far behind in the payments?'

'Two months,' Fran replies before Jake has a chance to say anything.

'Two months. Gosh. Well. Um, he did jiggle things around a bit, I know that, paying bits off the mortgage when he got a bit of extra money. Maybe . . .' I stop. I can't think of an explanation as to why we'd be behind on our mortgage repayments. 'Forget it. I'll pay it,' I say firmly, dreading the idea that Jake might try to bail us out again. 'I'm still working. I'll sort it, don't worry.'

'Honey, it's a pretty fucking hefty mortgage. And interest rates are going up,' says Fran with a laugh, and I feel another twinge of annoyance that she has an opinion on my private finances. 'Do you know what your monthly repayments are?'

'Yes,' I lie. Shamefully, I have no idea. I stare down at the oily slick of salad on my plate, no longer hungry. 'If the worst happened I could sell up, buy somewhere cheaper.'

Fran smiles at me pitifully. 'It's all in his name, hon. You can't.'

'Oh.' I bite down on my lip hard.

'He bought the flat before you met,' Fran points out, eyes narrowing, looking more serious now.

'But we're married,' I point out.

'There's no death certificate. It's going to be very hard to do anything until they've got one.' Fran exchanges a look with Jake. 'You've got to go and talk to the lawyer about this as soon as possible, hon.'

'I've got an appointment with the lawyer.' I'm pleased that I can say this, that I don't appear to be a complete airhead. 'Tomorrow lunchtime.'

'Great. I'll come too,' Jake says decisively. 'I'll bring all the papers.'

'Jake, my mother is coming up tomorrow,' says Fran coolly. 'Birthday lunch. River Café. Remember?'

'I can go on my own, it's no problem,' I say quickly.

'Thank you.' Fran repays me with a smile. 'If you're sure.'

I smile back. Even though I don't particularly like her, I want to please her. She's one of those women.

Jake's face darkens. 'There is one other thing, Gina.'

The way Fran averts her eyes, I can tell it's going to be bad.

'Raf called me this morning.'

'Oh.' Fat Raf. Your colleague, Rex, the one who spent most of the time searching for you at the bottom of a beer bottle in José's bar. He was never going to be much use finding you, was he? Maybe that's why you invited him along. 'How's Raf?'

'He says he's learned about a conversation that took place at KPHI about a month before we all went to Spain.' I've never seen Jake look more troubled than he does now. He takes a deep breath. 'Rex knew he wasn't going to be made a partner, Gina. He'd been told before he left.'

'*What?*' I shake my head, thinking of all the times you'd talked about becoming a partner. That was the plan. You'd become partner, earn shitloads, retire early, be free. 'But . . . but . . . he *was*, Jake. He absolutely was. That was why he worked so hard. He mentioned it the morning he went away, I'm sure he did.'

'Raf is adamant that he'd already been told it wasn't going to happen when he left for Spain.'

My breathing starts to quicken. I close my palms over my belly to protect it.

'Look, I'm going to speak to KPHI senior management. But it seems Raf got this from a source close to the top. He says confirmation will only be a formality. I'm sorry, Gina.' Jake shakes his head as if he can't quite believe he's telling me this. 'I thought you should know.'

Seventeen

The last time I went swimming with you was in Atlantic waters off Ile de Ré last summer. I had a burn where the cold water met the ache in my sit bones from the sex and the bumping of the hard leather bike saddle. I was less fit than I thought I was, trying to keep up with you. I tried to hide it by not screaming when I sat down and being enthusiastic when you suggested another twenty-mile killer cycle route across the island. But you guessed anyway. The next morning you let me sleep in late and when I woke there were yellow flowers from the market on the table, blushed peaches and warm croissants and, leaning against the gnarled olive tree in the garden, a newly rented tandem. God, I loved you for that.

'I'm feeling good!' Lucy bobs up out of the water in a boa of bubbles. 'Thank you for turning me on to this place, Gina.'

'Glad to have turned anyone on to anything other than a stiff course of Prozac.'

She laughs, tosses her hair off her face, releasing a rainbow of droplets into the sunshine like a girl in a cheesy shampoo ad.

'The Serpentine was one of Rex's favourite places. I used to find the idea of grotty London fish nibbling my toes a bit grim. Now I like it.' I lean back into the cold green bath, thinking about the baby swimming inside me, too. My pregnancy calendar tells me that soon the baby will practise breathing under water, inhaling and exhaling amniotic fluid, a true water baby.

'Off downstream. Need to pee.' Lucy launches herself off the wooden pole, her pale hair roping down her spine. I lower myself further into the water, mouth tightly closed, nostrils just about the surface, like an old croc.

I look at the other swimmers. I look for you.

And there you are, pounding towards the other bank in a front crawl, wearing a blue swimming hat. There you are, a lean figure silhouetted against the sun on the bank, about to dive, your body and the water held in tense suspension, waiting for each other.

I see you everywhere at the moment: a head in a crowd on Marylebone High Street, a reflection in a glass window, the circular gleam of your bald spot as you lower your head over a coffee in Starbucks.

'Couldn't you just murder an ice cream?' Lucy clambers out of the water, then reaches down to help me up, her slim arms straining at my weight. People watch curiously, as if they've never seen a pregnant woman in a leopard print maternity swimming costume before (thank you, Femi). I'm relieved to hide my strange shape in a towel.

My bikini line hasn't been touched since you left, your absence marked in its wiry millimetres. Self-conscious, I turn away from Lucy in the cold, tiled changing room and rub vigorously between my toes. I can't not be aware of the contrast: Lucy, plucked and waxed, slender as a water nymph, me hairy, huge and neglected. Out of the corner of my eye, I catch an older lady with a topknot of long grey hair and mottled flesh watching me. I wrap myself tight in my towel.

What would you make of my body now? One of the first things you complimented me on were my 'lovely ankles, like the nicely turned feet of a piano'. Now if you press a finger into my ankle it dips about a centimetre, as if you were prodding an undercooked cake. My belly button protrudes like the tip of a pinkie finger and I have a tube map of veins on my breasts. You were quite disparaging of women whom you thought had let themselves go. I used to bring you up on that one, didn't I? (You had the good sense to keep any thoughts about Dawn's figure strictly to yourself.) Anyway, I forgave you – like I forgave all your little quirks – because your mother is such a cold, polished glamazon who seems to exist solely on wine, coffee and slithers of stinking blue cheese and has set the bar so ridiculously high for the rest of us that you don't know any better. When I think of it like that, I still don't know why you fell for me. But you did.

I'm thankful that wherever you are, Rex, you remember me as I was before the pregnancy. Even if it does mean missing my marvellous breasts, which, for the record, now appear to have stabilised at an extraordinary coned-shaped 32FF. Warheads ready to take out the free world.

'I feel properly alive now,' Lucy says, patting her legs dry. Her legs are so smooth and slim, I can't help but stare, nostalgic for my own lost legs, the slip of sex and skin. She notices me noticing. 'What?'

I pull my big black maternity knickers over my drum-tight bump. 'Just wondering if I'll ever have sex again, that's all, I guess.'

Out of the corner of my eye I see the older woman smiling indulgently.

'Don't be silly.' Lucy wrings water out of her hair on to the tiled floor. 'It's not over, Gee.'

'I didn't have sex for a year after my first baby,' blurts the naked old woman behind us.

'Really?' beams Lucy, who loves eccentric, outspoken older women and fully intends to be one herself.

'But then it came back.' She clicks her fingers and her long, tubular breasts shake alarmingly. 'One minute all you want is a good night's sleep, the next . . .'

Too much information. I shove my wet towel and costume into my bag.

'Your friend's right.' The woman dries between her toes, resting her wild breasts on her knees. 'It's not over, love. It's just the beginning.'

I'm out of that dressing room pretty quickly after that.

At the café beside the Serpentine we sit at a round metal table, handbags on our knees, licking our ice creams. We are surrounded by mothers and babies. The babies kick hot pink legs beneath the canopies of their prams. The mothers push broken bits of biscuit and bananas into their wet mouths as if feeding little pets. Will this be me? I can't imagine it.

Lucy smiles. 'I know what you're thinking, and you'll be totally brilliant.'

114

'Hmmm,' I say doubtfully.

'You will. And that woman, the woman in the changing room, she's right you know.'

'That I'll get my mojo back?' I let out a small incredulous laugh. 'Yeah, right.'

Lucy shrugs. 'Why not? You are beautiful, young—'

'Husbandless. Pregnant. Not exactly a recipe for hot sex, Lucy.'

'Nothing ever stays the same,' says Lucy cryptically. 'Either Rex comes back . . .'

I frown at her, unsure where this is going.

'. . . or you will move on, Gina,' she says determinedly, refusing to pussyfoot around me.

'Move on? I can't be with someone else, Lucy.'

She licks her ice cream nonchalantly and leans back in her chair. 'You won't always think that.'

'He's the father of my child. There's a certain finality about it. It's not like what . . .' My voice trails off, my brain not wanting to go there. '. . . what happened before.'

She frowns, opens her mouth to say something, then doesn't. We both know that there is nothing to be gained by going over catastrophic old love affairs.

'Anyway, he will come back,' I continue. 'He will come back for the baby. He's alive somewhere, Lucy. If he was dead I'd feel it.'

'You're such an old hippy sometimes.' She looks exasperated.

'I've been thinking about it. Rex would have been so humiliated not to be made a partner. It would have felt like it was all for nothing. That must be why he never told me.

115

And there's the debt. It all points to him running away. And if he ran away, he can run back!'

'He may just be dead. He may not have left you or run away. He may just be dead, Gee.'

'That soul-eating job. They wanted blood, honestly. He worked *so* hard. He was always trying to escape it. Maybe he felt he *couldn't* escape it? Maybe he . . .' I trail off, knowing that this tunnel of thought only leads to darker, colder places.

'It could be a coincidence, all of this, Gina,' Lucy points out carefully. 'That's all I'm saying.'

'You sound like Jake,' I huff.

'He could have had money worries, work crises, gone out into the sea and *still* got into trouble in the water. The two do not have to be connected.'

I look away, deflated. These are almost the exact words of the caseworker. Why won't anyone have a little faith?

'Oh, what do I know?' she adds resignedly, brushing away a wasp with her hand and returning to her ice cream. 'You knew him better than anyone.'

I think about this for a moment. 'Did I, Lucy?'

'Well, you did get married pretty quickly, that's for sure,' she concedes. And I hear an echo of her past reservations, the way she tried to persuade me out of marrying you so quickly. She didn't like the way you wanted all of me, worried that there wasn't much left over for my friends. 'Barely had time to buy shoes for your wedding,' she adds wryly.

'Me neither,' I smile, thinking of my teetering pale blue shoes, their hot pink lining, the way they pinched my toes cruelly at the church, but after our first dance – Elvis, 'Can't Help Falling in Love' – my happiness acted like anaesthetic and they felt like slippers. I wore a vintage thirties dress from a little shop at the dog-end of the Portobello Road in the palest petal-pink silk, set off by a small bunch of cherry pink Sweet Williams. You had wanted it small, fuss free, quick, Marylebone Register Office – you couldn't face the Catholic church in the end – then a small, intimate lunch upstairs at The Ivy. It was fleeting but perfect. 'The thing is, Lucy, when I met him I felt like I'd known him forever, so it didn't matter that actually I'd only known him six months when we got married.'

'When you know, you know, right? That's what you always used to say to me. Slightly smugly, I have to say.'

I laugh. 'Ah, but what if it's the *belief* that you know someone that stops you actually getting to know them?'

Lucy frowns. 'Give me a moment. Yes, I'm with you.' She nods. 'Good point.'

'Maybe Rex wasn't always upfront with me? I mean, I thought he was. But maybe he wasn't?'

She gives me a sharp look. 'And you were always upfront with him? Come on, Gina.'

I look down at my hands, my cheeks heating. 'No, I wasn't.'

'Look, I'm not criticising you for your . . . omission,' Lucy says softly. 'I understand why you didn't tell him about what happened.'

'Do you? Really?'

'Yes, of course I do. I'm female. What savvy female really believes honesty is the best policy? It'd be like telling a man the true number of men you'd slept with, rather than shaving off at least five.'

117

I smile, relieved. 'Thanks.' I rest my head on her shoulder. Her hair feels impossibly silky and smells lushly of river. We sit like that for a while until Lucy says, 'So you're properly skint, Gina? This is not good.'

I tense. 'Mum and Dad gave me some money to tide me over. I haven't yet told them I've worked through it, or quite how bad the situation is. I don't want to worry them. They've been so kind and have had more than enough on their plate in the last few months.'

'You definitely can't sell the flat?'

I shake my head.

'But you could rent it out? The rent should cover the mortgage.'

'But what if Rex came back and found someone else living there?'

'If he's staggered home from Spain after all this time, he'll find you, Gee.' She nibbles her lip thoughtfully. 'You could move to mine but I'm not sure sleeping on a sofa bed in Hackney is the best place for a woman in your condition. Although you would be well placed for excellent curry. Hey, what about Dawn's place?'

'It has been mentioned, yes. She's very keen to have me back in Derbyshire. On a matter of principle.'

'I sense a "but" coming.' She pulls out her retro tortoise-shell hand mirror and lifts it to her face. 'Something in my eye, sorry.'

'Looks like a midge.'

'Nice.' She pulls up the rim of her lid. 'And the but? You were saying?'

'Well, she's got her hands full with the twins and the

useless Gareth, hasn't she? She doesn't need another person in the house. Anyway, we'd drive each other insane within about twenty-four hours. And I need to stay in London for work. I can't give up my job, not now. I need the money.'

'I reckon Martin and Femi would happily have a word with Hector about you taking a wee sabbatical. Come on, he owes you, Gee.' She picks something out of her eye. 'Got it, the blighter. The thing is, Gina, Hector would have to be a right old wanker not to hold your job open. Considering the circumstances.'

'He *is* a right old wanker, Lucy.'

Our eyes meet and flash in her mirror. 'Yeah,' she says ruefully. 'Lest we forget.'

Eighteen

Mandy

His advances rejected, Mark put his arms behind his head and stared despondently up at the damp patch on the ceiling.

'I'm not sure why I can't,' Mandy sighed.

'We both know why you can't.' Mark refused to look at her. He hid his hurt with anger.

Mandy, suddenly tearful, looked down at the fleshy curves of her body, the swell of her boobs, the round hips, her pussy, and wondered what the hell was wrong with it all. This was the first time, apart from when she was pregnant, that she'd ever gone off sex. In fact she felt numb. Like someone had flipped off a switch. It wasn't as if she didn't still fancy the pants off Mark. It wasn't him. It was her. But that sounded crap. And now he was angry at her.

'You've got no room in your head for anything else, Mandy.'

'I'm sorry, honey.'

'I don't want apologies, Mandy.' He stroked her thighs,

his strong, skillful fingers unable to work their magic. 'I want us back.'

'I'm here. I've not gone anywhere.' She attempted a coquettish grin. It didn't work. Too old for coquettish, she decided.

'You don't think I know what you've been doing all day?'

'Working!'

'Googling, poking through . . . weird boxes full of *his* stuff.' A vein throbbed on the side of his temple. 'I'm not stupid. I know you've been obsessing, OK? This is not normal behaviour, Mandy, seriously. How would you like it if I started searching out memorabilia from my past relationships?'

Mandy was silent, knowing she'd been rumbled. 'I love you,' she said eventually. 'That's all I can say.'

He turned to face her, eyes glinting beneath their thick, paint-splattered brows. 'Then show me.'

'Through sex?'

He couldn't help but grin then, the grin she loved so much, wolfish and full of longing. 'Oh, twist my arm.'

'We can't just communicate through sex,' she back-pedalled, although it had worked pretty well up until now. 'We can talk?'

'Mandy, baby, I'm all ears.'

'Well . . .' She stopped. What was there left to say? He knew the story. Rex's disappearance had thrown up all sorts of feelings she'd thought were dead and buried long ago. More than anything, it had created a huge headache about what to do next. That was what hung over her so heavily. What to do. What to do . . .

'See? When I try to get you to open up you go silent. What am I meant to fucking think?' His eyes searched hers warily, scared of what he'd find in them. 'Are you really saying you're not still in love with Rex Adler?'

'That's exactly what I'm saying, Mark.'

He wasn't convinced. 'Since Rex went missing, a part of you has gone missing too, Mand. It's like you're not there for me. Or Ryan for that matter.'

His words hit the target and she closed her eyes, put her hand to her thumping, spinning head. 'I keep playing it all over and over. I don't know what to do. I normally always know what to do, Mark. You know what I'm like. But I haven't the foggiest.'

'Just do it, Mandy. Just bloody well do it. The guy is as dead as a dodo.'

'You really think I should tell the wife?'

'Yes, I do. Anything to put an end to this.'

'But the problem is, if I tell her it *won't* be the end of anything,' she sighed, already dreading the conversation. 'It will be the beginning.'

Nineteen

Not Mandy Mills? Yes, Mandy Mills. I read through the email again: it's from your ex, asking if I want to meet up. Not having the foggiest how to respond, I slide the phone back on the bedside table and close my eyes, knowing how tough my working day will be if I don't sleep. I must forget Mandy for now. I must sleep.

I don't sleep.

It's five am. It feels like the city has absorbed so much summer heat in the day it's now sweating it out through its concrete skin. It's very, very quiet. Like everyone has died. My brain leaps about in the silence, a crazed horse in an empty field. I don't know what to do for the best. I cannot stay here in our beloved little flat. But I cannot go to Derbyshire either. I have no money, no security. Things have been better.

Once you used to lift my hair on hot nights, kiss my neck, saying you could never get enough of me. On really sweaty, slippy nights it was impossible to tell where your flesh ended and mine began. You used to pant my name when you came. Now? It's just me talking to you, getting nothing back.

Emails from your exes. Yes, things have been better.

I heave myself out of bed and take refuge in the toilet, where I watch the sun rise behind the mottled glass of the bathroom window. I've been doing a lot of thinking here on the toilet. (It helps if I put slices of cucumber on my eyes before breakfast to bring the tear swelling down before work.) Other times when I cannot sleep, I dress, wait for the sunrise and head out to Regent's Park just after dawn, happy to be in the company of London's early morning runners, fellow insomniacs and saucer-eyed clubbers who haven't gone to bed at all.

In recent days I've also taken to hiding in your wardrobe, mad bat that I am. It's the place where you are most condensed. I step in, crouch down, the tips of your ties tickling my face, the expensive leather of your shoes stiff beneath my knees. It smells of you in there: spicy aftershave from that tailor's on Savile Row, polished leather and laundry. There it's easier to reach back into the past and find memory pockets to sustain me: running down the Strand in a rain storm, hand in hand, laughing hysterically; a stolen lunchtime at the National Gallery; your expensive jacket laid down on the damp ground of the Heath as a picnic blanket. Our romance compressed into a thousand brightly lit moments. But the questions still flutter out of the dark like moths. Why did you borrow money off Dom and Jake? Why did you not tell me that we were in financial difficulty? Why? Why? Why? I know that you wouldn't want to worry me about money. You were old fashioned like that, never wanted to discuss exes, politics or money, mine or yours. You wanted us suspended above life's crappy bits, a beautiful mobile – line figures making love – rotating slowly in the breeze. The problem is that without you I feel exposed and vulnerable, unprepared for life on my own. I'm terrified that I am turning back into the person we met, that pathetic woman crouched beside the road, trembling alone in the darkness. The woman I never told you about.

Twenty

'That lot, keep or storage, love?' Mum points to a mountain of clothes on the bed. Clothes that you once unzipped me from, clothes, it has to be said, that look unlikely to ever fit me again.

'Storage. I don't think I'll be seeing my waistline for a while.' I rest a hand on my belly and it judders strangely. Someone is definitely inside.

'Bah, mine never returned at all. All my old clothes ended up at the school summer fair.' Dawn tosses the parcel tape up in the air and catches it. 'There's still a thin waist inside me waiting to get out. She's just on a very long lunch.'

Mum smiles and starts folding up the clothes on the bed, laying them neatly in a cardboard box. 'Who are they, these renters, Gina?' she asks, folding.

'I don't know. The agency has sorted it all out. Media people, I think they said. God, it's so weird to think of them sleeping in our bed.'

'And pooing in your loo,' adds Dawn.

'Thanks, Dawn. Helpful.'

'That was the doorbell, wasn't it? I'll go.' Mum re-emerges

126

with Jake, smiling so hard that all the sinews in her neck pop up like piano strings. Jake is wearing jeans, a battered brown crossbody bag over his shoulder, a folder of press releases in his hand. His hair is spiking out at angles from his head as if he's been standing downwind in a Tube tunnel and he has a smudge of something dark on his cheek, the kind of thing you end up with on your face in London if you touch too many surfaces in public areas. 'Sorry I'm a bit late. Screening ran over.'

'No, perfect timing. We've just finished, haven't we, love?' beams Mum, flushing a little. She keeps going girlish around Jake. It's embarrassing. 'Always takes longer than you think, eh?'

'Always,' Jake reassures sweetly.

I smile apologetically at him.

'Cup of tea, Jake?' Mum asks brightly. 'It may have to come from the café opposite though. We've packed the kettle!'

'I'm fine, thank you.'

'Oh,' says Mum, looking a little put out. 'Coffee? I can nip to Starbucks. But you'll have to write it down. I can never get my head around these new-fangled coffees.'

'No, not for me, thank you. I'm fine.'

'Oh.'

The scene takes on the clunky feel of amateur dramatics, the boxes stage props, me pregnant, the disjointed family tableau.

'Well, you two better scoot along then. You'll get a horror of a parking ticket. They'll book you for anything around here.' Mum shakes her head.

'Like driving the wrong way down a one-way street.' Dawn hoots with laughter, her cheeks wobbling. 'I mean, shock*ing*!'

'There were no signs,' mutters mum, flushing.

Jake turns to me, eyes amused behind his glasses. 'Ready, Gina?' he asks, as if giving me one last chance to change my mind.

'Ready,' I say, trying not to look as nervous as I feel. It is a hugely generous offer, and one that I have to accept if I am to remain working in London.

'We're all so grateful, Jake,' Mum says breathlessly, making up for my reticence.

'Pleasure is all mine. I'm really pleased I can be of practical help for once.' He looks at the boxes, bemused. 'All of them coming with?'

'No, no. Just that one.' I point to the precious box of memories: photos; the business card you gave me on the Heath; the skeletal heart-shaped leaf you gave me last autumn; the pot of Carmex with your fingerprint in the lipsalve. It's funny the things that matter in the end, how something so big can be condensed to nothing. 'And the two suitcases.'

'That's all? I'm used to a woman who can fill a Boeing's hold with just her toiletries.'

'Ha!' Dawn laughs, hula hooping the parcel tape around her wrist. 'The moment the baby stuff starts to arrive you'll be grateful she packed small, Jake. Believe me, it'll be like having Angelina Jolie's nursery in your spare room.'

'Dawn, I won't be *with* Jake when the baby comes,' I correct quickly, mortified in case Jake thinks I'll be there forever, a petulant sitting tenant. 'I'll have sorted the finances out by then and be back in Marylebone. Please don't worry. You won't have to accommodate my baby stuff, too.'

Dawn and Mum exchange glances. For a moment, no one speaks, and I wonder if they all now see me as a slightly mad person who needs to be allowed to believe she's still sane.

Jake shrugs, picks up a box. 'You can stay as long as you like, Gina.'

'She'll have finished work by the end of October, very latest, wouldn't you say, Dawn?' says Mum. 'It's cutting it too fine to stay at work longer than that. You need to rest before the birth, Gina.'

'Bloody hell, yes. Six weeks before the birth I could hardly walk,' groans Dawn, doing a comedy stagger across the room, arms on her lower back, domed stomach pushed forward.

I smile apologetically at Jake on behalf of my family. 'Er, shall we go?'

As we drive away from central London towards the suburbs the roads narrow. The housing stock changes from regency townhouses to tightly packed Victorian terraces. Litter blows down the pavements. I notice mothers and pushchairs, groups of hooded teenagers on bikes on street corners. It reminds me of when I used to live in Hornsey, in the lifetime before you. How spoiled I've been in Marylebone, I realise, surrounded by designer boutiques and organic cafés and pavements filled with smartly dressed people who don't live there but are shopping or working before going home to places . . . well, like this, I guess.

'Our street.' Jake slows down, pulls up outside a pretty terrace.

I spot Fran walking back and forth in front of the bay window, a red dress draped across her fabulous body like a territorial flag. 'Welcome!' she says a few moments later, kissing me enthusiastically on the doorstep. 'Let's get you a cup of tea. Holy crap, what's this?' She looks down at the cat basket.

'Sorry, this is Whippet. Jake did say . . .'

'Shit,' he says, wincing. 'The cat. Forgot. Sorry.'

'Only you would forget to mention a cat, Jake.' Fran stares blankly down at Whippet. Then she looks at my bump, as if weighing the two up. 'You and me, we're going to have to bond, matey boy,' she says, kneeling down to Whippet's eye level. The cat's tail twitches.

'She's a girl,' I say, feeling sorry for Whippet and wondering whether I should have sent her up to Derbyshire to feast on country mice after all.

'She's a bit of an old dear, isn't she?'

'I don't know how old she is actually. She was a stray, turned up at the door of the flat last year. I took her in.'

Fran looks surprised. 'And Rex let you? Wow. That man sure loved you, hon.' She turns on her heel. 'Come in, I'll show you around.' Her voice cools. 'It is, after all, the first time you've visited, isn't it?'

'Yes, yes it is.' I blush, not wanting to explain that you always made excuses when they invited us over. It didn't seem natural to me to keep your own flesh and blood at such a distance. But you insisted that because we lived centrally they should come to a restaurant near us, that this was the

130

natural order of things. You were the oldest brother after all. Jake, you said, couldn't have everything he wanted when he wanted it. And nor could Fran.

'Sitting room.' She flippantly waggles her arm around the room as if showing round a prospective lodger. 'Jake's got all his crap in here, I'm afraid. Realise it could do with a spring clean by a team of guys in white protective suits.'

'Oh no, it's lovely.' I clock two comfortably battered leather sofas, a large red Kilim rug, Jake's surfboard leaning against a wall, shelves stuffed with books, the kind of scruffy paperbacks that I love, the ones that look like they might have been picked up from a secondhand stall beneath Waterloo Bridge, the kind that made you sneeze and banish from our flat.

Fran pads through the house on pedicured feet to the kitchen. I follow her, trying to ignore Whippet mewing pitifully in her basket and resisting the urge to retrieve her. 'You've seen a kitchen before,' she says, dryly.

It's nothing like ours. The kitchen is bigger than I expected, extended so that light pours through part of the ceiling. But it's still homely rather than modern and polished like our flat, the wooden kitchen units painted a comforting turquoise green, a silver pendant hanging low over the wooden dining table.

'And more crap.' She nods to the magazines and newspapers piled high on the table. 'Jake's one of those men who do not *see* their own mess, I'm afraid. He has a blind spot. Actually he has many.' I glance over at Jake who is smiling wearily like he's heard all this before. 'Now, I guess what you really want to see is your room.'

We all turn at the same time and collide awkwardly before threading up the narrow stairway to the top of the house. 'Love nest,' says Fran with just the faintest trace of sarcasm in her voice, pointing to the master bedroom. I glimpse it through the half open door. The bed is huge and covered in what looks like white sheepskin. I instantly think of them having sex on it and pray that I'm not going to be in the room next to theirs.

'One more flight up, if you can manage it, hon.'

'No problem.' I am puffing a bit now, the baby pressing down on my pelvis.

'Not exactly capacious,' Jake apologises, knocking the door to the attic room open with his knee. 'But I thought you'd prefer the privacy and quiet up here.'

'Lovely, thanks,' I smile at him gratefully.

The room is tiny, low ceilinged, clad in white-painted tongue and groove. There is one small double bed beneath a skylight, a small dresser painted grey, a metal rail for hanging clothes and, a sweet touch of Fran's, a stack of magazines beside the bed. There is something else beside the bed, too. It takes me a moment to comprehend what it is. My mouth drops open.

'I just couldn't resist. Do you like it?' Fran looks uncharacteristically sheepish.

The crib is made from wicker. It has a draped lace hood like something in a fairy tale.

'I'm sorry. It just makes it all so . . . so real, I guess. It's beautiful, thank you.' My voice breaks and I disguise it with a cough and bite hard on my lower lip to stop the unexpected swell of tears. A crib!

Fran, oblivious, claps her hands together. 'Great. I knew you'd love it. Let's go get a cup of tea.'

As she skips down the stairs like a sprite, Jake turns to me, looking concerned. 'Is it all OK, Gina?'

'It's perfect.' But something that I can't put my finger on doesn't feel quite right.

Twenty-one

Jake's house smells different to our flat. It sounds different too, what with all the twanging and glugging of unfamiliar pipes at strange hours. The bed, although I am extremely grateful for it, is not *my* bed. It's in a little nook, walls sloping to a point directly above it so that I bump my head if I get up too quickly. After five nights of sleeping here, I have a ridge of small bruises along my forehead. But it has made me realise just how little I really need: a bed, a bath, food and sleep. And you, of course. You. Us. Mostly I miss us, the people we were when we were together. Who I was when I was with you.

But am I depressed? Clinically not! The doctor made me answer a checklist of questions yesterday, peering at me pitifully over his bifocal glasses after I told him my story. I appear to be bearing up well, he remarked with some incredulity, as if I might be hiding suicidal tendencies in my handbag. I wanted to tell him that I'm not depressed because I know you are still alive, and that this faith still warms me like a fire. I didn't in case he thought I'd gone nuts and wrote something damning in my notes. So I stuck to the line, equally true, about the baby giving me a reason to carry on. (My pregnancy calendar says he has grown eyelashes. And he *dreams*. Isn't that incredible? What can he possibly dream about?)

You once told me that depression is a sticky, gluey grey hole, a quicksand that stops you doing anything. You vaguely mentioned you'd suffered a mild bout once or twice, long, long ago. I'm somewhere different to that. Maybe I'm just predisposed to cheerfulness. ('You and your pink sky thinking,' you always used to marvel.) Or maybe it's because I do, in fact, have more reason than most to get up in the morning: there is always the chance that this is the day that we will find you after all. Yes, I think it's that.

The police have no new leads but the private investigator remains bullish (and expensive). Your mother has been back to see the medium, who confirms that you're still very much alive, somewhere 'hot and high'. (Narrowing things down there then.) Every week someone from your past seems to pop up, not all entirely welcome. This week it's Mandy again. Yes, Mandy Mills, your ex. She emailed me a second time – I never replied to her first mail, couldn't think how to respond – asking if I want to meet up. Lucy sensibly points out that 'no good ever came out of meeting exes', but I'm curious.

'Gina?' The front door slams and the house shakes.

Jake's voice. Good.

I step out of my now-cold bath, puddling the floor with water. I throw on my dressing gown and thump downstairs.

In the hall, Jake unclips his bicycle helmet and grins, as if genuinely pleased to see me. 'You in bed already?'

'No, just had a bath.' I tighten the belt on my dressing

gown, feeling underdressed. It's not my home after all. 'I'll get some clothes on.'

'You don't need to dress up for dinner here. Ready to eat?'

'Always. When's Fran back?'

'Don't worry about her. Another shindig in Soho tonight. She'll eat out.'

'Oh, OK.' Even though I hope Jake's not here because he misguidedly feels that I need to be babysat, I am relieved that Fran will not be joining us tonight. I fear I've become one of her projects, Rex. Everything is about 'The Pregnancy'. She interrogates me on pregnancy symptoms, watches as I swallow the pre-natal vitamins she bought me in case I push the pill up my sleeve and flush it down the toilet when no one is looking. And I thought Dawn was controlling.

'Jake, do you like steak?' I have no idea what he likes or doesn't.

His eyes light up. 'I love steak. Why?'

'I bought some on the way back from work.'

'You angel.'

I look away; no one has called me that since you.

'I'll find a Jamie recipe or something and do my best not to turn it into a leather elbow patch . . .'

'Actually, Jake, I'd like to cook it.'

'You don't have to.'

'I want to. I haven't cooked for anyone since . . . well, since Rex left. Mum and Dawn have been cooking for me like I'm a child. I'm surprised my meals aren't puréed to be honest. And I'd love to cook for someone else. If . . . if you don't mind.'

'I'd love it. You can't be a worse cook than me.' He rummages in his bike saddlebag. 'I thought you might want to watch a movie later. Early dibs on the new American releases? I've got a few press copies.' He pulls out a bundle of DVDs. 'Er, there's a romantic comedy here somewhere. Sarah Jessica Parker . . .' He stops. 'Sorry, I'm being a presumptuous old git, aren't I? You're probably into Russian art house or something.'

'No, I'll watch anything with Sarah Jessica Parker in it,' I laugh.

He eyes me sceptically. 'What's your favourite movie?'

'*To Catch a Thief*. *Breakfast At Tiffany's* a close contender.'

He looks taken aback.

'You expected it to be *Legally Blonde*, didn't you? Admit it.'

'No, no, it's not that. Just that *To Catch a Thief* is one of my favourites, too.'

Cue a jarring moment. There is something intrinsically embarrassing about discovering we love the same movie. 'I'll get dressed,' I say quickly, stamping back up the stairs with all the grace of a wildebeest.

I change into a cool blue summer dress that lets air billow over my bump and get to work in the kitchen. Steaks. Buttered beans. Fried garlic and rosemary potatoes. I lay it all out on the wooden work surface and hunt through the kitchen drawers for the things I need. It's like the first time you cook in a rented cottage. I can't find anything. Jake tries to help, offering misguided pointers – nothing is where he says they are – and thirstily uncorks a bottle of wine. I notice that there is a big candle in the middle of the table, half melted. Even though I'd love to light it – my life has been strip lit since you left – I worry that this might make the dinner too intimate, especially as Fran isn't here.

Happy to be cooking again, I prod the potatoes with a wooden spoon, relishing the garlicky heat blasting up at my face. To cook is to live. Cooking is the opposite thing to dying. I cook, therefore I am married . . . Silly, but that's what it feels like.

We chat easily as I potter about the kitchen, Jake leaning on the countertop, chin in his hand, dryly recounting funny anecdotes about work, garlanded bad movies and debauchery at Cannes. In turn I tell him about Gareth's toy classic car collection and the beauty of Derbyshire in springtime and how my dad was offended that his future son-in-law never asked him for my hand in marriage and how my Nana was a code-breaker during the war and how my twin nephews are the funniest, most nutty five-year-olds ever. I start to slip into the chatty carefree Gina of old.

Jake seems more at ease too, notably more confident without Fran around, or you, come to think of it. And I wonder about families and pecking orders and whether we're all held in place by our siblings to some extent. Remove those siblings – or the long-term girlfriend – and we become a different version of ourselves.

'Steaks,' he nods, interrupting me mid-sentence.

'Shit!'

Almost burned. But not. Perfect. The beans are also delicious and the potatoes have just the right amount of crunch. You used to love my garlic potatoes. And steak. Yes,

I have served to Jake the dinner that I would have served to you. Is that weird?

'You look terribly serious again,' Jake says.

'Really?' I shrug. 'Just Rex, you know. I forget about him for a moment and I'm happy. Then I remember and I feel bad for feeling happy.'

'I know exactly what you mean.'

We sit in silence for a moment. The loss of you, the Rex-shaped shadow, sits beside us. The extra guest.

'Jake, do you remember Rex ever mentioning a Mandy?' Easy Gina has gone. Angst Gina is back. 'Here, finish the potatoes.'

'Mandy?' He looks up surprised, puts down his cutlery. I shovel the potatoes on to his plate. 'Yes, I do remember a Mandy. Old girlfriend. I met her a couple of times. Why do you ask?'

'She emailed me.'

He raises an eyebrow above his glasses. 'Really? Why?'

'Asking if I wanted to meet up. Didn't say much really.'

'Odd.' He cuts into his steak and the pink juices spread across the white plate. 'I guess people feel the urge to connect at a time like this.'

'Yeah, that's what I think too. What was Mandy like?'

'As far as I could make out, no horns or forked tail.' Jake grins. 'But I never got to know Rex's girlfriends well, so she could have been hiding them, you never know. Seriously, she seemed nice enough.'

'You must have met others too, apart from Mandy,' I probe, curious now. 'He was hardly short of female attention.'

'Yeah, women liked Rex. Lucky bastard. So you're going to meet this Mandy?'

'Well, it's a chance to fill in the blanks a bit, isn't it? I thought it didn't matter that I didn't know that much about Rex's romantic past. He always told me it was irrelevant. Everything was about the present. But now, well . . . it makes me wonder.' I stare down at my plate, feeling a bit foolish. 'I wonder if I was naïve not asking questions.'

'Er, it's called being in love. You didn't do anything wrong, Gina,' Jake says gently.

I swallow hard, appreciating the way Jake could choose to make me feel worse about you, but doesn't. 'Thanks.'

'More importantly, this is a bloody good meal. You've inspired me. I am a man of few recipes, Gina, cooked badly but enthusiastically. I'll subject you to my mint and pea risotto this weekend.'

'Oh, I won't be here this weekend, or most weekends. I'll go back to Derbyshire, stay with my parents, get out of your hair.'

He frowns. 'You're not a lodger, you know? Please don't feel you have to hide away. Fran is really happy to have you here.'

'She didn't need to buy the crib,' I blurt, the words shooting out before I can stop them.

He goes stony-faced. The mood dips. 'I know. It was presumptuous. Sorry.'

'No, no, I don't mean it like that!' I'm mortified that he thinks I'm knocking Fran. 'It's so generous of her. But just putting me up here, that's generous enough, really.'

Jake turns his wine glass round and round by the stem,

brooding for a few moments before speaking. 'Gina, there's something you should know . . .'

'Oh?' I am wary of more revelations. No more, please.

'That crib. Fran bought it six months ago.'

'But I wasn't pregnant six months ago,' I say, puzzled.

'Fran had a miscarriage.'

'Oh no! Jake, I'm so sorry.'

'It's alright, very, very early, you know.' A resigned smile. 'She should never have bought the crib at that stage. She just loves to buy stuff. She couldn't help herself.'

'Oh, but it must be awful for her having me here.' I crush my hands over my mouth. Poor Fran. Poor Jake! I think about the scan. How painful that must have been for him. I've been so swallowed up in my own problems, I've forgotten other people have them, too. 'I shouldn't be here.'

'Of course you should. She suggested it, not that I objected, of course. She was really keen to take you in.'

'That's so big hearted of her. Wow.' I feel humbled. I've misjudged her.

'We weren't sure we were going to have children at all.' He leans back in his chair, staring into the ruby red of his wine. 'She wants to concentrate on her career. Hell, she wants me to concentrate on my career. Wants me to earn double what I do now. In today's newspaper climate? Fat chance,' he adds ruefully. 'I'm afraid she's bound for dis-appointment. We know there are likely to be medical difficulties in that area, too.' He shakes his head, collecting himself. 'Sorry, the wine, the company, making me overshare. You don't need to hear this.'

'What about you? Do you want children, Jake?' I ask gently.

He looks puzzled, then sad. 'Well, the brutally honest answer is that I've never been sure about babies. It's the most important job in the world, I know that, and that's why I couldn't do it with any reservations. If I became a father I'd want to do it wholeheartedly. I fear I might be too selfish.'

'Oh.' I'm surprised. 'Really? I'm not sure life works like that. Look at me. Hardly ideal.'

He smiles and shrugs. 'Mitigating circumstances.'

'No, it just happened. It could happen to you.'

'Unlikely.'

'You never know,' I say and immediately wish I hadn't.

'The pregnancy was a mistake, Gina.' Jake stands up abruptly and pulls a beer from the fridge, muttering something about starting the film before it's too late. Like the fridge door, I sense the subject is now firmly closed.

Twenty-two

Mandy

Mandy was a tea woman herself but had stupidly ordered a coffee because she was sure that Rex's wife would be a cappuccino drinker. She scooped the foam off the top with a teaspoon. Noxious black coffee beneath. Yuck. The undrinkable coffee was somehow typical of a day that felt rushed, badly prepared. And the longer she sat there waiting for Gina, the more it seemed like a thoroughly barking idea that she should be sitting in that little café off Baker Street at all. When she'd emailed Gina she hadn't expected her to agree to meet so soon. Like that day. She'd spent the morning running around like a mad thing, getting her hair and nails done, only to go out in the drizzle without an umbrella and ruin a twenty quid blow dry, chip one nail and to arrive here, damp, frizzed and – she glanced at her watch for the umpteenth time – early.

Rex's wife would no doubt be the type of woman who was fashionably late. A designer, it had said in the paper. She imagined a painfully thin blonde dressed in black, dangling one of those enormous handbags that cost a month's mortgage repayments from her skeletal arm. She imagined a woman who would look down on someone who worked as a PA. And she imagined a woman who would not believe her.

But she had to try. Didn't she? Mark was right. It *was* hanging over them. She had to tie this up. And it would never be the right time, would it? All these years she'd waited and bloody well waited for Rex to give her the sign. The sign had never come and now the bastard was dead.

No, she must not lose her nerve. She must tell Gina.

Clinking her teaspoon anxiously against the side of the china cup, she decided that she'd go in softly, softly. That's what she must do. Tread carefully, making sure the poor woman was stable enough to take it in before she blew her world apart. She was pregnant after all.

'Excuse me, are you Mandy?' asked a high, girlish voice behind her. 'Mandy Mills?'

Twenty-three

Mandy startles when I say her name. In the millisecond before she whips around, I sweep my eyes over her coral dress, fake-baked arms, nails painted the exact shade of her dress, one chipped. Not what I was expecting.

'Gina?' Hers is a wide, warm smile. Oh, not as beautiful as I'd feared. Gorgeous yes, twinkly, blonde and warm, but not beautiful. She's older than I imagined, too. Her hair is overprocessed. And she has pretty, lived-in green eyes. This is all immensely reassuring.

'Hi,' I smile back shyly, noticing the lack of a wedding ring. She notices me back, her eyes flitting from my expensive watch to the blue ring you bought me.

She pulls a chair out from under the table. 'You sit down, take the weight off your feet.' An estuary accent. No, she's not as posh as I imagined either. God, I'm so glad she's not posh. 'Beautiful bump.'

'Thank you.'

A waiter comes over straightaway and I order tea. We smile at each other blankly for a moment across the table, like we're on a blind date. 'It's so terrible about Rex,' she says, with flat sincerity. 'I'm deeply sorry, sweetheart.'

'You're not what I expected,' I blurt, before I can stop myself.

She laughs. 'Nor you! You are so *young*!' The mood pops and lightens.

'Thirty, not that young. I feel ninety.'

'*Young*!' she exclaims. Her eyes brighten to an unusual grass-green. 'And what amazing red hair!'

I touch my hair, wilder and thicker than ever in pregnancy. 'I spent my whole life wanting to be blonde and sleek like Grace Kelly.'

'And I always dreamed of having long red hair. Like that woman from T'Pau.' She ruffles hers. 'Got stuck with mousy mouse instead. Blonde from the bottle, in case you couldn't guess.'

Not all women declare themselves bottle blondes within the first five minutes of meeting – Fran likes to pretend she's a natural – and this makes me warm to Mandy. 'Thanks for getting in touch.'

She takes a sip of coffee, winces and puts it straight down again. 'You don't mind? It must have been a bit of a shocker getting a blast from Rex's past like that.' She winks at the waiter, hands him her cup of coffee. 'You couldn't swap it for a nice cup of tea, could you? Thanks so much.' She leans forwards across the table towards me, pushing her gold bangles up her wrist. 'I just thought that if *I* was in your position . . .' She stops, catching herself. 'I might want to meet his . . .' She slaps her forehead. 'This is all coming out wrong. Sorry.'

'Oh, please don't be sorry. The email came at exactly the

right time. I've been thinking about Rex's past a lot recently, wondering if it could shed light on anything that's happening now. I . . . I know it sounds silly.' I hesitate, embarrassed. 'It's just that we haven't been married that long. There are a few . . . blanks to fill in.'

The waiter brings Mandy a cup of tea. She looks up at him, winks. 'Lovely. Ta very much.' She looks back at me. 'Blanks? Aren't there always, eh?'

'You see the thing is, part of the reason I want to know is that I'm sure Rex is still alive, Mandy. Missing, not dead. Any clues as to his personality, his state of mind, could help us find him.'

She freezes, her cup in mid-air. 'Alive?'

'Definitely.'

'Woo. OK. I'll be honest with you, Gina, I took it he was dead.'

'Dead men aren't very good at burying themselves.' I nick Raf's line.

'You've got a point there.' She puts her cup down, listens to me carefully, head cocked slightly. There's something about her that I instinctively trust.

'Sometimes I feel like the only one. The only one who still has faith he's out there, Mandy.'

Her green eyes fill with pity. I worry that I've come on too heavy too soon. 'You keep that faith, sweetheart. Probably wouldn't approve of us two having coffee, eh?' She grins. There is mischief in that collusive grin.

I smile. 'Probably not.'

'Well, he's not here, sweetheart, so feel free to ask me what the hell you like.'

Faced with an open invitation, my brain seizes. 'Um, so you were together two years?'

'About that.'

'Do you mind me asking why you split?'

'Oh, it's never one thing, is it? There are some men who suck you in and it's hard to know which way is up, which down. He was one of those, I guess.' She studies me intently, weighing up what else to reveal. 'I was in that relationship longer than I should have been, Gina, let's just say that. He didn't want to commit. Blew hot and cold. All that clichéd stuff.' A quick tight smile. 'Look, you've got enough on your plate, I can see that. You don't want to hear me moaning on. It's in the past anyway.'

'No, please. I want to know.'

'Well, I always hoped he'd grow up one day, to be frank. I always knew it would take the right woman. What I didn't know at the time was that woman wasn't me.' She smiles, more warmly now. 'It was you.'

I stare down at the table, feeling an irrational shot of guilt for being the one you married. Mandy seems so lovely.

'That was one of his many contradictions, wasn't it? He was this brave adventure boy and yet . . . oh blimey, he was shit scared of the things he wanted most.'

I look up at her quizzically: what did you want most?

'Stability, commitment, a family of his own. Like a normal guy. Most guys settle down and commit by their thirties, don't they? He couldn't.' She smiles and frowns at the same time; different feelings competing to express themselves. 'He needed someone who would totally blow him away and

148

make him forget his fear of commitment, I guess.' She smiles, rolls her eyes. 'Now I am banging on.'

'*Do* bang on. Please. It's so good to talk to someone candidly about Rex. Hardly anyone will, not now. It's as if no one wants to speak ill of the . . .' I can't say it.

Mandy twists the gold bangles on her wrist, picks up the stalled conversation. 'The longer we were together, the happier we were, the more tricky he became. That was the funny thing. It's like he didn't *want* it to work, Gina. His finger was always hovering over the destruct button.'

Things fall into place in some dark, shadowy corner of my brain. Did your fear of commitment perversely explain why you wanted to get married so quickly to me, to seal the deal before the typhoon of endorphins wore off? Did love only make sense to you at full pelt? Is that why you had to believe I was perfect? You were a man of extremes. There was never a middle way. Absolute commitment within a few days of meeting on one side of the coin; a fear of commitment on the other.

'But all men can be changed by a good woman, they really can. And that was you, Gina. You must take comfort from that.'

'I do.'

Mandy sighs, looks away. 'It was like pressure building up in his head, that's what he said. I'll never forget the words. Made me feel like a deep-fat fryer.' She smiles. 'He never changed his mind after ending it. Never looked back, never showed the slightest wobble.' She sips her cup of tea, adds without pity, 'He was going out with someone else within the week.'

'I'm sorry.' We've all been there. 'That must have been gutting.'

'Rex is Rex. He can't be anything else, can he?' She fiddles with the teaspoon, rolling it on the side of the saucer.

'No,' I agree thoughtfully. 'No, he can't.'

She shakes her head again, whistles beneath her breath. 'And those moods! Up and down. I tried to get him to go to the doctor but of course he refused point blank. He had no time for . . . cod psychology he called it. But I didn't think it was right, you know, that someone should feel like Superman half the time, so down the rest.' She frowns, trying to gauge my reaction. 'You look surprised. Was he not like that with you?'

'No, not really. Ever since I met him he's seemed pretty happy, full of beans, apart from when he worked too hard, of course. His work definitely wore him down. But he escaped it by doing all his adrenaline hobby things, getting away.' I remember with a pang the pile of surf gear by the beach cabin door. That was all it was meant to be, a windsurfing holiday. Now we're here. It's still incomprehensible.

'You know what? It sounds to me like he was on one long high with you. You were . . . sorry, *are* good for him.' She watches me for a moment. 'I can see why he fell for you, Gina, you and your lovely hair.' She puts a hand on my sleeve and the physical contact shocks me a little. 'He must have been dead chuffed to know he was going to be a father, eh?'

I swallow hard. 'No, no, that's the worst thing, Mandy, I never got to tell him. He didn't know.'

'Oh.' Mandy bites her lip now, flecking her front teeth with pink lipstick. 'I'm sorry.'

'But he'll be so happy when he gets back. He'll love being a father.'

Something about her tightens. For a beat, I feel uncomfortable.

'He will come back. He can't have just . . . just . . .' I start to sniff. Oh no. I really don't want the waterworks to come on in front of Mandy.

She pulls a tissue out of her handbag and hands it to me. 'Thanks.' I blow my nose. 'He can't have just sunk to the bottom of the sea without a trace. He was a brilliant windsurfer. There wasn't a storm, high winds, nothing like that.'

'And didn't he win some gold medal when he was younger? I never heard the end of that one.' She beats her chest like a silverback. 'The Windsurfing Champion.'

'Medal?'

'Gold, wasn't it? I'm sure it was gold.'

I puzzle over this for a moment then dismiss it. You must have told me and I forgot. 'Jake thinks there's a possibility he could have windsurfed to Morocco.'

Mandy's eyes flash. 'Jake, the brother? How's he doing then?'

'OK. He's been amazing. Spearheaded the campaign to find Rex, flown back and forth . . .' Just saying it out loud makes me realise how much he's done. 'I'm living with him and his girlfriend now.'

'Good man that Jake.' She hesitates, as if wondering how candid she should be. 'Rex never appreciated him.'

'No, I don't think he did. It's a shame. I never understood why.'

'Competitive. Rex was bloody competitive. I think he always thought Jake had it easy.' She frowns, the furrows in her forehead pooling foundation. 'Isn't Jake's dad wealthy?'

'I don't know. But Jake doesn't seem particularly wealthy.'

'The rich ones never do, do they? Or maybe it was something about Jake having a dad around. Rex didn't have that. I don't know. But there were tensions alright.'

I nod, trying not to feel peeved that Mandy knows so much about your family dynamics. You never spoke about your father to me – or Jake – for long without closing the subject down pretty sharpish. Why did you speak to her?

'And the mum.' Mandy whistles. 'There's more warmth in my son's goldfish.'

'Anything else, ladies?' asks the waiter.

'No, just the bill please.' She applies a slick of lip gloss expertly, without a mirror. 'Got to pick up my son from football. Footie mad.'

'Right,' I say, trying to hide my disappointment. There is so much more stuff I want to ask. I like Mandy. I feel like we could talk for hours.

'I've probably said too much. I could talk the hind legs off a donkey.' She tucks a fiver under her saucer. 'I'll get this. My treat.'

'Thank you, thank you for suggesting we meet too.'

'We'll stay in touch now, shall we?'

'I'd really like that.'

She looks chuffed. 'Really?' Unexpectedly, she crushes me to her in a bear hug. 'Whatever happens, Gina, you've got to be strong, eh?'

'I'm trying.'

'That's the spirit.'

She holds me firmly by the forearms, fixes me with these grass-green eyes. 'I don't mean to belittle your predicament, but I'll tell you for free, Gina, that men let women down in all sorts of ways – they go missing, they have affairs, they walk out without a backward glance – and the best thing any woman can do is make sure they can survive on their own.' She gazes down at my tummy. 'Especially if kids are in the picture.' There is something steely in her voice now. I wouldn't want to be on the wrong side of her. 'Promise me you won't spend the rest of your life waiting for Rex to come home, eh?'

Of course I will spend the rest of my life waiting for you to come home.

'If he doesn't want to be found, he won't be.' She pulls her hefty bag over her shoulder, smiles kindly. 'If there's one thing I know about Rex, sweetheart, it's that.'

Twenty-four

'Crockery flying yet?'

'Oh, they're having a right humdinger, Lucy.' I whisper into the mobile phone and perch on the edge of my bed. 'I'm never going to get out of here.'

'Do you think they'll shag and make up?'

'Oh God, I hope not. How will I escape then?'

Lucy laughs. 'Through the skylight?'

'I've got a train to catch to Derbyshire in forty minutes.' I glance at the clock. Shit. I can hang on for another few minutes but no longer. Wedging my mobile between my ear and shoulder, I walk back to my bedroom door, open it another inch. Fran is still shouting. I hear my name.

'Lucy, I just heard my name,' I whisper frantically.

'What do you mean?'

'They're arguing about me. I've outstayed my welcome, I knew it.' Your disappearance has changed so many lives already, Rex. It's like a boulder rolling downhill, going faster and faster. When will it stop?

'I'm sure they're not, Gee. Fran invited you to stay, remember?'

'Bet she's regretting it now.'

A door slams.

'Oh, did I just hear—?'

'Door. Slamming. Hard. Lucy, I think they've finished. I'm going to run for it while the coast is clear. I'll see you next week for lunch.'

I creep out of the bedroom and down the stairs with my bags, cursing each creaking stair tread. To my surprise I hear them behind their bedroom door – no one has left the room – having a heated, hushed conversation.

'You've got to tell her,' Fran is hissing.

Tell her. Me? What?

'She seems to be totally clueless, Jake. It's not fair. All the decisions she's making about this baby are based on—'

Jake interrupts in a low, angry growl. 'Can you just leave the baby out of this, Fran?'

What about the baby? What the hell are they talking about?

'I think it's imperative that we *do* talk about the baby, Jake.'

'Fran, for fuck's sake,' says Jake in a voice that I haven't heard him use before. 'Stop it.'

Knowing that I've got to get as far away from this bedroom as possible in the shortest amount of time, I start to creep down the corridor. But it's too late. The bedroom door flings open. Fran's glare catches me like a blinding prison searchlight.

'I . . . I . . . I was just heading to the train station. I'm going to Derbyshire.'

'Right.' The way she's looking at me, she knows I've been listening.

'Do you want a lift to the station, Gina?' calls Jake from the bedroom in a tight voice.

'I'm fine, I'll hop on the Tube.'

Fran is still glaring.

'It's no bother, I'll take you.' Jake is by the door now, tucking a crumpled blue shirt into the waistband of his jeans. Fran turns her searchlight glare to Jake; she clearly does not want him to take me to the station.

'Honestly, I'd rather get the Tube. The traffic is bad at this time, I might miss my train.'

Jake's brow furrows. He knows I've heard them too now. He winces apologetically.

'See you Sunday night,' I say as brightly as I can.

'Enjoy the Brecon Beacons, hon,' calls Fran as I hurry down the stairs with my bag. I don't stop to correct her.

Twenty-five

I lean back on the deck chair, watching a blood orange sun sink behind the forbidding escarpments of green and grey stone. I never get bored of the view. You loved those peaks too, the earthy lanolin smell of the surrounding fields, the epic cloudscapes of the Derbyshire skies. The last time we were here at Dawn's? January, I think. We lay in bed in the spare room, giggling and whispering, you telling me how to survive outside at night – build up a mattress from sticks and leaves, the worst cold comes from the ground, have sex – and were unable to keep our eyes off each other in company. The second morning you alarmed my family by nonchalantly going off on a walk on your own after breakfast, not telling a soul where you were going. There was no mobile reception and you didn't come back in time for lunch. I had to reassure my parents that you did this kind of thing quite a lot. You always turned up in the end. Nothing to worry about. But even I watched the swirling soup of steel grey clouds with trepidation – you wouldn't have been the first person to have got lost and hypothermic up there in bad weather – and when you finally breezed in at tea time, as if you'd just popped out to buy a pint of milk, you were astonished that we'd all been worried about you.

'Aunty Gee, can I feel the bump?'

'Hey, Danny.'

Danny is pink cheeked beneath his wild windswept mop of butter-blond hair. There are leaves stuck to his blue fleece, like he might have rolled around in the compost pit, which he most probably has. Happily neither him nor Tom have succumbed to their mother's attempts to civilise them. Despite all their neatly pressed clothes and early bedtimes and banned toys – guns, swords, anything with a hint of violence – they always manage to get a streak of mud on their cheeks, tear the knees of their trousers, and have the ingenuity to transform anything – barbecue skewer, stick, toothbrush – into a weapon.

'Baby's moving. Here, give me your hand.' I press his small hand to my tummy. The baby shifts a limb beneath it.

He looks unsure. 'Feels bit strange, Aunty Gina.'

'Feels stranger when it's in your tummy.'

He swiftly removes his hand and digs a sandy half sucked lolly out of his pocket. 'I saved it from Kit's party yesterday,' he grins, exposing one dark tooth, blackened after a tumble from the apple tree. 'Lick?'

'Not this time. Thanks, though.'

He sits down next to me, picks a blade of grass and holds it up, watching an ant march along it. I remember sitting in a garden just like this – half a mile away – as a child, watching ants climb up my white nylon lace socks. For the first time in years I get a pang of yearning for the landscape of my childhood. We could have done this together, Rex. We could have come back here together, stole it from my past, made it our own . . .

'Aunty Gina, now that Uncle Rex is dead will you come and live with us?'

I take a sharp intake of breath. 'He's missing, Danny, not dead.'

'Mummy says he's dead.'

'No. He's missing.'

He ponders this for a moment. 'Mummy has put hot air balloon wallpaper in the spare room. She says my cousin will sleep there.'

I smile, trying to avoid straight answers. 'It's cool wallpaper, isn't it?'

'Too babyish.'

'Way too babyish if you're five.'

Danny puffs his chest out a little. 'It'll be fun to have a cousin to play with, though.'

'He's going to be very, very lucky to have such lovely cousins to play with.'

'It could be a girl. That's what Mummy says.'

'It could. I just think of it as a boy, a boy like you.'

'Me too. I'd hate to be a girl.'

I laugh. 'Luckily you're not, eh?'

Danny looks thoughtful. 'I wouldn't like not having a daddy either.'

'Sorry?' Although I heard it right the first time.

'My cousin won't have a daddy, will he?'

This floors me. I can almost imagine a future for myself without you, Rex. But I can't go there with the baby. I'm protected by these, the darkest of thoughts, by the fact that

159

the baby is still a pregnancy rather than a child. But Danny reminds me that one day he will be a little boy just like him, a boy who needs guidance, who wants to learn how to ride a bike, how to build a bonfire and kick a football . . . You need to come home. Soon.

Danny shoves the lolly into his cheek. 'He can share my daddy if he likes.'

'That's very kind of you.' I pull him towards me and kiss the top of his head. 'You are such a lovely boy, Danny.'

'Lunch!' bellows Dawn from the back door of the house, wiping her hands on her striped apron. She can probably be heard in Yorkshire.

'We better go.'

'I'm taking my ant to lunch.' Danny holds the blade of grass in front of him as he walks.

As we amble through the garden towards the barn, through the tunnels of lavender, the low gnarled branches of the apple tree, the wooden climbing frame, I am whacked by a powerful sense of déjà vu. I look up the lane that runs alongside the house and I can almost see you walking through the beech trees, swigging from your camelback water bottle, compass dangling from your neck. *See, no need to worry. I'm back safe.*

'What a treat, eh?' Mum says cheerily, determined that nothing will overshadow Sunday lunch, this prized family occasion, especially now they've snatched me back from the city so they can put more meat on my bones.

The wooden outdoor table is covered with a navy and white polka dot tablecloth, sprigs of meadow flowers in little jam pots, the usual abundance of food. It is like something from a catalogue, a reward for a life lived well. Would we have had this one day, too? Was this the pay off? Or are you too fiery, too restless to be happy with simple pleasures and polka dot tablecloths? 'It's gorgeous, Dawn.' I sit down.

'Better than the old smoke, eh? You know what, it's been blissful out here this summer. We've had so many butterflies this year, haven't we, Gareth?'

Gareth, who is seated next to my mother, nods obligingly, eyeing me warily, as if I might just blow at any moment. He hates dramas of any kind. 'A lot of cabbage whites,' he confirms drolly.

You were imperiously amused by my family's reliance on small pleasantries, but funnily enough I value them now more than ever, the picket fence of politeness that protects us from my anguish.

'You look a picture in that frock, Gee,' says Dawn, digging into the breadbasket with gusto. I'm wearing the dress she bought me in Hennes, a custard-yellow maternity sundress that is at odds with my situation, and my red hair for that matter. 'Here, help yourself to tomato salad, sis.'

'I'll do it.' Mum tongs tomato slices onto my plate. She'll be cutting up my food next. 'Dressing, love?'

'Please.'

'So how's life at Jake's?' asks Dad, watching me eat approvingly. 'Looking after you, eh?'

'Absolutely.'

'Good, promised me he would.'

'Don't tell me you had a word, Dad?'

Dad grins in reply. Oh, Dad.

'And how's Princess Francesca?' Dawn puts on a snooty

voice. She's still annoyed that I am living with Fran and Jake rather than her and Gareth, irrespective of practical considerations.

'Busy. She works long hours.'

'Look at you, trying not to sound relieved about that,' laughs Dawn.

I shoot Dawn a dark look, but she's right. Somehow Dawn's always bloody right.

'Now I really must give her some of my damson jam,' says Mum, adding a surreal fête-flavoured twist to the proceedings. 'I'll be eating it until I'm ninety at this rate. I made far too much last year.'

'Jam! Fran won't eat jam, Mum!' Dawn hoots. 'She might just inhale cottage cheese. Perhaps a raisin if she's *really* going to have a blow out.' Dad guffaws into his salad, dribbling dressing into his beard. The twins jump up from the table and dart towards the nearest football in the garden.

'Boys!' shrieks Dawn. 'I'm not running a zoo here!'

'Let them go, Dawn. Good to have some grown-up time, yes?' Gareth speaks in a cryptic, loud self-conscious whisper, as if trying to impart a coded marital message that I don't understand.

Dawn's eyes dart towards me, back at Gareth. 'Oh, yes, right. Yes, of course.'

A tension descends. More glances are exchanged. Over the hills I hear the faint drum roll that tells me that you are about to be mentioned, laid out on the table for discussion. Dad clears his throat and sits more upright in his chair, spreads his thick-fingered hands in front of him.

Mum clears her throat, too. 'Daddy's been digging around

a bit more.' The tip of her nose pinks as it always does when she's nervous. 'Haven't you, Teddy?'

Dad winks. 'One ear to the ground at all times, Gina.'

Dawn and I look at each other, our mouths twitching. The idea of Dad – who can barely follow the plot of *The Bill* – sleuthing is funny.

'You better give her an update, Ted,' says Mum, nervously twisting a crust of bread in her fingers.

'Well, it's a tricky old business alright.' He checks me for signs of hysteria before continuing. Mum gives him an encouraging nod from the other side of the table. 'It's a bit of a bureaucratic mess, involving different police forces, different territories. Grey areas. It gives me a blinding headache just thinking about it.'

'Do get to the point, Teddy,' mutters Mum, dabbing at the corner of her mouth with a napkin.

'Right, well, the thing is . . . if Rex were a fishing man and his boat went down, even if his boat wasn't found, or his body, we might be able to get a death certificate after six months. *Might*.'

I look at Dawn. She won't meet my eye now. Gareth has gone scarlet and is pushing down his cuticles. 'Where's this going, Dad?'

'The lawyer we've been using in Malaga, love, the one the missing persons' charity put us in touch with, he explained that there's a small quirk called, er, one second, I forget.' He pulls a crumpled bit of yellow notepaper out of his corduroy pocket, pulls his reading glasses up on their chain. 'An interim "declaration of absence",' he reads in his posher reading voice. 'But I'm afraid it's complicated.'

'Dad, please . . .' My heart is starting to slam.

'We've really got to prove he's dead, otherwise it's a ten-year wait, love.'

'There's no straightforward way round it, sis. We'll need to do some serious jiggery pokery.'

I look from one of them to the other, puzzled, spotting a conspiracy.

'We're terribly worried about how you're going to support yourself without his life insurance,' Mum says quietly.

'Life insurance? Mum, we could get a call any minute saying he's in a hospital somewhere. What are you talking about?'

'Oh, Gina. Not that again. Please.' Mum drops her forehead to her hand, knocking over a glass of water. Dawn jumps up and frantically dabs at it with a tea towel. 'Gina, you are going to have a baby,' Mum continues wearily. 'A baby, love.' She repeats it, as if I might not know what she's talking about.

'Children don't come cheap, you know,' Gareth offers. 'I should know.'

'Doesn't anyone understand? I don't want Rex's life insurance, I just want him home,' I cry.

'Of course you don't *want* him dead, no one's saying that, Gee,' says Dawn, starting to pile strawberries into a bowl. 'Don't be daft.'

'Three-quarters of missing people are found in the first forty-eight hours,' Dad says in his softest bedtime-story voice. 'He's been gone months, months now, Gina. There comes a time—'

'Why do I feel like the last person to believe in fairies

around here? There's no body, in case you haven't realised. Until then he's *not* dead.'

'For God's sake, sis, how long are you going to keep this up for?' groans Dawn. 'It's getting ridiculous.'

I stare down at my strawberries in fury, trying to stop myself from yelling at them all to fuck off. I know they're only trying to help.

'Think of the baby,' whispers Mum. 'Just think of the baby.'

'I'm going to have that tattooed on my fucking forehead.'

'Language, Gina!'

A nervous giggle explodes from Dawn, masking the ringing sound coming from inside the conservatory. She tilts her head in its direction. 'Your phone I think, Gee.'

'Don't run so fast, love,' Mum shouts after me as I bolt towards the phone, kicking over my chair as I run. 'You're pregnant.'

It takes me a few moments to find the damn thing in the back of Danny's toy cement truck. It could be you. It's not, of course. 'Jake?'

'Gina . . .' His voice sounds strange and thin.

'Jake, are you OK? What's the matter?'

'Someone has phoned the missing persons' hotline.' His voice wavers. 'There's been a sighting.'

Twenty-six

Mandy

The goal was two muddy coats on the wet park grass. Ryan and his friend Ty scrambled, rolled and kicked around it, oblivious to the rain and cold. Mandy, watching them from a damp bench, hunkered down under her umbrella and rearranged her scarf to protect her nostrils and mouth from the wind. It was like winter already. Where had the time gone? And still she'd not had the balls to tell Gina.

'Watch this, Mum! Goal kick,' Ryan yelled, sensing that his mother's attention was wavering. He planted the ball a few metres from the goal, charged at it, head down like a baby bull. Ryan's ability to focus solely on one thing – whether a ball, Lego or a packet of football cards – and forget about everything else was one of the many things she loved about him; she lacked those qualities herself.

What would her life have been like *had* she had some focus, rather than muddling through? She'd be earning a lot more money, that's for sure. But money wouldn't have given her Ryan. And marrying a wealthy man hadn't helped

Gina. No, it wasn't looking good for Gina.

'Goal!' whooped Ryan, arms in the air. 'Goal!'

Mandy clapped, trying to disguise the fact that her mind was elsewhere.

She still half expected Rex to pitch up on her doorstep – the way he'd used to before she met Mark – eyes glittering, face contorted with stress that came not just from his job but something deep inside of him that couldn't be contained. She'd always invite him in, even if it were the middle of the night, putting aside her own anger at his past behaviour. He wanted to sit on the sofa and listen to her babble on, silly stories about her day in the office, the neighbours, Ryan, trivial domestic stuff; it had a soothing effect, as if there were a part of him that craved humdrum ordinariness in his frantic, high-pitched life. He told her so little about his own life in return, though. She used to think he held it back so that she'd have less of a claim to it. A couple of hours later, longer sometimes – he'd been known to conk out on the sofa – he'd sink back into the night, calmer than when he'd arrived. She wouldn't see him again for weeks. Until the next time one of those moods hit.

Funny that Gina didn't recognise that version of Rex. Something about Gina's ignorance worried her. Did she actually know her own husband? She'd put money on the fact that Rex wouldn't have remained on a stable high indefinitely, however madly in love they were. At some point his spirits would have come crashing down around him. And then what?

Mandy couldn't stop thinking about that day in the café, the way that poor girl's tired, haunted eyes had lit up when she talked about Rex not being dead, saying that if he were she'd feel it or some such. There was something so sweet, loyal and innocent about her. Rex must have had her eating from his hand; she was just the type. She'd seen those relationships before – older guy, sweet young girl – there was always an imbalance of power somewhere if you dug deep enough, a willingness on the girl's part to believe that the man was somehow a bigger, stronger human being than he actually was; that was part of the transaction. Those girls sensed that they shouldn't question things too much. And they were right. The more you questioned Rex, the less he gave. He was always looking for unconditional acceptance. Is that what Gina gave him? No wonder it was Gina he married, not herself. She never could keep her trap shut. She'd always asked too many questions.

'Goal!' shouted Ryan.

But Mandy didn't hear him. She was too busy typing out a text message to Gina. She had to try one last time.

Twenty-seven

Fran is standing in the hall, right in front of me, stark naked. The front door shuts behind me with a clunk. She laughs, not attempting to cover herself up, giving me a chance to admire her body. 'I'll make myself decent and be down in two secs.'

'Jake,' I call again, desperately hoping he's not naked too and I haven't interrupted them shagging. Not that I care that much. 'Jake?'

I find him in the living room – dressed, thankfully – and throw myself into his arms. 'Thank you. I knew he was alive! I knew it, I knew it, I knew it!'

'Gina, it may not be anything,' implores Jake, pushing his hair off his face. 'It was a man resembling Rex with longer hair and a beard. It doesn't mean . . .'

'But he would have longer hair and a beard, wouldn't he?' I beam at him. 'Oh my God, Jake, it all makes sense, perfect sense. Who spotted him?'

He sits down on the edge of an armchair, takes off his glasses and rubs his eyes. I notice how drained he looks. 'It was a tourist, British, a woman, a pensioner. She'd seen a leaflet at the airport a couple of days earlier.'

'So the leaflets did work! All your hard work paid off.'

I am about to hug him again when Jake says, 'It's not that simple. Sit down a sec.'

I sit down on the sofa opposite him, my enthusiasm deflating out of me like air from a balloon.

'You didn't need to rush back from Derbyshire like this, Gina.'

'I couldn't stay there. I couldn't sit still. Tell me it all again, please.'

He slips his glasses back on, peers at me bookishly from above their frames. 'This woman, a British tourist – she sounded like an older lady on the phone – she believes she saw a man who resembled Rex in a souk in Marrakesh. She didn't realise until a few hours after spotting him who he was, but thought his face was familiar at the time for some reason, like she might have met him once. Those were her words.'

'Oh my God.' I can't help the slow smile spreading across my face. 'This changes everything, Jake.'

'No it doesn't, hon.' I whip around to see Fran standing at the door of the sitting room, dressed in a dove grey silk dressing gown now, the sash belt tied tight around her slim waist. 'It doesn't change anything. It just makes things more complicated.'

Jake glances at Fran wearily. 'Fran doesn't think I should have told you, Gina.'

'What?' I feel anger bubble up inside. 'Why not, Fran?'

She sits down next to me on the sofa, too close to my side, smelling of soaped clean skin. 'Honey, there are false sightings all the time. There must be a million men in Morocco who

170

resemble Rex, you know, tourists, hippies, hirsute travellers.'

Jake says nothing. Is he not convinced by the sighting either?

'All this is going to do is make the lawyer's job even more of a pig's arse.' There is a whine in Fran's voice now that is getting on my nerves. I wish she'd just butt out. 'That's the problem. You need closure, Gina. Not this.'

'Clearly he's not dead, Fran,' I say curtly.

'Oh for goodness sake,' she groans, as if I'm totally impossible. 'Tell her the other details, Jake.'

'Other details?' My heart starts to thump excitedly.

Jake's shoulders hunch. 'There is one thing I didn't mention on the phone. This man, the man who resembled Rex, he was with another woman.' He lets the word hang there for a moment.

'With? You mean . . .'

He averts his gaze. 'Yes.'

'This is not good for the baby,' says Fran. 'I told you, Jake. I told you that you shouldn't have mentioned any of this stuff to Gina. You never listen.'

I sit very still, trying to take in the implications of what Jake's saying. Tears sting my eyes.

'Gina,' says Jake softly, crouching down opposite me so that his head is level with my knees. 'Look at me. Fran is right, I'm afraid. It may be true. But we have to remember that there are false sightings all the time. People mean well, reporting it, but it's not necessarily Rex.'

'It's not him,' Fran is gently saying over and over, like a lullaby. 'It's not your Rex, hon. He wouldn't run off with another woman, would he? You know that.'

I wipe my eyes on my sleeve, ignoring Fran. 'What does your mother think?'

'She wants to believe it's him,' says Jake.

'If you told Clarice that Rex had been spotted on the high wire in Cirque du Soleil she'd believe it. Catholics, even lapsed ones, have enormous capabilities for faith and denial, isn't that true, Jake?'

Jake smiles. 'And the rest.'

Fran pulls me towards her, pushing my face into her damp hair. 'You've just got to take it one step at a time, hon. Let's all just get to your due date, eh?' She rubs my arm. 'We're here for you, really here for you. Aren't we, Jake?'

Jake gives me an encouraging smile, but he looks quietly devastated in a way that I've not seen before. And I wonder if his hopes are being smashed by Fran's persistent cynicism, too.

'I'm going to fly to Marrakesh and find him.' I sit up, brightening. 'That's what I'm going to do.'

'Not in your condition,' Fran says sternly. 'I forbid it.'

I turn to Jake. 'Will you go, please? One more time.'

'Hon, think about this,' interrupts Fran. 'Think about it for just one second. Do you know how much time Jake has spent on this campaign? How many hours? Days? *Weeks*? It's taking over our lives. Your life. Think about it, what's Jake meant to do? Wander around the souks for days and days on the off chance some dozy OAP has spotted a man with a beard?'

'We can't just sit here doing nothing!'

Jake walks to the window, parts the blinds with his fingers and looks out at the autumnal sky darkening behind a frame

172

of vivid ginger leaves. 'I'll go.' He whips around to face me, eyes blazing. 'Of course I will.'

'Oh, for fuck's sake,' groans Fran.

Securing a cheap, last-minute ticket, Jake leaves for Morocco at the crack of dawn the following morning. I hear him banging around downstairs, trying to be quiet, and seize my chance to talk to him alone. 'Jake!' I hiss from the landing as he reaches for the front door, bag over his shoulder.

He looks up. 'What are you doing up at this insane hour? Go back to bed.'

I creep down the stairs to the front door, desperate not to wake Fran. 'Can I ask you something?'

'This already sounds like a question I won't be able to answer.'

'It's not about the sighting. It's about something else.'

He looks curious. 'What is it?'

'Did Rex win a gold medal for windsurfing when he was in his early twenties?'

'A medal?' He looks puzzled. 'Unlikely. He only learned to do it when he was about thirty.'

'You're sure?' Mandy said you'd mentioned it many times.

'Pretty sure. I doubt Rex would have wasted an opportunity to inform me if he had won a medal, Gina. Why do you ask?'

'Oh. Someone has got their wires crossed, that's all. I keep thinking about it for some reason, but it's not important.'

He glances at his watch. 'I've really got to leave.'

'Sorry.' I crane up and kiss him on the cheek. 'Come back with my husband, please.'

Twenty-eight

I've designed a pink striped tea towel. That's it, all day. No wonder Martin looks so pissed off. I suspected it was only a matter of time before the dramatic frisson of my situation wore off and he became frustrated at my rubbish output. I hope he hasn't reported it to Hector, although I can't really blame him if he has. Ever since Jake left for Morocco I've been in a fog, unable to concentrate, counting the minutes until he calls. Tea towels no longer impinge.

I've been producing Hollywood scenarios of your return, Rex. My favourite involves you thrusting open Grey Home's double doors, striding into the studio, all tanned limbs and wild piratical hair, scooping me up and carrying me back to our beloved little flat in your arms. My least favourite involves you and another woman kissing beneath Marrakesh's arched doorways, rolling on a bed covered in sequined Moroccan throws, heat and cinnamon in her long sun-bleached hair. But even this can be explained: you were bumped on the head by a windsurf sail, lost your memory, have been picked up by a fishing boat, deposited in

Africa where, alone and vulnerable, you've fallen into the arms of a rich female bohemian traveller who wants to nurse you back to health. Very soon something will trigger your memory. And our wonderful life will come flooding back to you, like the ocean seeps through the smallest hole in a boat's hull. Or maybe Jake will just amble round a corner in Marrakesh – I can see him now, straw sun hat on, glasses misting up, wearing his cobalt-blue crumpled linen shirt – and there you will be.

'Heard these are vitally important for the growing baby's brain development.' A handful of Quality Street chocolates scatter across my desk. I look up. Femi grins back at me. 'News from Jake?' she types.

'Not yet,' I type back.

'Bah.'

'Fran's given him a HUGE list of rugs and cushions and stuff to buy from the souks! Will be miracle if he finds any time to look for Rex.'

'Ha! Canny woman – why waste retail op? How feet today BTW?'

I stick a puffy foot out from the side of my desk.

Femi bends down to look. 'That's nothing. I got so water-filled I had stretch marks on my ARMS.'

'I reckon I'm going to get stretch marks on my toes. Is possible?'

'When it comes to pregnancy ANYTHING possible.'

'Fem, do you think lots of men lie about their achievements?'

'What do you mean? What sort of achievements? Size? ☺'

'Do you think weird if someone says they've won a medal for something, something sporty say, and haven't?'

'If man lies about little things I'd worry he lied about BIG things too.'

'☹'

'Oh dear – wasn't the answer you were looking for? What's all about?' Femi cocks her head around the side of her Mac, directing my attention to the corner of the studio. 'Wait a minute. Who IS that? Wild shoes. And Hector!?!? I thought he was safely back in Hong Kong this week?'

Outside the glass meeting room, Martin and Hector are shaking the hand of a lithe young woman in canary yellow heels. She looks like she could be a member of an Indie girl band, the feisty beautiful type who plays drums at the back. Hector opens the door for her with exaggerated chivalry, then glances over at me with the tiniest of smiles as if he knew he'd catch me looking. I look away quickly and return to fiddling with the striped tea towel design. I add tassels.

'Gina?' There's a block of striped candy pink shirt directly in front of me. I look up: Martin's smile displays teeth so white they have a strange grey tinge to them, like they've been peroxided down to the dentine. 'I think you may as well call it a day.'

'Oh.' I swallow my mouthful of toffee half chewed. Something tells me that this comment doesn't come from a concern for my pre-natal welfare. 'But it's not even five o'clock, Martin.'

'You've done enough.' We both know that what he really means is, you've done f–all, just go home and come back in fresh tomorrow morning.

'I'm happy to stay.' In the middle of a recession you can't

afford not to appear willing and hard working. 'Really.'

'No need.'

'Oh, OK. Um, thanks.' I take the order sheepishly, gather up my bag, shut down my computer. Femi shoots a quizzical look across the desk. 'Sorry if I've been a bit distracted today, Martin.'

His nose wrinkles: this is a frown. Since he's had Botox his wrinkles have migrated to odd places. 'Well, not long now, Gina, honey. Then you can put your feet up and have a proper rest.'

'See you next week then,' I say brightly, trying to sound like a professional designer, not a woman in crisis who he can't fire without facing a lawsuit. 'I've got some great ideas for the linen collection.' I hope he doesn't push me on this because I haven't.

'Great. That's great.' He puts his hands on his hips. 'Just so you know, I think we've found your maternity cover. Lila. She's just popped in to sew things up.' He does a small torso jiggle, like he's warming up to dance. 'And the boss says yes.'

Hector likes her? Well of course he does. She's pretty, blonde and looks like she was born in the eighties.

'I'd be very grateful if you could show Lila the ropes before you go.'

'No problem.' I don't really like the idea of being replaced by someone called Lila. I don't like the idea of being replaced at all.

'I am so in love with her portfolio. It's very . . . *woo*! Ex St Martins, of course. But she'll be able to do the more bog standard stuff, too. Young, hungry, comes with super duper references.' He cocks his head on one side in a gesture of exaggerated empathy. 'If you *do* decide you don't want to come back . . .'

'Martin, I will definitely—'

He puts a finger to his lips, zips them. 'Say nothing! I know it's your legal right not to tell me now, Gina. All I'm saying is that, hypothetically speaking, *should* you decide you don't want to return to this job, which would be perfectly understandable given all the horrific turmoil you've suffered in the last few months, totally understandable, no one would blame you, least of all me, and if that were the case, hypothetically speaking again, I'll have Lila all trained up and ready to go.' He puts a hand on my lower back. 'I want you to know you can sleep easily, Gina. That's all. Oh, wait a minute.' His nose frowns again. He is looking in the direction of the senior offices. 'Hector wants to see you.'

My heart sinks. 'Now?'

'Hector doesn't do later, honey.'

Hector's door, usually closed, is ajar. 'Come in.' He is facing the window on his black egg chair.

'Hi, Hector.'

He swivels very slowly to face me, as if allowing me to admire his face in profile, three-quarters, then finally straight on. I notice that he is wearing new glasses, black with a ring of horn-rim. They draw more attention to those marker pen eyebrows. No tie, of course. Regulation white Prada shirt. A slash of hot pink silk socks beneath his lime-green desk.

'Close the door, Gina. Thanks.' A minute nod of the jaw requests that I sit down on the leather chair opposite. I shift under that piercing stare.

'How many weeks?' He rests his chin on threaded fingers and speaks softly in the manner of an expensive gynaecologist.

'Twenty-nine.' Annoyingly, I blush.

'I see.' He leans back on his chair, keeping his eyes fixed on me. 'Pregnancy suits you.'

My gaze drops to the large silver-framed photograph on his desk: a beautiful raven-haired wife, two gorgeous kids huddled together, laughing in their vineyard in southern France. Shame rises up from my throat in a hot flush. I look away from the photograph quickly.

'Gina, I want to let you know that I'll be returning to London on a more permanent basis in a couple of weeks.' He raises that eyebrow. 'Don't look so shocked. You will soon go on maternity leave. We don't have to bump into each other beside the water cooler.' A smile warms the gas ring blue of his eyes.

'I can't work here if you're here.' I look down at my hands. I have fingers like raw sausages. 'You know that.'

'Oh come on. We're grown-ups.' He stands up soundlessly and glances out of the window at the hunk of grey stone building opposite. 'By the way, I've made personally sure you've got a very generous maternity package. I'll keep your job open if you should want it, too.' He is all measured sincerity. I know better than to trust it. 'Don't worry about Lila.'

'Thanks, but I know what I'm entitled to.' I better get Dad to find out sharpish. 'You don't need to treat me like a special case. I've never wanted that, Hector.'

'Now is not the time to be proud.' A smile curls the corner of his mouth. His eyes are amused; nothing I can say will ever penetrate deeper than the silk lining of his suit. 'I do wonder what you take me for sometimes.'

I stare down at my swollen feet, wishing this meeting over.

'Look, Gina, I know that Rex was tricksy, to say the least.' His voice drops to that silken whisper, the quietest one that forces you to strain to hear. 'And dead.'

I look up, incensed. 'He's not dead!'

'Oh come on, he's dead, Gina. Let's not pretend otherwise.' His features soften. 'Look, I just want to help, OK?

I grab my bag with shaking hands and try to leap out of the chair, although of course I can't because I'm the size of a baby elephant so I have to heave myself up using the sides. Not quite the effect I was looking for. 'I don't want your help. Ever,' I hiss.

'Is that any way to talk to your boss?'

Twenty-nine

'Gina, I'm home!' Fran's voice wakes me from a horrible dream in which you are metamorphosing into Hector: Hector's black eyebrows and silver hair, your dark eyes and wiry mountaineer's body. I get up, steady myself on the banister, the unsettling dream sticking to me like the sweat. 'Hi, Fran.'

'Haven't woken you, I hope.' She looks unusually smiley, her hands pulled down by two heavy shopping bags. 'Fancy a nice girlie dinner before Jake gets home later?'

There are no precedents for this girlie dinner. Fran has been out socialising such a lot for work that we've avoided each other quite successfully in the last few weeks. I've got used to hanging out with Jake, watching the same movies over and over – *The Apartment*, *Lady and the Tramp*, *North by Northwest*, *Casablanca*, *Brief Encounter*, *Gone with the Wind*, *To Catch a Thief* – in the dim light of their sitting room with a lime soda and a tube of Pringles. It's there that I've found most comfort, temporarily suspended in someone else's story. I'm not sure I'll find it in a girlie dinner with one of the most ungirlie women I've ever met. 'Great,' I manage.

An hour later, I stand at the kitchen door and my jaw drops. The kitchen has been transformed. The table – cleared of books and newspapers – is covered in tea-lights, small vases of pretty white flowers, bowls of olives and crackers and bread. Romantic and pretty, it flings me right back to Valentine's Day last year with such force I have to put a hand to the doorframe to steady myself.

Knowing you were likely to be in the office until ten pm and were cynical about all things Valentine's, I'd come home expecting a night alone in front of the telly. Instead, you'd managed to leave work early and filled our flat with white roses, fairy lights and candles. I'd opened the door and my jaw had dropped then, too.

'Scrubs up OK, eh?'

'Amazing.'

'You look dumbstruck!'

'I wasn't expecting this, that's all.'

'I forget you've got used to Jake's terrible hospitality. Let me make up for it. Here, a cheeky half glass.' She holds out a glass of what looks like champagne. 'No, don't worry. One half glass in nine months isn't going to hurt the baby, promise. Don't fret, I've Googled it. You know me, neurotic to the end.'

Fran seems to almost glow in the candlelight, the white of her shirt reflecting the clean underside of her throat and jaw. I've never seen her this upbeat and friendly. 'I've also brought some Pringles. Plain salted OK? Jake told me the pregnancy has turned you into a crisp monster. I don't normally have them in the house, as you know.' So she's unaware that Jake keeps a stash for me in the tins cupboard. 'But what the hell, eh? Let's live a little! Drink.'

The champagne smells sour, bad breath sour, but after I've got over the olfactory assault it tastes nice. And I feel the effect of one sip almost immediately. It's like meeting up with an old friend. 'You really didn't need to go to all this trouble, Fran.'

'So did! I've neglected you, Gina. I work so bloody late all the time.' She slaps her hand to her chest. 'I hope you forgive me.'

'Don't be silly.' I think about the crib. The miscarriage. 'I don't know how I'll ever repay you for your kindness, Fran.'

She raises her glass, smiling sweetly. 'To good things coming out of bad things. Now, park that belly.' I sit down. She brings two large bowls of salad to the table: avocado, cherry tomatoes, a jungle of green leaves scattered with toasted seeds. 'This is just the starter, don't worry. There's some fish for main. You like fish, don't you? It's very good for babies' brains.'

'I know, you bought me those fish oils, remember?'

'Doh.' She slaps her forehead klutzily. 'I'm micromanaging again. Jake says I get worse as I get older. Water? Sparkling? Still? Me too. Can't do bubbles and bubbles. Help yourself to salad dressing. It's lemony, though. Do you like lemony dressing? Oh, good, good. Don't stand on ceremony. Start, please. That's not enough, Gina, not nearly enough! Seriously, pile on those tomatoes, they're totally fantastic. You know, I cannot *believe* we've not done this before, can you?' She takes a sip of champagne and leans back in her chair, grinning. 'It's silly isn't it, only to do things with the blokes? We so need girlie time. More tomatoes?' she adds, with a slightly manic edge.

'Lovely. Thank you.'

'Fill your boots.'

Over the roasted fish we chat families – hers, 'cursed by its own success!' – and the beauty of autumn, London's, according to Fran, far outstripped by America's. 'New England. Heav*en*,' she sighs, draining her glass of champagne and swiftly pouring herself another. 'Have you been there?'

I shake my head. I haven't been anywhere compared to Fran. 'I've been to Newhaven,' I joke lamely.

She tosses her hair back and giggles. 'Do. Not. Mention. That. Place. Jake took me to Newhaven once. Some *seriously* dodgy relative.' She waits for me to laugh. I laugh. 'That said, it beat the week holed up in a village outside Lyons. Jake has a thing about provincial France.' Giving me a sidelong look, she adds, 'In case you haven't noticed we're opposites in lots of ways.'

'Opposites attract.'

'True. Although I don't believe in analysing these things *too* much, do you?' She hovers her fingers over a tea-light as if testing how close she can get to the flame before it hurts. 'It works, that's all that matters.'

'Do you think you'll get married?' I am emboldened by the champagne and Fran's ebullient mood.

'Marriage?' She flushes and her smile flatlines. 'We'll get round to it when there's a break in my bloody schedule, which is unlikely to be before 2020! But the most important thing is that we are a stable unit, a seriously stable unit, whether we're married or not.'

'Yes, of course.' The word unit makes me think of alcohol

units or Ikea storage solutions. 'You're lucky to have each other.'

'We are indeed.' She rests her chin in her hands, gazes at me, a smile playing around her full pink mouth. 'Now, *here's* a question to reflect on. Do you think you are lucky to have Rex, Gina? To be married to him?'

I'm a little startled by the question. 'Well, yes. Yes, of course,' I reply, bemused.

'Even though this has all happened?' She leans collusively across the table. 'You know, I was thinking about this the other night. If one had complete knowledge of what lay ahead in a relationship, would one embark on it in the beginning? It would be like getting on a ship, knowing it was going to sink, wouldn't it?' She giggles. 'Marrying Rex would be like getting on to the *Titanic*!'

I flinch at the comparison. 'If we were scared of getting hurt, none of us would fall in love.'

She sighs wistfully. 'You are *so* sweet.'

'I'd do it all again.'

'With perfect foreknowledge?' She narrows her eyes, unconvinced. 'Come on.'

I nod. 'Totally.'

'You know what? I admire you. I admire you for taking on someone more complex than Newton's Law, Gina, I really do.' She raises her glass. It wobbles in her hand. 'Hats off.'

'It didn't feel complex. Being together felt . . . simple.' I struggle to explain it.

She takes a swig of her champagne. Considering I've only had half a glass, she's doing pretty well at vanquishing it. 'I can see why he fell for you.'

'Oh.' Her words echo Mandy's. What do they mean?

'Here, bread. You must eat bread. If there's one time in your life you can gorge on bread . . .' She watches me eat approvingly, her eyes focused on my tummy, which is pushing against the edge of the table now, hard with baby, gas and food. 'It must be so difficult, having to do this all on your own, Gina. Even considering having a baby in these circumstances.'

'It wasn't considered.'

'No, of course not. An accident!' Something lively sparks in her eyes. 'But the upshot is he's left you unable to grieve, unable to move on. To cope with all that whilst bringing up a baby,' she enthuses, warming to her theme. 'I mean, how on earth are you going to *manage*?'

'I'll have to,' I say tightly, feeling a growing sense of unease. I wish that Fran would back off a little. It's all too intense.

'Manage isn't a good word, is it? I've banned my team from using it. I noticed it always preceded failure.' Fran stands up, brushes down her trousers. 'Right, I think it's time for pudding, don't you?'

Pudding is lemon tart, perfectly gooey inside, the pastry as thin and crisp as an autumn leaf. It is delicious, but the tired heaviness that hit me earlier in the day returns and I yearn to escape this dinner and hole up in my attic bedroom alone.

She takes one bite of her tart and puts down her spoon. 'Have I been too blunt, hon?'

'No, no, not at all!'

'I've never been one to skirt around things. I don't believe in pretending everything's OK when it isn't, that's all. You

186

know me, mouth like an advertising hoarding. I'm sorry.'

I smile. 'I'm grateful for your honesty, Fran, really. Lots of people would rather pretend everything's OK.' I think of my mum's and Dawn's well intentioned but slightly maddening efforts to make this pregnancy normal. 'Pretending is actually harder.'

'You're *so* right. The God's honest truth is that it's going to be horrific bringing up a child without a father. It's so very hard without a male role model, honey. So very hard.' Her words hum above the table for a moment. 'It's well documented. I mean, look what it did to Rex.'

'Lovely tart,' I say, changing the subject abruptly. What on earth does she mean? 'You know, Fran, I'm very tired. I hope you don't mind if I turn in.'

'We have tried you know,' she says, ignoring me. 'For kids. It didn't work out.'

'I'm sorry, Fran, I really am.' I say quietly. Dawn always says there's one thing worse than giving birth and that's not being able to give birth. 'It must be so hard for you having a pregnant woman in the house.'

'Gina, please. It's quite alright. Really. I'm made of pretty steely stuff.'

'Women do have repeated miscarriages and then go on to conceive.'

Her face thunders over. Oh no, what have I said?

She puts down her spoon. 'How did you know I'd had a miscarriage?'

'I . . . I . . .' God, I'm such a buffoon. I could kick myself.

'Jake blabbed?' For a terrible moment I think she's going to explode but she seems to pull it back just in time. 'No, no

187

need for you to feel embarrassed,' she says with a strained smile. She refills her glass. The bottle is now empty. 'Look, Gina, there is something I've been meaning to suggest to you for some time now.'

'Oh?' I say, hugely relieved that she's changed the subject.

'Look at us. Look at me.' She pins me with a stare. I blink first. 'The house.'

'Lovely house.'

'I've got a perfect home to offer a baby, Gina. I've got a lot of love to give.'

'Of course you have. You'd make a totally brilliant mother,' I say, although I wouldn't want her to be mine.

'Thank you, thank you, Gina.' She looks relieved. 'That means a lot to me. And there's no easy way of suggesting this, so I hope you don't take it the wrong way, hon.' She takes a deep breath. 'But I want you to take some comfort from the fact that I'd take the baby, your baby, Jake and I would. We'd take it to our hearts.'

I've misheard her. 'Sorry?'

'We'd give the baby an awesome life. I'd give you access, of course, and . . .'

All the blood rushes to my head. 'You don't mean *my* baby?'

She leans forward keenly, trying to close a deal. 'Think about it, Gina, it would be the natural solution, wouldn't it? We'd adopt the baby – we'd marry first if you'd prefer, no problem at all – and you could be . . . an aunt or something?'

I put a protective hand on my bump, unable to believe what I'm hearing. 'Stop, Fran. Please stop. There's been a terrible misunderstanding.'

'You could start again!' she enthuses manically, shooting a fine shower of spit over the table. 'You're young. You—'

'Fran, please, stop.'

The front door slams. Stunned, I listen to the sound of a bag dropping to the floor, Jake's heavy footsteps on the floorboards. He appears sunburned, tousled at the kitchen door. 'Man leaves, tea-lights appear,' he jokes, looking from one of us to the other, his smile slowly flattening. 'Oh dear. Was it something I said?'

Thirty

'I know you're in there, Gina . . .' Jake begs, his voice ragged. 'I'm coming in.' He pushes open the bedroom door. 'I'm so sorry. I'm just so sorry. I don't know what to say.'

I refuse to look at him.

'I want you to know that Fran's . . . suggestion. It had nothing to do with me, Gina.'

'Really?' If he is lying it will totally destroy the precious, delicate friendship we have salvaged from the horror of everything. It will destroy everything.

'Really,' he answers solemnly. 'On my mother's life.'

My relief is short-lived, overtaken by anger. 'Does Fran really think I'm the kind of woman who would just hand over her newborn baby? I mean, Jesus!'

Jake sits on the corner of my bed, shoulders stooped in apology. 'All I'll say her in her defence, Gina, is that in her misguided way Fran felt she was doing the right thing. She really believes that by putting the offer out there it gives you . . . options.' He winces as he speaks, forced to defend the indefensible. 'She's used to pitching ideas at work, winning people round. I know this sounds ridiculous but

190

sometimes that voraciousness spills over from work.'

I shake my head in disbelief. 'Voraciousness? Come on, Jake. She really thought I'd give up the only thing I have left of Rex? That I'd be that fucking heartless?'

He rubs his face with his hands, knocking his glasses crooked. 'She's lost her sense of perspective. God, I can't justify this. I'm just so sorry.'

'Me being here is not helping. I'm going to move out.' Enough is enough. I must leave Grey Home early. I must leave Jake's. I must start again.

'Not over this. Please, Gina,' he implores, looking desperate. 'Don't go yet. Not yet. I'd feel like I'd failed you and Rex horribly.'

'I can't stay now, Jake. It's not fair on Fran. You. Me. Nobody.'

'If you'd talk it through with her? She's all hot air, Gina. Fran immerses herself in things, but the moment they've gone, they've gone. She's like a child. She only thinks about the things right in front of her face.'

'How can you *be* with her?' I burst out before I stop myself.

He visibly flinches.

'Sorry. I didn't mean that.' I did.

'It's a relevant question, considering what's just happened,' he says quietly. 'I can't answer it, not now. But I still ask you to give her, and me, another chance, Gina. Not to move out.'

I look at him, your lovely, big blond brother, this man who scooped me up and gave me refuge. He is the person who wants you back as much as I want you back, who will search to the ends of the earth for you. To not be around him fills me with panic. 'OK.'

'Thank you,' he says simply. 'Thank you, Gina.'

We sit and stare at each other in silence for a moment with a collective relief.

'I'm sorry about not coming back from Morocco with better news. Well, any news.'

'The detective hasn't got any new leads either?'

He shakes his head glumly.

The baby gives a sharp kick. Then another. I put my hand on my bump and feel something sticking out. A hand? A heel? I take Jake's hand and place it there. 'This will cheer you up. Can you feel it?'

The baby greets his hand with another kick. Jake grins his biggest grin, the kind of grin that makes me think of him in dungarees swinging his legs from a hay bale. 'Fuck!'

'Language. I don't want "fuck" to be his first word, thanks all the same.'

He laughs, bends down towards my bump so his mouth is millimetres away. 'Hello baby,' he whispers softly. 'Hello.'

'So there you are, Jake.' We both swivel round to see Fran standing in the open doorway, her face tight and white with fury. Jake pulls his hand away from my belly in a flash. But it's clearly too late. She saw us.

Thirty-one

'Surprise!' Lucy removes her palms from my eyes. My mouth drops open. Dawn and Femi grin back at me like loons from Lucy's pink sofa. Balloons. Cupcakes. A mountain of wrapped presents. 'Oh my God. What's this?'

'Your baby shower, doughnut.' Dawn grins, resplendent in a vast orange sundress.

'No way! Was Jake in on it, too? I wondered why he was so keen to give me a lift halfway across London.'

'Naturally he helped mastermind the entire clandestine project.' Lucy raises an eyebrow. 'He's quite the girl.'

My eyes fill stupidly with tears. 'I can't believe it.'

'Now sit, eat cake, don't move under any circumstances. This is your baby shower and you *are* going to enjoy it. That's an order,' says Dawn. 'And you're not allowed to cry by the way, sis, hormones or no hormones. Someone pass my leaking sister a tissue immediately.'

'To Gina and her wonderful baby,' says Femi, after the pink champagne has been poured. 'To the future.'

'To the future,' we all repeat, with slightly manic teary smiles.

'Right, presents,' says Lucy quickly, none of us wanting to dwell on the future for too long. She hands me a beautifully wrapped box. 'From yours truly.'

'Lucy, you are naughty.' I peel back tissue paper to find a set of newborn baby clothes: all white – Lucy's not bought into my boy theory – babygrows, crocheted booties, hats, cardies, vests. I hold the impossibly small booties up. 'So it wasn't a wild rumour, I *am* having a baby. And this is the proof. Thank you so much.'

'Glad you've finally got your head around it, sis,' Dawn quips, rolling her eyes.

'You like it?' Lucy looks very pleased with herself. 'I did my research – well, I spoke to the breeders, stand up, Femi Johnston – and tried to get everything you might need to clothe the baby for the first six months.'

'What she's trying to say is that if we left it to you there was a small risk that the baby would end up sleeping in a sock drawer swaddled in a tea towel.' Dawn winks at me. 'Your present from me and Gareth is behind the sofa, sis.'

'Behind the sofa?' I peer over to see a large object wrapped in brown paper. 'Oh, that is a very big present, Dawn.' I pull away the paper in strips to reveal a gleam of metal, neon yellow fabric. 'A pram! Oh, Dawn, this is so generous.' I leap up and kiss her doughy cheek. 'Thank you. Thank you so much.' I touch the pram's bouncy yellow canopy and silver wheels, grip its foamy black handle and push it ineptly across the sitting room. 'Do I look as weird as I feel?' I giggle.

'Yes!' they all cry, as I crash the pram into the coffee table.

I start opening the other presents, amazed to find that there are gifts here from girlfriends I haven't seen in an embarrassingly long time. (You wanted me all to yourself, Rex. And I colluded with that, loving the feeling of being wanted so exclusively.) How little I've put into my old friendships since getting married. Yes, I am that terrible example of womankind who neglects their girlfriends, and sister, as soon as she falls in love. But here they all are. Still. They didn't give up on me. Touched, I pick up a strange squashy tube. 'No, no idea. What is it?'

'That's an on-the-go bottle warmer,' says Femi with authority.

'You won't need it straightaway. You'll be breastfeeding,' Dawn says with equal authority, not to be outdone.

'Will I?' The truth is that the prospect of a real-life baby landing in my disseminated life in less than two months' time is still unimaginable. 'I guess I will.'

'OK. Tell us about the birth plan, Gee.' Femi settles back in the sofa with a glass of champagne. 'Aw, this is taking me right back. I wish my babies hadn't grown into stinky tweens.'

'The birth plan? Well . . .' I can't explain that my birth plan is focused on your heroic eleventh hour appearance. 'I haven't got *quite* that far. But I do like the sound of a water birth.' A water birth, oceanic and primal, the baby's head popping up from the water like a seal: I'm sure you'd approve.

'Always struck me as a tad unhygienic.' Dawn licks blue icing off her upper lip. 'But your call, sis.'

'And have you chosen the hospital?' asks Femi.

'If Rex isn't back . . .' No one dares look away, their smiles frozen on their faces. '. . . as soon as I start my maternity leave I'll move back to Derbyshire.'

'Yay!' shouts Dawn, a little sozzled. 'Come to the hills!'

It's been a tough decision. But I cannot possibly stay any longer at Jake's. Things have not been harmonious in the house since the incident. Fran and Jake are rowing all the time. All too often I'll walk into a room and the conversation will finish abruptly. Jake will stare at the floor. Fran will busy herself noisily at the sink or bury her head in a magazine. (Interestingly, she's now stopped offering vitamin reminders and pregnancy tips. Was I only ever a surrogate?) I need to let them live their lives, get out of their relationship and out of the postcode.

'Good food. Walks. Fresh air. I like the sound of that plan, babes,' nods Femi. 'But what about the hospital? Can you transfer?'

'Oh, I'll be able to secure one of those oversubscribed pool delivery suites at our local hospital by battering them into submission with newspaper clippings about Rex's disappearance. They can't say no, can they?' shrugs Dawn.

'What about drugs?' says Femi. 'I hope you're planning to take lots and lots, Gee.'

'No, I'm going to do without drugs. I want to feel every second.' What can hurt more than I've hurt already?

'Insanity!' Femi slaps her forehead with her hand.

'I feel I owe it to the baby to be . . . I don't know . . . present. God knows I haven't been up until now.'

'You owe it nothing of the sort,' says Dawn crossly. 'Just get it out into the world with as little pain as possible, that's my advice. It's alright, I know you won't take it.'

'Well, if you've got it all worked out, maybe you won't be needing this after all.' Lucy hands me a fat hardback book. 'It's a how-to baby manual. My sister swears by it.'

'This is exactly what I need, thank you. I'm clueless.'

'Ooh, don't you worry. There will soon be nothing you don't know about episiotomies, placentas and dilating cervixes!' Dawn crows with too much relish.

'And my last present is a promise,' announces Lucy solemnly. 'Gina, I give you the gift of my amateur babysitting abilities.'

'Me too,' says Femi, raising her hand.

'Gee, you *will* live to see another happy hour.'

The tears that I've been holding back start to pour out of me. Dawn lunges towards me and thrusts me into her huge bosom. 'You're not allowed to cry at your baby shower. It's against the rules.' She kisses the top of my head like she does the twins. 'Shush, now, sis.'

'A baby shower wouldn't be a shower without some dancing, would it?' Femi leaps off the sofa and starts to pull me up by my arms. Lucy turns the music up. Kylie.

'Femi, I can barely walk, let alone dance!' I protest, wiping away my tears with the back of my hand.

'No excuses.' She starts wiggling my arms back and forth and I have no choice but to dance, eyes closed so that the music pools around me. Time slips in the rhythms. I don't know how long I dance. But as I dance the absence of you falls away. Fran's proposal falls away. Hector falls away. It's just me and the women I love, back in a world I was in terrible danger of losing.

Thirty-two

An early evening firework hisses across the skylight. I text an excuse to Mandy cancelling lunch tomorrow, and slump horizontal on the bed with an earth-fissuring groan. I've been feeling strange all day, hormonal and weepy, with an overwhelming urge to burrow into a dark corner and remain there. I'm thirty-four weeks pregnant and it's the fifth of November. A year ago we stood hand in hand in a long, brick-walled garden in Dalston and watched a Simon Cowell effigy whoosh up in flames, assuming we had decades of fireworks nights ahead of us, endless Cowells to burn. How I wish we could return to the innocence of that smoky, starlit night in the East End. The flesh and blood reality of you seems further away than ever today. It makes me wonder how long it takes before someone is erased from the lives of those they left behind. Ten years? Twenty? When do we stop missing the missing? There must be a line that you cross.

I wonder if you know when you cross it.

'Supper, Gina,' Jake shouts up the stairs. Relieved to be shaken out of my darkening thoughts, I heave myself off the bed.

'Given that it sounds like Kabul and you won't be able to sleep anyway, I'm afraid the only thing to do is to come with us to the fireworks party.' Jake ladles lentil and hock soup into my bowl.

'I'm dog-tired. I was thinking I'd just watch a movie. This looks very tasty, thanks.'

'If you're not careful you'll end up growing a film critic's goatee,' Fran says with a barely detectable snort. 'Look, hon, the Simpsons blow a grand into the air in twenty minutes just to outdo the neighbours. I promise you that it really is a spectacle worth witnessing.' She gets up, leaving her soup half eaten.

'Why don't you see if Lucy and her other half want to come too?' Jake suggests cleverly.

'OK,' I say to appease him, sure that Lucy and Christian, the most-invited couple I know, will not be available.

Lucy and Christian arrive an hour later. Lucy is wearing a black fur Cossack hat, startling against her pale blonde hair, and a fake fur coat, which looks like it will go up like a torch if an ember settles on it. Christian is wearing his usual cool boy gear: trilby, red jeans and a tightly cut smoking jacket. Fran, on meeting them both, looks put out by their edgy glamour, and changes from her coat – black, A-line – into something knitted, long and glamorous. 'Holy crap.' She steps into the street with a swoosh of knitwear. 'It's like a warzone out here.'

She's right. Orange sparks crown the chimneys. The sky bangs. We walk through smoky flashing streets for about fifteen minutes – each footstep leaden with the full weight of my body – before we arrive at a large Victorian terrace directly overlooking Queen's Park. In the glass panes of the front door I see the shadows of bobbing heads. The urge to burrow somewhere quiet and dark is almost overwhelming. I am about to tell Lucy and Jake that I've changed my mind when the front door flies open and escape becomes trickier. Inside the house the hall is a milling throng, adults laughing, clutching wine glasses that are knocked and spilled by steaming crowds of children. A woman wearing a black dress and a slash of red lipstick emerges from the swell of people, 'Welcome!' She looks at me, at my belly, and smiles that slightly embarrassed smile of recognition that is so familiar to me now. 'You must be Gina?' She offers a hand, holding on to mine for a bit too long after shaking it. 'I'm Izzie.'

'Hi, Izzie,' I smile determinedly.

She looks relieved at my smile, as if she feared I might just walk through her door and start sobbing in a ball on the floor. Not wanting to get involved in an actual conversation, just in case she feels, as so many do, that they must force themselves to mention *it*, we push through the crowds to the kitchen. The house is amazing – the walls are dark, punctuated with startling orange lampshades and vast works of colourful abstract art – and the garden is magical, a towering bonfire burning, excitable children looping their sparklers into figures of eight. They remind me of the type of children we sometimes use to model in the Grey Home catalogue, the boys with long hair, the girls with wild goldilocks curls. I immediately see that this crowd is different to our old crowd, mine and yours, Rex. Far more family orientated, this lot are at a different life stage, although they are about your age.

Your bachelorhood definitely lasted much longer than most.

'Alright?' whispers Jake. 'Just say if you need to sit down. If you want to go home I'll take you back, no big deal. And what's this? Is that all you've got?' He pulls at my cape. 'You're going to freeze.'

'Nothing else fits.'

'Do you want my coat?'

'No, I'm toasty. Interior heating system. Don't worry about me.'

'You alright for a minute then? I will return with liquor. What would the ladies like?'

'Glass of red, please,' Lucy smiles, clapping her hands together to keep warm.

'I'll hunt you down a lime soda,' Jake says to me before I get a chance to tell him that's what I want. 'Now, Fran . . . Fran?' He looks around. I spot her first: she's curled into a dangling wicker chair, suspended off a wooden beam, surrounded by a huddle of adoring men. He looks away quickly, nudges Christian. 'Come on, give us a hand. We want to get back before they let the big guns off.'

As Christian and Jake sink into the crowd, Lucy turns to me, slowly lifts one eyebrow.

'Why the eyebrow?'

'Nothing too much trouble for Jake, I see.'

'Lucy, he's getting us drinks!'

'He is very protective over you, Gee.'

'Well, yes. He seems to think that pregnancy is a debilitating illness.'

'He can't take his eyes off you.'

'As I said, he's a bit of a mother hen.'

Lucy's eyes glint. 'Well, I can certainly see why Fran's getting uppity.'

'Don't be silly.'

'God she's annoying, isn't she?' Lucy glances over at Fran. One of those women who feel entitled to everything. You can just tell. I mean, look at her tossing her hair in that chair. It's ridiculous. No woman should toss hair like that. She's not a horse.'

'Shhh, Lucy.'

'God, I wish you'd come and sleep on my couch. I promise I won't steal your baby.'

'Another two weeks, my maternity leaves starts and I'm out of there.'

Lucy studies me for a moment. 'Jake is going to miss you.'

'Miss me? He's hardly going to miss having his brother's weeping pregnant wife knocking around the house. He'll have his old life back, as long as I haven't completely destroyed it.'

'I don't think he'll want you to go.'

Something about the way she says it makes the hairs stand up on my arms.

'It's just the way he looks at you.' She covers her face beneath her eyes with her scarf and flutters her lashes. 'Eyes don't lie.'

'Don't be daft, Lucy. Stop it, please. You're doing my head in.'

She stares at Fran again. 'But what does he see in her? How can he *bear* her? They don't seem the least suited. Such an odd couple.'

'Come on, she's beautiful. Clever. Successful. And she has legs up to her armpits.'

'Yes, but the energy is all wrong. No wonder he doesn't want to have kids. Not with her.'

There is a bang and a pulse of light. A sea of heads tilt upwards, eyes fixed on the showers of gold falling from the sky like rain, a collective 'Oooh.' Fireworks launch without pause then, bang, bang, bang, so loud they make the baby jolt in my stomach. I get a twinge of pain – a foot on my spine? – and put my hand on my bump to reassure the baby.

Christian and Jake return with drinks in their hands, beer bottles wedged beneath their chins. Lucy drops her head back to rest on Christian's shoulder. He slips his hand around her waist. I glance over at Fran again. A man is holding the chain from which the chair dangles, gently rocking her. It's a very public flirtation. I glance at Jake, feeling for him, wondering if he's noticed. He catches me looking at him. Lucy's comments still fresh in my mind, I quickly look away.

There is a loud whistling and the sky explodes into a sea of pink. With it comes another twang of pain in my tummy, this one harder than the last. I gasp.

'What's the matter?' Jake asks.

'One of those pelvis stretching pains, I think. Maybe I'll go and sit down.' The pain makes me feel vulnerable. I desperately wish I hadn't come out, that I'd trusted my gut instinct and gone to bed.

'Shall I take you home?' he shouts, straining to be heard over the rat-a-tat-tat of the rockets.

'No, no, you can't leave the party now. It's only just begun.'

Lucy takes her head off Christian's shoulder. 'You alright, Gee? Tired? Maybe you should wait for the curry. Food might help.'

I shake my head, knowing instinctively that curry won't help.

'I was just saying I'll walk her home,' says Jake to Lucy.

I want to get out of here, this noisy, sulphuric, crowded place full of strangers. A black thought – I need you *now*, I need you looking after me – hits me like a lobbed firework.

'Christian and I will walk you back.' Lucy tugs at Christian, who doesn't look particularly thrilled by the idea.

'You stay here, Lucy.' Jake zips up his jacket. 'I'll walk Gina home then I'll get my bike and cycle back round. I'll return in no time.' The arranging goes on without me. I say nothing, oddly passive, as if I'm retreating into myself, turning inward to protect something. Perhaps I'm saving the last kernel of energy I've got for the walk home.

We have to push through a crush of people to get out. Feeling claustrophobic and panicky, I keep myself focused on the back of Jake's jacket. Follow the jacket. This is all I need to do. If I follow Jake's jacket it will all be OK. Finally we're out of the party. I breathe a sigh of relief, link my arm through his.

'I guess it must all be a bit intense if you're pregnant. I feel bad now. Sorry.'

'No, no. It's just me. I'm sorry to drag you away from the party. It felt like I hit the wall, you know, like marathon runners do, only without the marathon bit.'

Jake laughs. We carry on walking up the main road, traffic roaring past us. The more we walk, the better I feel. I want to keep walking forever, moving forward, one foot in front of the other, weight going from hip to hip. Our rhythm is only halted by traffic lights.

The traffic lights take forever. As we stand there I become aware of a peculiar, warm sensation between my legs. A patch of damp heat starts on the gusset of my knickers, spreads to my thighs, calves. Something is running down the inside leg of my maternity jeans. Shit. There is a puddle of oil-black liquid on the pavement.

Thirty-three

Mandy was piling peas on to Ryan's plate when her mobile beeped with an incoming text. 'Bollocks,' she muttered beneath her breath. The peas shimmied off the spoon. Ryan giggled as they rolled across the floor.

This was the second time Gina had cancelled lunch. Heavily pregnant and tired, Gina said this time (a headache the time before that). Poor thing. If she was feeling that drained it would be cruel to say anything now; she was only six weeks off her due date after all. The shock could be too much. Maybe it was just as well she'd cancelled lunch. Yes, just as well.

Funny that she felt so disappointed. She'd been looking forward to seeing Gina. She liked Gina. There was something endearing about her, something sweet and rare, maybe a bit naïve, but not stupid, not at all. She'd never expected to feel maternal towards Rex's wife but she did. She wanted to protect her, which was ironic, because if she needed protecting from anyone . . .

'Peas everywhere, Mummy!' Ryan cried, delighted. 'Little green balls.'

'I know, I know.' Mandy clicked her tongue in the way her own mother once had, and kneeled on the floor, trying to scoop up the blasted peas with an ineffective bit of kitchen roll. Every time she reached for one it rolled away and she ended up having to go deeper under the table where Ryan's little feet swung in their cobalt blue trainers. Oh, bless his feet. It was always these things – the size of his diddy feet, the scuffed knee – that came at her sideways and made her heart lurch with love.

'Now there's a sight to cheer a man after a hard day's work.' She felt a hand on her butt. 'Ry, do we know why Mummy is hiding beneath the table?' asked Mark.

Ryan giggled and shook his head.

'Peas. Flaming peas,' Mandy muttered, crawling out from under the table, pushing her hair off her face with the back of her hand.

'They don't look flaming to me. They look kind of soggy.'

'Shuddup.'

'Oh dear.'

'One of those days, sorry.'

'Here, I'll do it.' Mark started sweeping the peas up with the broom. 'Now sit down, have a cup of tea.' He gave her a sidelong glance, sensing something was amiss. 'You alright?'

'She's only gone and cancelled again, that's all.'

Mark's face clouded. It always did whenever the subject of Gina came up.

She sat down heavily on a kitchen chair. 'Eat your tea, Ryan, OK, one more fish finger. Yes, one. It's good for you.' She turned to Mark. 'I was looking forward to seeing her, that's all. Silly really.'

Ryan picked up a fish finger for inspection. 'Mummy, who's Gina?'

At the mention of her name, Mark turned his back, wide shoulders tensing.

'Gina is, um, a friend of Mummy's,' faltered Mandy, feeling strangely guilty. 'We were going to meet for lunch this weekend. But now we're not. It doesn't matter, Ryan.'

Mark ruffled Ryan's hair. 'We can still go carting, don't you worry. We'll have our boys' one.'

'Yay!' said Ryan, leaping up from his chair, having not eaten his fish finger, and bolting from the room.

'Carting, Mark?' Mandy frowned. 'Really?'

'We did discuss this a couple of nights ago, Mandy.'

'Did we?' Mandy looked blank. Had they? Why couldn't she remember? She'd been so preoccupied.

'Oh don't look like that. He'll love it. You know he will.'

'He's so little, Mark. Couldn't you do something, I don't know, slower? Safer?'

He pulled her towards him, feeling for her curves. 'It's perfectly safe, I promise. I'd never take him somewhere that wasn't. You know that.'

She winced. 'I do, but . . .'

He held her firmly by the arms. 'You've got to let go of him a bit, Mandy. Just a teeny bit. You can't keep him wrapped in cotton wool. He's a boy. Boys need to do stuff.'

'It's just . . .'

'Trust me, OK?'

She looked into Mark's flecked eyes. She loved him so much. No, she couldn't let everything be coloured by the past. 'OK.'

'And forget Gina, will you? Just for this weekend. There's nothing you can do until after the baby's born now. You've cut it too fine.'

She nodded, feeling the pressure in her head ease a bit as she always did under Mark's touch. 'I know.'

'Good. Now give us a snog.' Cupping her face in his hands, he pulled her towards him.

Thirty-four

'You won't be going home just yet.' The nurse, an angular woman with thin lips and cold fingertips, glances at the thermometer and tosses it into the bin.

It is two am. I am in a cubicle of four pale-green curtains, a transitional ward off the maternity ward, where it seems pregnant women come, looking anxious, and then leave again after a lengthy check up, looking more anxious.

'But nurse . . .' Jake says in a croaky, dehydrated voice. He is slumped on the hard plastic chair beside my bed, the strain of the last few hours dug in lines across his forehead. I am so relieved that he is with me, even if he has no idea what is going on either.

'Gina's waters have broken.' The nurse scrawls something on my hefty wedge of notes. 'We need to keep an eye on you, Gina. You're at risk of infection, I'm afraid.'

'It's just that I know I'd feel much better in my own bed. That's all.'

The nurse ignores me and checks my blood pressure for the third time since we arrived. 'Low,' she says, not explaining further, scribbling again.

'So how long will I be here?'

'I can't say. The doctor will need to see you.' She doesn't look up from the notes.

'When will we see the doctor?' Jake asks politely, stifling a yawn. He has a grey firework ember in his hair, proof of the existence of the world we were in before we stepped into this bleached parallel universe.

'Morning. About eight am.'

'*Eight am*?' I am about to protest, but exhaustion rolls up my body and over my head in one large lick. I want to be horizontal with my eyes closed. I don't really care where.

The nurse, giving up on me, addresses Jake. 'We'll move her to the ward now. You can come back in the morning.'

I'm seized by panic. 'He has to go? He can't go. I want him to stay with me.'

'Visiting time's in the morning,' she says in the manner of someone who has had this conversation a hundred times on her shift already.

After saying goodbye to Jake, I lie in a different bed in the pre-natal ward, trying to take in the speed with which my circumstances have so dramatically changed. I wish you were here, Rex. You'd know what to do. You'd know how to comfort me. You'd reassure me while my womb leaks. It's horrible. It really is. My hospital sanitary pad is sodden with this clear, scentless fluid within minutes. I've given up going to the bathroom – the shower is splattered with blood, like someone's been murdered *Psycho*-style – and have perfected the technique of changing my pad while lying horizontal, a task helped by the fact that the hospital nightie has no rear to it, giving me another reason to avoid the public parade down the ward to the bathroom.

Still, I recognise my luck in getting a bed beside the window. London is spread out like a blanket of fairy lights, the sky quiet now, smoky but no longer splattered with fireworks. It's a great view. The view to my right is less picturesque. The mountainous snoring silhouette of a heavily pregnant woman is cast on the curtain by the harsh beam of her sidelight, making sleep even more elusive. The other women on the ward haven't drawn their curtains at all, as if they've given up on privacy altogether, or are acknowledging the curtain's futility. It certainly provides no respite from the machines that constantly beep, nor the flashing lights, the ringing buzzers, the mobile phones vibrating with incoming text messages on hard plastic surfaces, or the rumble of trolleys on corridors deep in the bowels of the hospital.

I want to be asleep – if only to get to morning quicker – but I am wide awake, heart pounding, unable to get comfortable. I play with the buttons on the side of my bed, changing the angle of the headrest, the puff of the pillows, anything to stop my mind leaping through the events of the last few hours and arriving at more and more worrying conclusions. I press my hands against the hard hot skin of my belly. This doesn't reassure. The baby doesn't move. He normally moves at night and he isn't moving at all. Should I ring the buzzer? Yes, I must ring the buzzer. Now is not the time to worry about making a fuss. My fingers search for the buzzer in the gloom behind me, find it, hesitate. I wonder whether I should hang on a little bit longer because then the nurses will rotate and I might get a nurse who is less like the current one, an old warhorse with breath that could strip paint.

To be honest, Rex, I am scared. Properly lump-in-the-throat scared. I can just about cope with you going missing, but not my body going off before time like a faulty firework, blowing up in my face like this without you. I glance at my mobile phone: four am. Four hours until Jake can come back. This is what I focus on, the only thing that keeps my spirits up. Yes, I will awake to see Jake's face and he'll get me out of here, I think, aware that this is my last thought as sleep crashes down on my head like a dumper of clay-black soil, burying all other thoughts alive.

It is pain that wakes me. A pain right inside my pelvis, like a period pain. It tightens then relents. I glance at my watch: six thirty am. I pull open the window blind fully, revealing grey smoky London in slices. A smell of toast mingles with the smell of something else, bodies, I think. Someone rattles back the curtain beside me, exposing the lower half of my bed. It is the snorer next door. The pain comes back again, stabbing at me in sharp little points like a scalpel, before all the points join up and create something more tidal, more thunderous.

I ring the buzzer. It's the abrupt nurse again, sounding more tired and more cranky. She tells me to 'keep an eye on it' and inform her if it gets worse. 'It's getting worse!' I hiss through gritted teeth.

'Shhh,' says the woman mountain next door. 'Some of us are trying to sleep.'

Finally the nurses switch. This one is nice. She is Filipino and has lovely shiny black hair pulled into a ponytail and a smile that reduces panic. I'm ridiculously grateful for her smile, even as she sticks her fingers inside me and tells me I'm in labour.

'I can't be! I'm not due for six weeks!'

'I'll get the doctor, sweetheart.'

'Get Jake!'

'Jake. Right. Have we got Daddy's number?'

'I . . .' The explanatory words are sucked out of me by another cramp. It's like someone has a belt around my insides and is tightening it. 'Fuck! Fuck, this hurts. It really fucking hurts.' As soon as the pain recedes, I scrabble inside my bedside cabinet for my phone, flick up Jake's number and thrust the phone at her before another squeeze of agony hits me. I want to give her Mum's and Dawn's too but she's gone.

The pain becomes so bad I wonder if I'm dying.

The doctor takes forever. I hate him. I hate him for making me wait while I am dying. And I hate you, Rex. I hate you for not getting home in time, for disappearing in the first place. Where the hell *are* you? I hate Jake, too. Where the hell is he? I hate everyone who is not feeling what I am feeling.

I stumble out of my bed, pace around it. 'Drugs!' I shout, pressing the buzzer frantically. 'I need drugs.'

'Oh, 'ere we go,' groans the fatness on the other side of the curtain.

It feels like I'm riding this pain alone for years. It's soaring, crushing, constricting. It takes my breath away, makes me forget who I am. I care about nothing, not even you, only this pain and the means of its removal. I look up through the blear of it all and there are faces. One of them is Jake's. I have an overpowering rabid urge to bite him. But he isn't close enough to bite. He is standing beside a ridiculously young doctor, and looks shit scared. The doctor is talking very fast. The only words that pierce the pain that is eating me from inside are 'premature' and 'emergency caesarean'.

'Do you understand?' says Jake. 'They're going to have to give you a caesarean, Gina.'

'What? Fuck . . .' The pain flies in again for another attack, like a bird picking out eyes from its prey. I grab Jake by the forearms and groan. 'I want a fucking water birth!'

'The baby is premature, Mrs Adler,' smiles the doctor patiently. 'A C section gives it the best possible outcome.'

'I want a fucking water . . . drugs! I want drugs, get me drugs.'

'Get Mrs Adler ready for theatre,' the doctor tells the nurse briskly, turning on his heel.

There is a sense of urgency now. Hands pulling me and pushing me on to a wheelchair, which is wielded by a surly porter in a blue convict-like overall. We rattle through the wards into a stainless steel lift where other patients wearing dressing gowns stare at me. I grip Jake's hand tight, tight, tighter. Someone says something to the porter. Now we are moving faster. He is almost running. I can hear his breath above my head. Jake is saying something, something about Dawn and my mum and trains. White double doors fling open. The smells change, become sharper, more clinical. Faces, more faces, green masks. It's like being beamed up into a UFO. An anaesthetist introduces herself with a smile and a handshake like we are at a cocktail party. This is the lady who is going to take my pain away. I smile back through gritted teeth. I'd do anything for this woman. Jake is wearing scrubs now, his hair poking out wildly from the taut pull of the mask elastic, his eyes bright with panic. The pain is

215

galloping faster and faster and I now have an overwhelming urge to poo.

'Don't push,' says a man in a mask. 'Don't push. Pant, Gina.'

The anaesthetist acts quickly. There is a jab in my spine. It takes seconds. Miraculously, the pain is sucked out of me, exorcised like a ghost. Oh my God, it's gone, it's gone. I sob with relief.

'Alright, Gina? Alright?' Jake begs. I nod. The pain has been sucked out of me. Now I am invincible.

The doctor presses something into my tummy. 'Do you feel this?'

'Sort of.' My mouth is very, very dry.

'This?'

'No.'

I can finally take in my surroundings, the alert eyes above the masks, and the green barrier that sits over my ribs like a windbreak on the beach, hiding whatever the surgeon is doing to my insides. I cannot bear to think about the baby. Oh God, the baby, not due to be born, spat up by my stupid body so early. Images assault me, my life since you left literally flashing in front of my eyes: taking that first terrible phone call from Jake at the crack of dawn, the ground coffee in the grinder that I can't throw away, the pot of Carmex lipsalve, the document on your laptop, Mandy spooning the froth off the top of her cappuccino, Fran, Jake in his puffa jacket, fireworks sprayed behind his head . . .

'Alright?' Jake mouths. I shake my head. Not alright, no. Not actually.

There is a tugging sensation deep inside of me, as if I'm

being attached to a hook and dangled from it. 'Won't be long, Gina,' says the surgeon, his eyes focused on the other side of the windbreak.

And it isn't. It isn't long at all. There is a commotion, more tugging, and the surgeon is pulling something out of my tummy, something tiny, covered with white waxy stuff, the size of a tiny rabbit. Is it a baby? Jesus, it's a baby! It makes a noise, a mew more than a cry. And the surgeon's eyes smile above his mask. 'Congratulations, you have a little girl.'

'A girl! Our boy is a girl!' I grasp Jake's hand and start to sob.

Jake is invited to cut the cord. He looks at me helplessly.

'Do it,' I cry. 'Do it for Rex.'

Jake snips the cord. And the teeniest baby I've ever seen is wrapped up in blankets and handed to me. She is weightless. Scentless. Even though I have no idea what to do with her I know she is mine, absolutely mine. And yours, Rex: her face is scrunched creating a dimple, your dimple, on her right cheek, a mirror image of you.

'We need to keep baby warm because she's so little,' explains a nurse, plucking her off me and whisking her away someplace else.

'It's alright. They need to take her to the NICU,' explains Jake softly. 'To put her in an incubator.'

I have had a baby and already she's being taken away from me? Nothing makes sense. I look from Jake to the nurse, who has run off with my baby. Like Fran wanted to. 'My baby . . .'

'It's OK, you'll see her very soon.' Jake puts his hand on

mine. It trembles against my skin. 'She's beautiful, Gina. She's the most beautiful baby.'

That pathetic mew again. I turn my head and see the nurses are bent over my baby in the corner of the room as if they're about to do something horrible to her. 'Go with the baby, Jake, please. Make sure she's OK. I want someone to be with her.' I am scared to be separated from this person who is barely separate from me. It feels wrong.

An hour later I am in another ward in another bed, chained to it by a catheter and a drip and tubes piped full of ruby red blood. I feel no pain, although there are bandages around my deflated empty middle – where is the bump? where is the baby? – and, confusingly, I am bleeding between my legs, even though no baby appeared between them. I've had a little girl. She is somewhere. A wave of panic convulses in my chest, sucking the air from my lungs. I try to push myself up on my bed to get a better view, looking for the baby, for Jake. I try to imagine where they are and I imagine a huge Victorian room full of cots and babies – could they get muddled up? stolen? – and untrustworthy people. I try to move again, straining my neck to get a view, to find a nurse who can take me to my baby, the tears streaming so fast they are pooling behind my ears.

'Gina.' Jake pulls me into his arms and I hold him very tight around the waist, breathing into him, gulping for air, holding on for dear life. 'You've been sleeping.'

I don't remember sleeping, or waking up. Time has smudged. The tears become a torrent, wild, fierce and endless, like they are coming from a place deep inside that won't be plugged.

'I've come to take you to the baby.'

I smile.

A nurse helps move me into a wheelchair along with all my tubes because it is agony to walk, even though I'm strictly told that walking is exactly what I need to do. The nurse starts to push the chair. Jake says, 'I'll do it.' There's a part of me that flinches at the indignity of it all, me in my bloodstained rearless nightie, trailing drips and bags of pee. But I don't care because I'm almost demented with yearning to see my baby. It is how I imagine I'd feel if I were going to meet you right now, Rex; that intense, more than that.

Our daughter is in a plastic transparent cot like a fish tank, bundled up in a white holey blanket and a white cotton hat, as if she were going skiing. Her pink skin is almost transparent, like a prawn's. I can see a tributary of veins across her temples. There are alarming tubes going into her nose. She is wearing a bracelet that looks too big and too stiff for her fragile wrist: 'Baby of Adler', it reads, and my heart breaks instantly. Her limbs are not rounded like babies' limbs should be but chicken-wing-skinny, all kneecaps and ankle bones and chalky flaking skin. Through the cloth of her hat, the ridged plates of her skull, which have not yet moved into their final position, are clearly visible. They are like the earth's tectonic plates, her head the world, my world now. 'She's too small,' I say. Looking at her makes my breasts throb. 'She should be inside me.'

'Baby's just under five pounds. That's not bad given she's six weeks early,' says the nurse nonchalantly. 'She'd have been a good size if she'd gone to full term.'

Still, she looks tiny. None of the photographs in the baby

manuals I pored over bear much relation to this scrappy pink thing. I stare at her, transfixed, scared of touching her, and cannot help but feel that my role has been stolen by this heated cot and the nurses who know what they're doing so much better than I do. I cannot ever, ever imagine being competent enough to mother this vulnerable baby alone.

'Do you want to hold baby?' Without waiting for me to answer, the nurse lifts the baby out of the cot and places her gently over my shoulder. I inhale the skin of her tiny head. 'Hello,' is all I can manage.

The nurse smiles. 'You two going to give her a name?'

'I thought I was having a boy. I was going to call him Rex.'

Jake crouches down to my shoulder height and gazes wondrously at the baby as if she's the first baby he's ever seen.

'We should put baby back in the cot now before she gets cold,' says the nurse, turning to Jake. 'Do you want to do it?'

'Um, er, OK.' Jake picks her out of my arms, nervously supporting the back of her head.

'A natural,' the nurse grins conspiratorially to me. The baby kicks her stick legs in the cot, then curls up like a small animal. 'Now Mummy, you need to get yourself into the pump room and stimulate some milk.'

'Pump room? What's a . . .'

The nurse explains the rigmarole of the next few days, weeks even. They won't put a time frame on it. She explains how they will feed the baby through the tubes in her nose, ideally with my milk if I can get it flowing. In order to get my milk 'in' I need to pump every couple of hours, even at night, like all the other premature baby mums: the pale, tear-puffy, shocked-looking women gazing into the fish tank cots. I need to pump out this precious milk and store it in the milk fridge. She makes it sound simple. When I'm not in the pump room I can come and sit with baby, 'to bond'.

The NICU is tropically hot, guarded by locked doors with strict visiting times and instructions not to enter unless you've washed your hands, left your bags outside, are only in perfect health. The strictness is both reassuring and alarming, a reminder of how vulnerable these babies are. With a swell of pride, I note that in comparison to some of the others my baby does look relatively robust. Some of them are too raw to even look at, their skin leaf-thin, their eyes still fused together, like they should exist only in the deepest and darkest of ocean depths.

Jake sits quietly beside me as I watch the air travel in and out of the lungs of 'Baby of Adler'. I cannot breathe myself until I see her chest inflate again. I'm told an alarm will go off if she stops breathing. And alarms do go off all the time, but in other cots, and they are mostly false alarms, a result of the baby moving on the sensor pad. But one time an alarm screams and a baby is rushed into theatre and this makes all the prem mothers, including me, cry. It could be us next.

I don't know how long I sit watching my baby, waiting for the alarm, stroking her back, feeling the fairy buttons of her spine. I wonder where she thinks she is. I wonder if she knows she's out of me. If she knows that we have been separated. I sit there until I become aware of the pain returning, a flare of heat in my stomach. The drugs are wearing off.

221

'Painkillers,' I say, turning to look at Jake for the first time in what feels like hours. He is ashen-faced, red-eyed, looks like he hasn't slept at all. He pushes me back to my ward in the wheelchair and bashes into a bin – 'Christ! I'm sorry!' – and I yell out with pain. Back at my bed, already missing the baby – how can you miss someone you've only known for a few hours? – I neck more drugs, until I am numb and the bed swings like a hammock.

'Gina, love. It's me.' The voice registers slowly. It is not Jake's voice. I become aware of the pain again. My insides feel scratched out. Time for more drugs! Oh yes, baby. I've had a baby. Bewildered, I open my eyes.

'Oh, Gina!' Mum tries to hug me but my tubes get in the way and she pulls the drip in my arm. 'Oh God, sorry. Did that hurt? You're sure? I got the first train I could.'

'The baby . . .' I start to cry. 'Where's—'

'She's sleeping. I've just had a peek, she's beautiful, so beautiful.' Mum strokes my hand, her face bearing down on me, her eyes large and full of tears. 'Dawn and Dad will be here any minute, too. Oh my poor love, my poor love. Those bloody fireworks. They must have given your body a right shock.'

'Where is he? Where is Jake?' I croak. I am thirsty, devilishly thirsty.

'I sent the poor man home. He was gibbering with exhaustion.' She pats my arm, right where the drip enters it. 'I'm here now.'

Dawn and Dad arrive. Dawn brings *Grazia*. Dad brings a tin of Celebrations. They all gasp when they see the baby. Dad says he's seen bigger guinea pigs. Eventually, many hours later, they are all firmly instructed to leave by a nurse called Brenda – Irish, loud, two front teeth that collide at an angle – and I get a chance to be alone with our baby again. I am determined to manage the walk to the NICU on my own, not in a wheelchair, so that I don't have to depend on anyone. This seems more important than ever. My legs are shaky and the scar bites like a wild dog. It takes forever but I manage it, slowly, slowly, trailing my tubes on a wheeled trolley like a macabre dinner lady.

Gazing at the baby, I decide, on a drug-woozy gut feeling rather than reflection, to call her Hope. It's an old fashioned name. But she is my hope, the little person who kept me going through all of this. Mum tells me 'not to rush into the naming thing', which is her way of saying she'd rather I named her after Nana, but I know that the name fits.

I ask Brenda if I can pick her up – 'Jeez, you don't need to ask' – and hold her warm weightlessness close to my chest. I feel Hope relax in my arms, her breathing deepen and slow. I dare to wonder if there is the tiniest chance that I might actually be providing her with something that she needs that she cannot get from anyone else, apart from colostrum. She nestles closer. And I am completely unprepared for the feelings that crash over my head: everything in the world that I never knew I wanted is in my arms, wearing a white bobble hat.

I am in love.

Thirty-five

The pump room is a female, gynaecological space: small, musty, painted skin-pink. It contains a fridge, wall to ceiling shelves lined with large white plastic vats of sterilising liquid, breast milk storage bottles, stacks of white labels, a selection of breast pumps and a comfy 'nursing' chair. Most of the prem mothers absolutely hate it – it does make you feel a bit like a sow sitting here attached to the electric pump – but I find it easiest to talk to you here, undisturbed, nipple distended in the pump's mouth, listening to the repetitive whoosh and suck of the machine and seeing my milk accumulate in the bottle. Here I can measure out my days in fluid ounces. It feels like I've achieved something.

When I'm not in the pump room, I'm attending to a constant stream of surprisingly time-consuming tasks: for one thing there's all the visitors, each one requiring my birth story told afresh, or numerous times if they're Dawn, with sound effects; there's all the waiting, for the shower cubicle to free up, for the tea trolley, for the meds; the rush to the loo in the morning so I get to it before Big Sue in the adjacent bed. Big Sue's family bring her KFC chicken buckets for lunch every day. She has guts like Hades.

So while the minutes drag here, the days go by in the blink of an eye. The exhaustion that comes with getting up every three hours in the night to pump milk means that most of the time I feel out-of-body, so tired I'm not sure that I'm tired at all. I'm just in a new zone altogether. This is why sometimes I cannot summon the energy to talk to you at all. Sorry, Rex.

There, three ounces. Result. I hold the bottle up to the window, sluice it in the sunlight. It's not white. I thought milk would be white, like the stuff you pick up from the supermarket. But this is pale green. The nurses had to reassure me that I wasn't radioactive.

I love the nurses, especially Brenda, who has the honkiest laugh you've ever heard and rolls her eyes at the snootier doctors behind their backs. In fact already I can't imagine life without Brenda. I'm fully institutionalised. While all the other mothers here are yearning to take their babies home, I'm struck dumb with terror at the idea. It's not just that I no longer have an obvious residence to discharge to, but also because I kind of like it here. I really do. I like the ward's anonymity, the way it shifts every few hours – beds empty, fill with new voices and bodies. Everything happens one day at a time. This is how I've been living since you vanished, one day at a time. And I'm not imposing myself upon anyone here. I've paid my taxes. I don't have to worry about crashing someone's breakfast or using up the last bit of milk in the fridge.

All I have to do is be careful not to let my mind wander

treacherously back to our Marylebone flat, our days in bed, listening to the shop grille rattling up in the morning. More than anything I have to stop myself imagining you lying back on our bed and wheeling Hope above you. That kills me.

Hope is living up to her name. (By the way, your mother has asked me to give her Marie – your granny's name – as a middle name. For the sake of diplomacy I've also added Dorothy, after Nana.) She is putting on a bit of weight. Her lungs are stronger every day too, which has pleased the doctors a great deal. Her eyes are still closed most of the time – she's not ready to open up to the world yet – but she's more responsive, more aware. She twitches her toes when she hears my voice. Still no red hair, though. No black hair either. No hair at all.

Five ounces! I'm done. I write my name clearly on the bottle in large clear writing – I live in fear that a nurse who can't read English well will feed my baby Big Sue's KFC milk instead – slide it on to a fridge shelf and hobble back to the ward. It still feels like a great white has breakfasted on my abdomen.

On the seventh day, a few minutes after my family leave, Lucy blasts into the ward in a parrot-green dress, black patent handbag swinging off her arm. The tired, bloated mothers on the ward eye her suspiciously: it is like a visit from another species specifically evolved to make us feel bad about ourselves. 'Brought you Pret salad!' She wings her bag on to the bed, unclips it. 'And treats.'

'Ooh, thanks, Lucy. Would it be rude to eat the chocolates before the salad? Breast pumping is like liposuction.'

'You halve your body weight every time I see you. Eat chocolate.'

'I had a lot to halve, let's face it.'

Lucy laughs and empties a pile of glossy magazines on to my bed, the latest must-read novels that I won't have the attention span to read, and some premature baby clothes as the newborn ones swamp Hope. As she opens the box of chocolates, a warm smell of cocoa fills the area around my bed, happily masking the smell of bleach. For a rare fleeting moment I feel what I can only describe as true happiness, the first I've felt for months, like the sun on your face after a cold winter. Then I remember that you are missing and the temperature drops again. 'Close the curtain,' I whisper, protecting both my privacy and the chocolates from Big Sue who is eyeing them hungrily. She is a piranha of a woman who can strip a giant slab of Dairy Milk to the wrap in seconds.

'I've got some news,' Lucy blurts suddenly. She holds out her hand. A large, boxy diamond blinks back at me.

'Ring? A ring. Oh my God . . .'

'Christian has asked me to marry him.' Her eyes shine, unable to hide her joy.

'That's so wonderful, Miss Lucy I'll-never-marry Wilson.' I touch the cool diamond. 'Gosh, it's beautiful.'

She blushes again. 'I didn't think he was the marrying type either.' She grabs my hand suddenly, blinking furiously. 'It was Rex, you know, Rex going.'

Big Sue farts on the other side of the curtain.

'Sorry.' I roll my eyes. 'What do you mean it was Rex going?'

'It made us realise, and I know this sounds corny . . . but I want you to know how it made us realise that if you find someone you love . . .' Lucy uncharacteristically stumbles over her words. '. . . you make the most of it.'

'Before they disappear?' I quip.

'No, I didn't mean that!' she gasps.

'It's alright if you did,' I shrug, picking a truffle out of the box. It's covered in edible glitter and shaped like a heart. 'I like that Rex going is the catalyst for something nice happening as opposed to something crap actually.'

'Good! Well, it is.' Lucy smiles with relief.

The chocolate tastes how violets smell. 'But will you wear red? You always said when you got married – not that you would, of course – you'd wear red tulle like Paula Yates did when she married Bob.'

'Absolutely.' She nibbles her truffle delicately. That eyebrow lifts. 'Gee, will you be matron of honour?'

'Me?'

'Come on, who else, div?'

'I might bring bad luck.'

She hugs me tight. 'Don't be a berk.'

'Will you make me wear scarlet?'

'Peach. You're not getting off that lightly.'

We start to giggle in the bleak face of it all, cheeks ballooned with truffles, spraying cocoa powder all over the hospital's starched white sheets.

'You can bring Jake if you like,' Lucy says when we've calmed down.

'Thanks, but I don't need a stand-in let's-pretend husband.'

'I don't see why not. Weddings must be tricky with a baby. I'd hire him.'

228

I shake my head, reach for another chocolate. All I want to eat for the rest of my life is chocolate.

'Oh, just bring him to piss off Fran. Go on.'

I stiffen. I don't like thinking about Fran too much. Part of me fears that she'll still steal off with my baby. If what happened to my husband can happen, anything can happen.

'At least when you get out of here you don't have to go back to that house.' Lucy flicks over the page of a magazine, scans it casually. 'You'll go to Dawn's, won't you?'

'I will.'

'Don't sound so happy about it.' She looks up, eyeing me curiously. 'Is the thought of leaving Jake's that terrible?'

'No, no, it's not that, more that I don't know how it will work out at Dawn and Gareth's. My future is so uncertain. That's all.'

'It will work out. Do you know why? You're bloody marvellous, Gina. Most people would have had a breakdown. You have been cut open, had a baby and your husband has been . . .'

'. . . mislaid.'

'Mislaid?'

I get this absurd inappropriate urge to giggle again. It's as if I'm constantly teetering on the verge of either tears or hysterics. Perhaps it's the lack of sleep. I swing my legs on to the bed and rest my head on the pillows with a sigh, gazing up at where damp has bloomed across the tiled ceiling. 'I guess I will miss Jake too though, you're right.'

Lucy goes quiet, not wanting to stop what might be coming next.

'He's been through it all, the pregnancy, the birth.' I glance at her. 'He cut the cord you know,' I say as casually as I can manage.

'He cut the cord? Blimey. No you did *not* tell me that, Gina Adler.'

'Well, I was meant to be having a water birth with Dawn, wasn't I? I hadn't planned for a C section. And Jake was there.'

'I can imagine . . .' She chooses her words carefully. '. . . that it must be kind of confusing for you and Jake, the way the roles here have been muddled up without Rex.'

'No one can fill the gap that Rex left,' I say quickly, thinking of Jake's large hands cradling my tiny baby as if she were made of hand-blown glass.

'I know that. You can't compare them anyway, chalk and cheese.'

'Meaning?'

'Well, Jake's a more straightforward personality, isn't he?'

'Straightforward? I don't know. I thought he was. He's more complex than he might appear. In a good way.'

'With Rex there was always a sense, oh I don't know, of holding back,' explains Lucy. 'Reticence, I guess. Like I never felt I knew him, none of your friends did.'

'Didn't they?'

'No, Gee, they didn't.' She smiles at me kindly. 'Anyway, Jake is different.'

A junior nurse walks over, holding an enormous bunch of pink peonies. 'For you, Gina.'

'Oh, big bunch,' coos Lucy. 'Somebody loves you.'

230

'Gorgeous, aren't they?' I read the note. I read it again.
'Who are they from?' Lucy frowns. 'Gee?'
'They're from Mandy.'

Thirty-six

'Good news.' The doctor rises self-importantly on his heels. 'I'm pleased to say you are well enough to go home, Mrs Adler.' It takes a moment for it to sink in that he means *me* going home, Hope staying here. Some mistake, surely. I explain that I need to be here to express milk. I need to be with Hope. The doctor clutches his clipboard tighter against his chest like a shield. No, there is no mistake, he says. The hospital needs my bed. I must go home and visit Hope like all the other mothers of premature babies. He looks at me as if to say, 'What's special about you?' then politely moves on to another patient. After Brenda has hugged me and cursed the doctor and dabbed at my eyes with a scratchy paper towel, I phone my mother. She has a small fit and passes the phone to my father who phones the hospital, blasts the ear off some poor trainee nurse at reception, and gets nowhere. I pin all my hope on Jake. He hunts down the elusive discharging doctor and tries to rationalise with him in his warm, firm journalist voice while the doctor tries to extract himself and go home at the end of his shift. Then I become someone else's problem. His replacement apologises but still won't let me stay. Rules are rules. There are no spare beds. And the hospital needs mine. I must leave without my baby as Hope cannot be discharged until she can suckle on her own and at the moment she's too young for the sucking reflex, or showing no signs of it. I must be patient. I have to hold myself back from pulling out the feeding tubes from Hope's nose and running out of the hospital with her bundled in my arms.

Oh, what do I do? What can I do? I cannot go to Derbyshire as planned, because it is too far away. I have to stay in London, near the hospital, to be close to Hope. I could stay in a hotel but the costs will spiral and I can't afford it. There is only one answer. Pushing thoughts of Fran out of my mind, I accept Jake's offer as the most practical option, with as much gratitude as I can muster, promising him fervently that I will go as soon as Hope's released. I will have to face Fran again.

It is a wrench leaving the safety of the ward and stepping into the world outside. Having got used to the tropical hospital microclimate the air feels cold and dirty. London looks different since I gave birth, a harder, more inhospitable place, the loiterers on the streets more menacing, the shop fronts shabbier, the sky greyer. The further we get from the hospital the more traumatised I feel, the ache inside me every bit as physical as the cut of the surgeon's scalpel. When we finally enter the house, it feels as if someone's taken my heart beating from my chest. I miss her that much.

Jake stops on the path. 'OK?'

I reach for his arm to steady myself. I'm not OK at all. I have never felt less OK. Something feels terribly, catastrophically wrong.

In the living room, Fran sits on the sofa, feet curled beneath her, cradling a cup of tea. 'Welcome back, hon,' she says coolly, getting up, explaining that she was about to pop out. Do I need anything? As I need everything and nothing, I shake my head, experiencing an upswing of relief when I hear the front door close, swiftly followed by guilt when I notice that the cup of tea she has left is full and steaming.

'A well earned drink?' Jake asks. Back in his domestic surroundings, he looks different from the Jake on the hospital ward, older, drawn, more tired somehow. Despite the draining hospital lighting, he has a purposeful radiance about him when he's with me and Hope that he doesn't have around Fran.

'No, I'm fine thanks. I just love the idea of sleeping on a real bed again. The one in the hospital was so rock hard and sweaty. Like sleeping on a slab of old cheese,' I try to joke but my voice is unstable, listing. I cannot believe how far I am from Hope. 'Would you mind if I had a lie down?'

Giving me a concerned sidelong glance, he swings my hospital bag in his hand. I follow him up to the attic room, hit by how much the house smells of food and perfume after the bleached toilet scent of the hospital. The stairs feel different than I remember too, perhaps because up until this point I've only ever walked them heavily pregnant. But even without my weight – the baby lost from its host body – I am wobbling, my knees threatening to buckle. I grip the banister with white knuckled hands.

Jake knocks back the door of the attic room with his knee. 'Your old bed, waiting.'

'Thanks,' I manage in a reedy voice.

The room is bones-bare since Gareth drove my stuff up to Derbyshire three weeks ago; it has the air of a room speedily vacated, a room with a story. I stare at the bed beneath the skylight where I spent so many bewildered hours. At first I don't know what it is about the room, the house, being *here*, that is so bloody strange. Then it hits me: I am no longer the person who slept in this room only ten days ago. I am different. I am already different! My God. I am changing without you. We are growing apart, Rex.

'You sure you're OK, Gina?'

I nod. My heart starts to slam.

He hesitates. 'You want me to give you a moment?'

I nod again, unable to speak, steadying myself with a hand on the wall. Jake backs away. Our gaze locks until the final moment he closes the door. I listen to his familiar lollop of footsteps and I want him to come back. I don't want to be alone with myself. There is the sound of a door shutting downstairs, then silence. My nipples start to tingle as if they've got pins and needles. Confused, I look down and see two spreading circles of milk on my T-shirt. My body is crying tears of milk for my baby. 'Fuck.' I rummage through the bag on the floor, trying to find the hand pump that Dawn gave me. 'Fuck. Where is it?'

When I finally find the pump I can't work out how to assemble all the little bits, which valve goes where. My breasts are dripping now, rivulets of milk running down the inside of my blouse, pooling along the waistband of my jogging bottoms like blood from a wound. I give up, throw the contraption on to the bed, crouch to my knees and sink my head into the stiff fabric of the holdall. Pain rips along my caesarean scar, then routes deep inside of me.

I have lost you. I have lost Hope. And I have lost the person I was before all this happened. It is all over. All over. I have never felt so wretched.

I sob, nose and mouth against the hard zip, my milk splashing on to the floorboards. I want Hope so much it is unbearable: the smell of her, her body slumped over my shoulder, her dribble against my neck. I imagine the number of busy roads separating us, the endless red traffic lights, the dirty miles, the single footsteps, and a groan escapes from my mouth. I want to rip my skin off, anything to escape the pain. The groan becomes a sound I've never heard before. It goes on and on. And I can't make it stop.

Someone is pulling me up under the armpits like a rag doll.

'Gina, Gina.' Jake tries to cradle me in his arms but I grapple, not wanting anyone to hold me, anyone but you. The more I struggle the firmer he holds me. I can smell my milk. All I can smell is milk.

'Gina, please.' He holds my head, one hand on each side of my face, stilling me, as if he's holding me up over a precipice. I know that if he lets go now I'll fall to my death, that everything rests on him holding me here. We stare at each other, panting, struggling to regain control of our breath.

I don't know who kisses who first.

Thirty-seven

Ten kisses

1. The kiss on the cheek to greet me on our first date in that little Italian off Beak Street, the evening of the day I met you on the Heath. The brief meeting of your cheek against mine. Yours was smooth and warm, as if it had been shaved and sunned. You smelled subtly of lemons. I wore tan leather wedges and a white broderie Anglaise dress and worried that you could see my flesh coloured knickers beneath the white. (Much later, you told me you could, and would I wear the ensemble again, please?) I had sea bass and fennel, wrapped in a sleeping bag of foil, which was totally delicious except I'd lost my appetite and I didn't know what to do when I felt the spike of a fish bone in my mouth, not wanting to take it out and put it on the side of my plate and turn you off me. In the end I swallowed the fish bone. I decided you were worth the risk.

2. The kiss after the Beak Street meal. The way it started out on the cheek, and then, in a sweetly teenage fumbling

way, misfired to nearer my mouth so that our noses knocked and we giggled. No tongues. Just as well after all that fish.

3. Date two, day two: tongues. Beside some wheelie bins on Great Portland Street, although I had no idea at the time. Wonderful things were swirling around our heads, butterflies and petals, trumpets blowing, the works. You tasted of coffee and something else, something sweet. I was so relieved that you were a good kisser, that I hadn't fallen for someone who couldn't kiss. After the tongues, I wondered what it would be like if you went down on me. That would come two days later, a different kind of kiss.

4. That different kind of kiss. Always.

5. The kiss after you'd been away skiing a month after we met. I greeted you at Heathrow. You'd been away five days. It felt like five weeks. People stared at us as you came out of Arrivals and we kissed. Someone clapped.

6. When you asked to marry me. I wasn't sure if you were joking. I kissed you and said yes anyway.

7. After I met your mother for the first time and I spilt my tea in her lap by knocking it over with my ridiculous draped sleeve and it ruined her pale silk dress. I almost cried, I was so embarrassed. You kissed my nose afterwards and said I'd been perfect and your mother loved me, a white lie for which I was grateful.

8. The 'I can declare you man and wife' kiss, even though I can barely remember it because I was such a bundle of nerves. But I remember it through the wedding photograph, my proof it happened.

9. The kiss on the doorstep the morning you left to go to Tarifa. Our last kiss.
10. TBC. A slot reserved for the home-comer.

Thirty-eight

I open my eyes as sunlight spills across the bed. The first thing I see is one wavy golden hair lying on the pillow next to me.

So it really did happen.

It comes back to me then: Jake peeling my arms from his neck and shutting the bedroom door softly behind him. Before that, the kiss. Oh my God, that kiss, the unexpected force of it, the way we collapsed to the floor, locked. Afterwards, pulling back, desperately pulling back, we lay panting in each other's arms on the bed as the night threw itself around us. My body is still humming from that kiss, cranked into life after months of neglect, alive and tingling. But my head is still screaming, 'Wrong, wrong, wrong.'

I do not know who made the first move. All I know is that it just happened, with the speed and power of something that was meant to happen, even though clearly it was not. None of this was.

Oh God. What have I done?

Is this it, Rex? The end? Do I end my one-way conversation with you now? We always said, no secrets, you and I. No secrets, don't you remember? I'm not sure either of us really honoured that, did we?

And now?

The problem is I don't want to stop talking to you. It is all I have left. This one-way conversation has become part of me. You are like a diary. A counsellor. The face in the mirror that talks back.

I have no choice but to carry on and tell you everything. And if one day you come home, I will tell you to your face. Because without truth there is only uncertainty, feet wheeling mid-air. And I cannot bear more uncertainty.

I slip back into a troubled sleep only to wake to a door slamming somewhere, milk-sodden sheets and tortured breasts. My mind jackknifes to Hope, alone in the hospital while her mother cavorts with her uncle and shame shivers across my skin like a fever. I jump out of bed and throw on some clean clothes, calculating that if I get to the hospital straightaway I'll be able to pump my breasts there. If I don't my breasts will surely explode. Unable to find my breast pads in my flustered haste, I slip two slender sanitary pads into my bra and, determinedly pushing thoughts of the kiss out of my mind, run downstairs. I am being tugged towards Hope on an invisible rope. The house is empty – Jake and Fran must have left for work by now – so I throw open the kitchen door carelessly.

Jake and Fran are sitting at the breakfast table. Jake's face flames. Fran's eyes sweep over me coolly. 'You look knackered, Gina.' She flicks her hair and a smooth blonde curl bounces on her shoulder. 'Coffee?'

'No, no thanks,' I stutter, unable to look at Jake. 'I'm

241

going to shoot to the hospital straightaway to see Hope.'

She smiles, no doubt grateful that I'm not going to gatecrash their breakfast. 'Will I see you later? I'm off to San Fran tomorrow.' Jake looks down at the newspaper on the table, shielding his face with his hand, allowing me to stare at him for a moment before I quickly look away. 'More mobile phone nonsense,' she adds.

'Oh, right. No, I won't see you later. I . . . I'm meeting my parents. I won't be around tonight, I'm afraid.' Jake is looking elsewhere, anywhere but at me. It is bad enough with Fran here, but after last night it strikes me that Fran not being here will be even worse. *What have we done?*

'Don't look so freaked out, Gina. Jake will look after you, won't you, Jake?'

Jake forces a smile. It is my turn to stare at the floor. I kissed Fran's boyfriend. In her house. Oh God.

'Just don't leave him in charge of the baby. He's not exactly what you'd call paternal, are you, honey?' Jake stands up and fusses with the coffee machine. Fran turns her attention back to me. 'You really do look so different without your bump. My eye can't get used to it. Amazingly, you look quite slim.'

My hand instinctively travels to the fleshy bagginess that is my stomach and I miss Hope with a fresh pang.

'There's a brilliant Pilates centre down the road. All the mums round here go after sprogging. You should make sure you take time for yourself, Gina.'

'Yes, yes, good idea.' I know as I say this that I will never make the Pilates centre. That if I can just get to the end of the day, the week, the year, without cracking up completely, I will have achieved more than enough.

242

'Although I guess you won't be here then, will you?' Fran adds with an unexpected coolness that cuts through the buttery breakfast air like a chilled knife. 'When the baby is out of hospital, I mean? You'll be in Yorkshire, won't you?'

I rock Hope in my arms, focusing on her tiny pink face, trying not to think about the kiss. Blame me, blame my momentary madness, my hungering for human flesh. The boundaries have all smudged since you left. Your disappearance blew apart life as I knew it. Don't hate me, Rex. Just come back for your daughter. Please, I beg silently, tracing the exquisite lines of Hope's cheeks with my finger. It is then that it happens: her eyes open slowly, as if breaking through the bonds of glued lashes. They are blue-black, focused, searching for my face.

'Hello!' Our eyes lock in mutual wonderment. A crunch of wind pulls her tiny red face into a smile. She doesn't look away.

'Aw, just you look at that,' croons Brenda, walking up behind me. 'I wondered why your mama was grinning like a loon today, Hope. Lunch, baby.' She fixes the milk-filled syringe to the end of Hope's nostril tubes, opens up the valve and starts to push milk slowly into it. I have to look away. It's a process that still upsets me, the medicalisation of something that should be natural.

'Going to try and breastfeed her again?' Brenda asks.

'She won't take it, Brenda,' I sigh despairingly. 'She's just not interested.'

'And she never will if you don't keep trying, will she? Come on, Mummy. Don't give up yet.'

Brenda finds me a small nook on the ward with an armchair behind a stained blue curtain. Feeling like a foolish teenager who has no idea how to look after the baby she has produced, I yank up my top and try to manoeuver a nipple into her mouth without asphyxiating her. It takes some time. Hope looks astonished by the nipple, sniffs, but as usual will not suck. 'Just *try*, please, then you can come home. We can leave London. We need to leave London, Hope. We really do.'

I hear muffled voices outside the curtain.

'If you could give her a few minutes,' I hear Brenda say a little briskly. 'She's trying to feed.'

Who's that? Any excuse to give up breastfeeding, I push my boobs back into my bra. As I do, I catch sight of myself in the mirror opposite and start. For the first time in weeks I'm not horrified by what I see. Weirdly, I do not look like a woman who has been up most of the night. My eyes are bright, my lips full and red as if I'm wearing make-up, which I'm not. I look alright.

'You can wait, that's no problem,' says Brenda.

I push back the curtain and peek out.

There is a woman standing at the reception desk, her back to me, bleach blonde hair pouring down her back, wearing a long coat, glossy brown riding boots. 'Mandy?' I call, standing up, Hope draped over my shoulder.

Mandy turns to me with a wide smile and those grass-green eyes. 'Hey!'

'Hi!' I walk over, pull the blanket away from the baby's face and smile. 'This is Hope.'

'She's tiny!'

I pull her back. Such a comment strikes fear into the heart of the mother of a premature baby.

'And beautiful, simply gorgeous,' she says quickly, seeing the look on my face. 'Just look at her fingernails! A little doll.' To my surprise I see that there are tears in her eyes. 'Well done, Gina. Well done.'

'I didn't do anything. She was an emergency C section.'

'What do you mean you didn't do anything? A C section! That's hardcore.' She steps closer. I begin to feel paranoid about germs, Hope's immune system still vulnerable.

'I'm going to put her back in her cot. Shall we go and grab a tea? I'd love a cup of tea.'

'Here, I'll take her,' says Brenda, picking Hope out of my arms. 'You go and have a nice cuppa with your friend.'

The hospital café is a place of extreme emotion and extreme boredom, a hub in which parents of ill children bite down their fingernails over endless coffees, and noisy extended families sit for hours waiting for test results. We find a small round table in the corner. Mandy comes back from the counter with two cups of tea and packaged short-bread biscuits. 'I hope you don't mind me turning up like this, Gina.' Puzzlingly, she seems nervous. 'I did try to phone you a few times this morning.'

'Sorry, I've not been . . .' Gosh, this is the first morning since you left I've not checked my phone. 'We're not meant to have our phones on the ward and, oh I don't know . . .'

'I totally understand. Barely with it, I was. You seem much more together.'

'I'm not here anymore, not sleeping here. I had to leave the ward.'

'You're not here? What do you mean?'

'They needed my bed.'

'Oh no! That's a scandal. And Hope's here? Terrible, terrible. So where are you? Where are you staying?'

'I moved back to Jake's last night.' At the mention of his name the heat rises. There is a scent of him, I'm sure, around my lips. Who knew he could kiss like that? Jake. Sweet, diffident Jake. Bloody hell.

Mandy hunches forward over the table, hands entwined, thumbs anxiously circling. 'Gina, look, there is something I've been wanting to talk to you about. I just don't think it can wait any longer. Not now Hope's been born.'

'Oh?' Apprehension clenches my stomach.

'I've been torturing myself over the last few weeks, trying to work out if I should tell you or not.' She closes her eyes, as if gathering her strength. Her fingers tease the edge of the biscuit packet. 'But if I were you, I'd . . . well, I'd want to know.'

'Tell me what, Mandy?' I begin to feel really uneasy now. No more surprises please.

'I promised Rex I wouldn't tell anyone, that's the thing,' she says, her voice barely a whisper now. 'Least of all you.'

The clatter of the restaurant fades away. That familiar old dread balls in my stomach. 'Mandy, please. If it's something that could help with the search, you must tell me. It doesn't matter what it is. Please.'

'Oh, I see you and my heart breaks.' Her voice becomes low and hoarse and she wipes away tears from the corners of her eyes.

'What's the matter? Mandy, are you OK?'

'It's not fair, not fair at all, you being alone like this. Sorry, give me a moment.' She takes a deep breath. 'Gina, do you remember I told you I had a little boy?'

My rogue mind flips to Jake again. The scent of his skin as we lay, clothed, entangled, dawn smudged pink at the window. 'Yes, er, I think so.'

'My little boy, Ryan. How to say this? I'll cut to the chase.' She looks pained. 'My boy, Rex is his father.'

Thirty-nine

'When it comes to Rex, nothing would surprise me,' Dad growls.

I'm still too stunned to defend you.

Mum reaches over the greasy wooden table and grabs my hand so tightly her wedding ring digs into my skin. The pizza restaurant feels like a small, hot red box, claustrophobic and inescapable. My heart ba-booms in my chest. I feel sick.

'In my day we had a name for men like that,' spits Dad.

'Teddy,' says Mum. 'Please.'

'She's a chancer, Dad,' I manage in a hoarse whisper. 'A chancer.'

'But what if she's not, Gee?' Dawn's flushed cheeks are full of pizza, her mouth pursed as if she's about to blow a storm out over the table.

'Back off, Dawn.'

'Girls.' Mum's eyes are full of tears. 'We need to pull together as a family at a moment like this, not be at each other's throats.'

'If it *is* flaming true . . .' The tips of Dad's ears are red now, his rage spreading across his face like a rash. 'I'll flipping skin the bastard alive!'

A family at an adjacent table look up, alarmed.

'It's not true, Dad.'

'I'll personally enjoy wringing his neck!'

Mum puts a hand on his arm. 'Blood pressure, Teddy. Blood pressure.' She takes a large gulp of her white wine, kissing the glass with lipstick. 'Let's presume it is true for a moment, just a moment. Don't shoot me a look like that, Gina. We have to do this. We'll get the DNA thingy majiggy done, but we still need to do this. Now, what's she like, this . . . this Mandy?'

'I've only met her twice.'

'Instincts?' asks Dawn, picking the olives off her pizza and putting them on the side of her plate.

'I liked her before. Clearly, I was duped.'

'Well, it's a nice age gap, Gina,' Mum says thoughtfully. 'Between Ryan and Hope. There won't be any competition or anything. Not like there was between you two. Don't look at me like that! *If*, love, if.'

'Gordon Bennett! I think we're all jumping the gun here,' barks Dad, making the waitress flinch as she removes a dirty plate. 'One step, one step at a time. Our main priority has to be wee Hope. Only once Hope is out of that godforsaken place should we start delving deeper into this . . . business.'

'I can hardly pretend I don't know anything, Dad. I can hardly pretend it's not happened.'

Dad shakes his head and looks at me with a mixture of affection and despair. 'What is it about you, Gina?' He puts an arm around my shoulders and kisses the top of my head.

'But they say things come in threes. This is the third. It's got to be over, eh?'

'Third?' says Dawn, looking puzzled. 'What other mishaps has my little sis got herself into?'

I dip my head, ashamed again. Dad squeezes my hand and I know then that he hasn't told her. This would have been hard for him. Our family aren't meant to have secrets from one another. But I always was a daddy's girl, and I knew he'd stay silent if I asked.

'Who's up for pudding?' asks Mum with faux cheer. 'I rather fancy the cheesecake. I know I shouldn't but . . .' She tracks a cheesecake being delivered to an adjacent table with her eyes. 'My sweet tooth is aching for it.'

Dawn puts her fork down with a clatter on the table. 'Does Rex's mum know yet?'

I shake my head. I can only begin to imagine Clarice's reaction. Clarice. Oh my God. If she knew . . .

Dawn blows out pizza breath. 'Well, I'd like to be a fly on the wall for that conversation!'

'What about Jake?' asks Dad solemnly.

'I . . . I . . . I haven't told him yet,' I stutter, feeling my face burn up. Normally he'd have been the first person I'd have told. Now I am dreading being in the same room with him. This is all such a godawful mess.

'You haven't told *Jake*?' Dawn says, eyes widening.

I look down at the table, aware that my family are wondering about my furious blush. 'No.'

'Well, maybe that's wise. Perhaps you shouldn't. Not yet.' Mum knots her hands. 'Not until we know for certain, eh?'

'Don't be daft. She's got a duty to tell him as soon as possible,' says Dawn. 'She can't not.'

'This isn't about *duty*,' says Dad sternly. 'This is about Gina and the baby. Gina must take things at her own pace.'

I smile gratefully at Dad. He's not one for great displays of affection but on rare occasions his love for me hits me like a train.

'When you and Hope finally get to Derbyshire, Gareth could do a bit of detective work about Mandy. Don't look like that, Gina,' says Dawn.

'It's high time you moved back home, love,' Mum says. 'Away from all this madness.'

'She's right, you know.' Dawn picks a bit of pizza out of her tooth with the edge of her fingernail. 'The quicker you get away from all this, the better, sis. Fresh start and all that, eh?'

I pull back my chair and jump up. 'Sorry, guys, but I'm going.'

'What about the cheesecake? You can't go before pudding. Where are you going, love?'

'I'm going to tell Jake. You're right. I can't hide this a second longer. I've got to tell him.'

My hands tremble as I slide the key into the lock. It occurs to me that the easiest thing would have been to phone rather than tell Jake in person. I creep into the house. Through the half open door I see him in the kitchen, a lonely figure, slumped forward over a bottle of beer. Just tell him, tell him about Mandy and remove yourself upstairs, I say to myself. Pack. Pack your stuff and go.

On seeing me, his face shadows. 'How's Hope?'

'I tried to breastfeed her.' I stop and blush absurdly at the word breast. Why did I say that? 'She wasn't having any of it.'

'She'll get it, I'm sure. Give her time.'

'Has Fran gone on her trip?' Even mentioning her name makes me feel like a traitor to womankind. 'I'm sorry not to say goodbye. I had pizza out with my family.' Silence crackles around us. I shift awkwardly on my feet. Do we pretend it never happened? 'Jake, there's something you need to know . . .'

'Stop, please. Let me speak first.' My eyes are drawn to his hands, large, pleasingly symmetrical hands that grip his bottle. I remember the way they traced the dips in my clavicles. 'You must think I'm the biggest arsehole that ever walked the earth.'

'No, of course not, Jake.'

'I don't know what happened.' His face is taut with an emotion I've never seen in him before. I wonder if he hates me.

'I don't either.'

He looks away, and it hurts so much, him looking away like that. I've felt so close to him over the last few weeks and now we are like strangers again. The kiss has ruined everything. I am more alone than ever. I want to grab him and shake him and make what happened go away, erase it, this stain on our friendship. I cannot bear the thought of losing him.

'I'm not the kind of man who makes passes at his brother's wife, Gina.'

'I know that, Jake.'

'It would destroy me to think I've hurt you in any way.' He speaks in a hoarse whisper, the voice of a broken man.

'You . . . you of all people haven't hurt me, could never hurt me,' I say, hating his anguish, wanting to fold him into my arms. 'You've done so much to help.'

He shakes his head, as if answering a question to himself silently.

'It's been so . . . confusing.' I stop, not knowing how to express how deeply wrong the kiss was and yet, in a funny way, how it made me feel that I am not just a washed-up widow, or a wife waiting for her long-lost husband to come home, or a pair of tits that get sucked into a breast pump. But I cannot say this and I cannot allow myself to think like this. There are more important things to think about now. Mandy's revelation blows even the kiss out of the water.

'Can I just say . . .' he begins. He looks strange. Suddenly I don't know what he's going to say at all.

'No, there's something, something really big, that I need to tell you first, Jake.'

Forty

Mandy

'Argh!' Mandy pressed her face into the cushion in frustration. She felt like tearing through the fabric with her teeth and spitting out the feathers. She'd ballsed up, ballsed up big time. And still it went round and round her head, the conversation in the café, repeat, replay, like a video. And it always stopped and freeze-framed on Gina's face, her pale-faced horror, as if she'd been stabbed in the abdomen beneath the hospital café table.

'I conceived him towards the end of our relationship,' she'd tried to explain. It had all come out wrong, brutal and implausible. 'The baby was the end. Rex didn't want anything to do with the baby.'

'You're lying!' Gina had shouted, leaping up from the chair, her red hair flying.

'I know it must seem like that, Gina. Please hear me out. Sit down, please.'

'You're lying! Rex would never do that,' she'd screamed, eyes rolling back in her head like a frightened colt. 'He's going to come home because of my baby. Hope is what's going to bring him back! He would always do the decent thing.'

Mandy realised that she'd hit a raw nerve then. 'I promise you I'm telling the truth. He wanted me to have an abortion. Please,' she'd said super softly. 'Please sit back down.'

Slowly, reluctantly, Gina had sat back down. 'No, he wouldn't,' she'd whispered, shaking her head. 'He was anti-abortion. It was a Catholic thing, it was . . . embedded.'

'Not when it affected him personally he wasn't. I tell you, Gina, it was me who wanted that baby, with or without his involvement. Not him.'

Gina had looked at her as if she was a bit of dirt on her shoe.

'I never accepted a penny, if that's what you're thinking. Ryan was, is, my responsibility, always.'

'You're saying he knew, he *knew* he had fathered this child?' Oh, the betrayal on that beautiful freckled face. She'd see the expression on that face until the day she died. 'I don't believe it.'

'He did, Gina.'

'Rex wouldn't do that! Rex wouldn't not take responsibility for his own child.' She'd started muttering the same thing, over and over, like a mad woman. 'He's not a monster, he's not a monster.'

'No, he's not a monster, sweetheart. I'm not saying that. But he could be a total arse.'

'I can't listen to this.' Gina clamped her ears with her hands.

'Look, things were bad between us. He thought I'd tricked

255

him into it, into getting pregnant, Gina. He was furious. He never forgave me.'

'Did . . . did you trick him?' Gina had asked so quietly it was barely audible, eyes filled with tears.

'I didn't try to get pregnant but I didn't try not to get pregnant. I knew I was getting on a bit, that this pregnancy might be my last chance. To be fair to him, he'd always told me he didn't want kids, that he wasn't ready, least of all with me. I was never good enough for him, you see.' She'd reached across and touched Gina's arm. 'He didn't love me like he loved you, Gina.'

Gina flung her arm away. 'So you never told Jake? His mum?'

'I promised not to.'

'In exchange for what? What was in it for you to keep quiet?' Gina narrowed her eyes. They were scared, those eyes, the eyes of a woman who was having her life ripped up in front of her. Part of Mandy wanted to backpedal then, say it was all a horrible mistake, but of course she couldn't, not then. It was out of the box. So she'd staunchly continued, 'I thought that if I did things his way then he might come round. I didn't want to alienate him totally. I hated Rex in so many ways, don't get me wrong, but I loved him, too. I knew his failings, understood them, and . . . oh, he was one of those buggers that was always worth it somehow.'

'Always worth it,' Gina had repeated robotically, her face white and blank. 'He was always worth it.'

'I knew I had a bit of time before Ryan started asking awkward questions, you see. I was going to have to tell him when he was older. It is Ryan's right to know. But in the meantime I thought if there was just *one* chance, one little chance, that Ryan could have a relationship with his real father one day, I shouldn't be the one to scupper it.'

Gina held her hand up. 'Don't tell me any more. Please. Just stop.'

'I've kept stuff for Ryan,' she'd persevered, scared that Gina would leave before she had a chance to make her story believable. 'A box full of stuff about Rex, old photographs, letters he sent me, funny mementoes of our time together. I can show you if you like?'

'No, I do not want to see it!'

How stupid of her to assume that she could dig that little box out of the attic and prove anything. All those years she'd thought she was amassing proof. Stupid, stupid, stupid.

'You mentioned a guy, Mark? He is Ryan's father, isn't he?'

'I wish he was but no, he's not, Gina. We've only been together a couple of years. He moved in about the time you must have met Rex.'

'How do you know when I met Rex?' Gina asked incredulously.

'He told me.'

'Rex told you? Why would he tell *you?*'

'He still came round occasionally, just popped in of an evening. I know it might seem hard to believe, but we had a friendship of sorts. An understanding. I guess I was a bit of a safety net.'

Gina shook her head. 'He visited you? No. I don't believe you.'

'He liked to check in on Ryan, see him when he was

257

sleeping. And that's what gave me hope. It gave me hope that one day he'd step up to the mark.' Gina was biting down so hard on her lip it was going white. 'He just needed to find the courage to love. And to trust that we'd all muddle through and it would work out.'

'I'd have known if he'd visited you,' Gina said. 'I'd have known.'

'He'd stopped visiting me by the time you two got together, although we spoke on the phone once or twice,' she'd explained quietly. 'When I met Mark, he didn't like it, you see. He didn't like me having my own life, moving on, even though . . . there hadn't been anything, not like that, between us for years. But he was so jealous, so incapable of sharing anything even then, years later. And once Mark moved in, he never came round again. Then he met you.'

Gina started to sob quietly. And the sobbing gave Mandy a chink of hope because it suggested that a part of Gina might be willing to believe her.

'I'm so sorry, I wish I wasn't telling you this, Gina.'

She wiped her tears roughly away with the back of her hand. 'So why are you? Why now? There's no money, if that's what you're after.'

'I'm not after money. The truth is, I thought you had a right to know, now that he's gone. I thought Hope had a right to know, too.' She smiled hopefully. 'That she's got a big brother!'

Gina shook her head defiantly. 'No.'

'I always wondered if the day might come when Rex had kids of his own. I hoped that that would be the catalyst for him. That he'd realise what he'd been missing with Ryan.'

258

Gina stared back at her blankly. She remained silent for an impossibly long time. 'Say something, Gina, please.'

'He would have *told* me. He would have told me,' Gina repeated. 'There was no reason for him to keep it a secret. We were soulmates. Rex and I were soulmates.' She got up to leave. 'I don't know what you want from me, Mandy. Please go.' Her voice was clipped, more in control now. 'Leave me and Hope alone.'

'I don't want anything from you, Gina! Stop, wait . . .' She rummaged in her handbag and pulled a photograph out of her purse. 'This is my Ryan, take a good look at him, Gina.'

She wouldn't look.

'Please, Gina.' She had to shove it into her small, trembling hands. Finally, Gina looked down. 'The spit, isn't he?'

She'd just stared and stared, that white-faced red-haired ghost girl, before throwing the photo down and running out of the café.

'We're here if you want us! I want to help!' she'd shouted after her, then sunk back to her chair, head in her hands, wondering what on earth she had done.

Forty-one

I look up to see Lucy rushing towards me across the park, her black cape flapping like wings against the heavy grey sky. She sits down next to me on the bench, panting, pushing wisps of hair from her cold-pink face. 'Oh my God. Tell me *everything*!'

'I don't believe her. I cannot square the man I know with the man Mandy describes. It doesn't stack up,' I blurt, breath tunnelling out of my mouth. 'He wouldn't not see his child, Lucy.'

'No, no, we'll get to that in a minute.' Lucy dismisses it with a flutter of her gloved hand. 'Sorry, Gee, but we already discussed Mandy and Ryan into the small hours last night. I'm not trying to belittle it but we won't know for sure until there's a DNA test.'

I nod dumbly, still shocked to the core.

'The kiss for God's sake!' She bounces on the bench. 'You can't just drop that into the conversation before hanging up and expect me to not want to talk about it, Gee! Oh. My. God. Did I hear you right? What do you mean you and Jake kissed? You kissed! Bloody hell, Gina! *When?*'

I pull my coat tighter across my body. 'It was nothing, just a weird moment the night I was discharged from hospital.'

'Nothing?' gasps Lucy. 'This is not nothing! Why didn't you tell me straightaway?'

'I don't know.'

'Denial,' Lucy promptly decides.

'It's hardly significant now. Not after Mandy's bombshell.'

'Gee, what are you talking about? This is *huge!*'

'Look, Lucy, it was a terrible, terrible thing for us to do. It could have ruined everything. I still might have ruined everything.' What I don't say is that I've barely been able to sleep or eat since it happened. And my nights have been dunked in strange, haunting dreams that stick to me like burnt sugar for hours after I wake.

'You of all people don't need to feel any guilt,' she huffs.

'Lucy, if I lost Jake it would be . . . catastrophic. It's bad enough. Really, please, just leave it. It's dead. Gone. Buried.' Cold air ripples across the surface of the lake and snaps at our extremities. To protect my fingers I push my hands into the opposite sleeves like a muff. 'Lucy, all I'm thinking about right now is Hope.'

She laughs. 'I'm not entirely sure I believe you.'

'If anyone else spoke to me like that I'd deck them.'

'Well, I'm not other people, am I?' She grins mischievously, knowing she's pushing it and doing it anyway. 'If you can't confide in me, who are you going to confide in? In my opinion . . .'

'Please feel free to stay silent for once.'

'Oooh, Gee, look!' Lucy turns her face skywards, mouth dropping open. 'Snow!'

Oh yes. Tiny snowflakes polka my dark coat.

'Don't make any decision now based on the fact that Rex is coming back, that's all,' she says, still looking up at the sky. I clench my hands together tightly in my sleeve. My cold flesh stings. 'He's been gone months. There is no sign of him.'

'There was a sighting, Lucy. A sighting.'

She meets my gaze again with a determined expression. 'What if it wasn't him and he's dead? What if it was him and he doesn't want to be found?'

I bite down hard on my lip.

'You have to wait ten years before he is legally declared dead. Ten years is a hell of a long time. You will be over forty.'

I cannot imagine being forty. I cannot imagine being a week older. One day at a time.

'What about *your* life, Gina? Do you want to spend the next decade in limbo, not loving, not being loved back? Not . . . shagging?'

'Don't project your loved-up bridal gushiness on to me.'

She looks hurt. I feel bad. But I cannot give her what she wants. I cannot go there.

She studies me for a moment too long to be comfortable. 'You look different, Gina, do you know that? You already look different. Now that I know about the kiss it all makes sense. He's kissed roses back into your cheeks.'

'It's the cold.'

'Nah.' She kicks out her buckled brown boots and scatters a circle of pigeons. 'Happier is not the right word, given the circumstances. It's just that you've got light in your eyes again, that's all.'

'Don't be daft.'

'It's true,' she protests. 'I swear it's true.'

'Even if I did eventually move on, it wouldn't be with Jake, not in a million years.'

'Ah, you're saying it *couldn't* be with Jake.' She sounds pleased with herself. Like she's cracked it.

'I'm not.'

'My mother always says that fucked up men are no longer sexy once you're a mother.'

'Meaning?' Lucy's mother has pronouncements on everything. Lucy learned everything she knows from her mother.

'Those intense, dysfunctional power-hungry types . . .' She shakes her head, whistles beneath her breath.

I glare at my mouthy friend. I always loved her for her straight talking. Today I hate her for it.

'Those type of guys are just not good enough for you anymore. Jake *is*.'

'For fuck's sake! Apart from the small awkward fact he's Rex's *brother*, he's not . . . not my type, Lucy. You know he's not!'

She laughs. 'Just because he's nice.'

'Rex was nice!'

She shimmies slightly beneath her cape. 'Doesn't sound like he was that nice to Mandy.'

It is snowing harder now. The cold has really got to me. I start to shiver beneath my layers. 'You know I don't believe he'd do that.'

'Only because you've set all your hopes on Rex swooping back home when he hears about Hope. Rex the hero. Rex the overjoyed father. But maybe he'd be a fucking awful father.

Have you ever considered that, Gee? The worst kind. The one that doesn't *show*.'

'Stop it, Lucy! Just stop it!' I jump up from the bench. 'I'm leaving.'

'Don't go.' She grabs me, her blue eyes glossy with tears. 'I love you, Gee. I really do. You are my wonderful, life-affirming, madcap friend who has been through so much shit and doesn't deserve to go through anymore, OK? You need a break. I see Jake. And he's funny and kind and gorgeous and he's clearly head over heels in love with you. He adores Hope and you're perfect for one another and you know what? Fuck what anyone else thinks and guilt and loyalty, it's your *life*, Gee. Oh, I'm sorry. Don't cry, don't cry. Come here.' She hugs me tight and we sob into each other's hair. 'This is it, that was all I meant, Gee,' she snuffles. 'We get one life.'

Forty-two

Hector. Hector Grimes. On the doorstep. Stamping his black shoes in the snow, car keys dangling from his hand. 'Hello, Gina.'

'What . . . what are you doing here?' I stutter. Hector at my door!

'I wanted to see how you were.' He glances around him, noting the tight Victorian terrace, the scruffy children's scooters in the neighbour's front garden, the patches of snow scraped off car windscreens where children have scooped snowballs. A million miles away from Holland Park. 'Martin only just told me you had to move out of your nice little flat. I came to check you were OK.' He reaches for his most charming smile. 'So this is Harlesden, postcode gang wars land?'

I just frown at him. What the hell is he *doing* here?

'Even if I'm not about to be mugged, can I come in? I'm freezing my bollocks off out here.'

I step aside as he brushes past me, the smell of him just as it always was. In the kitchen he looks out of the window at the flat white sheet of a garden. 'Virgin snow.' Only Hector could say that and make it sound sexual. 'So how's the baby doing?'

'Good. Thank you.'

'Glad to hear it.' He leans on the wooden worktop with one hand, like he owns it. Like it's his desk at Grey Home. 'And you? You're looking good, Gina. Slim again.'

'Hector, what are you—'

'I'm impressed, Gina,' he interrupts. 'I'm impressed by how you've coped with all this shit.'

'Hector, if it's about work, I'm happy to tell you my intentions . . .' I say, knowing with certainty that I'll not return, that I'll make it work another way, somehow. Surely it's time for Femi and me to set up on our own, as we always said we would. I will make it happen. No, I can't go back to Grey Home if Hector's moving back to London permanently. It's never going to happen.

'You do what you like, Gina,' he shrugs nonchalantly. 'Whatever you decide you'll get stellar references.' His eyes grow amused. 'I'm not a total arsehole.'

'So you've changed?' I say, emboldened by the fact he is on my territory now.

He sucks in his breath. 'I wouldn't have actually done it, Gina, you know that, don't you? I did threaten it, you're right. I did. It was a low point, a very low point. Agreed. But I would never have given you a bugger of a reference just because . . .' His forehead crosshatches. 'I wanted you to stay, OK? I didn't want you to throw away your career because of me. If you'd left Grey Home then you'd have screwed up your CV. You know that. Besides, I was in Hong

Kong, it would have been pointless martyrdom on your part if you'd left then.' He steps forward. 'You'll thank me eventually.'

I step backwards. 'You are fucking unbelievable, Hector.'

He fixes me with those eyes: wolf-blue ringed with dark navy. And, like hypnotist's eyes, they transport me back, back, back. I look away to stop the past rearing up at me. But it doesn't work.

We are back on that narrow country road in Derbyshire, not far from my parents' house, although Hector doesn't know this because I haven't told him my parents live close by, fearing it will spook him. There are insects pulping on to his BMW's windscreen, veins pulsing in his short, thick neck. As we plunge through the rainy darkness our attempt at a stolen night away becomes ever more toxic, more unreal. It has been a disaster: Hector doesn't like Derbyshire, the place where I grew up, the place I wanted to show off. It is too far from London. It is raining, torrentially. There are midges. Bad food. Obese people in fleeces. The bed in the B&B we've fled was small and itchy and his wife Lena kept phoning, suspicious, talking about one of the children having a fever. I could tell he wanted to go home. When I accused him of spinning me a lie about leaving Lena, the room seemed even smaller, gloomier, and both of us wondered why we were there, how it came to this. So we left.

In the car we don't discuss how he'll explain to Lena why he's come back from a business conference in the middle of the night. We don't discuss how we'll face each other at work. I know for certainty now that the sex and the thrill and the speedy rushes of pleasure I mistook for happiness in the beginning were an illusion, just as Lucy always said. I know that this is the end. That the important thing I had to tell him I can't possibly tell him now. So I tell him he's an arsehole. Part of me still hopes that he will tell me he's sorry and that he loves me and everything will be OK again, but of course he doesn't say that because he doesn't feel that. Instead he starts shouting, if you think that little of me, Ginge – *Ginge*!, the bastard – you can get out of the fucking car and walk back to London! It's the first time I've ever heard him raise his voice. I scream back at him, stop the car, stop the car! I *will* fucking walk! Like a crazed redhead. He actually screeches the car to a halt. Not wanting him to get one over on me, I get out, slam the car door, call his bluff. He orders me to get back in the car. I shake my head, too furious, too proud, needing more from him before I do get back in, which I will have to eventually.

He drives off. Just drives into the night.

I watch the lights of the car shrink to red monster eyes. Alone in the darkness, shaking and terrified, I don't know who to call or who will rescue me. So I call my father. I tell him I am at the side of a road in the middle of nowhere. I tell him I am pregnant.

'I'm sorry, Gina,' Hector says now, running his fingers through his silvered waves. 'For the way it ended. For that appalling night.'

I am so grateful I listened to Dad and never told Hector that I was pregnant, just dealt with it as clinically and decisively as I could. Whatever the hurt and what-ifs involved, it was far better than the alternative.

'I tried to get you to get back in the car.' He uses that caramel cajole that used to do it for me every time. 'I called you, Gina. You didn't pick up.'

'I don't want to talk about it, Hector, really. It's all in the past now.'

He slumps back on the kitchen units. 'Lena and I are divorcing.'

It takes a while to sink in. 'I'm sorry.'

'Well, it was never going to work, was it? I guess that must have been clear to you back then.' He searches my face for something.

'I'm . . . I'm terribly ashamed of what I did, Hector.'

'You have nothing to be ashamed about,' he says softly.

'You have children.'

He looks away, darkening. Something desperate streaks across his face.

'I knew it was wrong in theory back then, but since having Hope, I know that what we did was wrong with every fibre of my being.'

'It wasn't anything to do with you, me and Lena splitting up, if that's any comfort. She never found out about us. No, this was . . . something else.' He looks away, flushes slightly. I know then it is another woman. Of course it is. To think that I thought I was the only one, the special one, the one who was going to save him from his dry, sexless marriage to the icy, beautiful Lena. What a berk. I want to go back in time and slap my own cheek until I see sense.

'I've never stopped missing you, Gina.'

I actually laugh.

'I've never stopped missing you,' he repeats, as if assuming

I hadn't heard it properly the first time. 'I miss your spirit, your laugh.'

'Don't be ridiculous.'

There's a peculiar neediness about him that disturbs me. 'What we had, Gina. That chemistry. It doesn't just go away. You can't turn it off like a tap.'

'You are joking?'

'Do I look like I'm joking? Sometimes life works in weird ways. We're both free now . . .'

'I am not the person I was with you. I am not that person any more. Don't you get it?' I look at him in bewilderment. 'So . . . so much has happened! Look at me, I'm a wife, a mother. I'm a different person. How can you possibly think that we would ever—'

'I'm alone, Gina. I'm forty-five and alone.' His face crumples, its once devastating handsomeness now puffy, middle-aged, disappointed. I'm surprised that this gives me no pleasure, despite everything. 'I miss my kids, I miss everything I pissed up the wall. I've fucked it all up, Gina.'

I'm stunned into silence. 'I can't help you, Hector,' I say eventually. 'I really can't.'

He is silent for a moment then pulls his car keys out of his pocket. 'Sorry, I don't know what I was thinking. I'll see myself out.'

I dumbly watch him walk towards the door. And for a startling second I see you, Rex. Not Hector but you. Walking towards the door in your navy suit. You. Hector. Big man boys in smart navy suits. Men who left me alone in the darkness, pregnant. Lucy's words wheel around my head: 'the worst kind . . .'

My body shaking with suppressed sobs, I run out into the snowy garden, needing to make my scorching hot body cold, needing to be washed clean of it all. I tilt my head back into the spirals of falling snow, spinning around, my mouth open, trying to catch the pureness, take it inside of me, make myself new again. I do not know how long I am there, all I know is that when Jake comes home he finds me in the garden, shivering on the bench. He doesn't say anything. He just wraps me in his arms, picks me up and carries me back inside like a giant baby.

Forty-three

Jake hands me a glass of red wine. 'Medicinal.'

'I'm sorry to be such a total liability.'

'I like nursing women back from hypothermia.'

'I'm a pain in the arse and I know it. I'm truly sorry.'

'It must have been a burden, carrying all that on your own.' He whistles beneath his breath. 'To not tell Rex.'

'Hardly anyone knew, only Mum, Dad and Lucy. I refused to even tell Dawn because I didn't want her wading in and judging me. I couldn't tell Femi because she worked at Grey. I'd got used to it being a secret, Jake. It had to be one, so it wasn't unnatural not to tell Rex, in a funny way.' I wince. 'Look, I'm aware that this doesn't sound great.'

'If I was going to marry someone I'd want to be totally open with them.'

'I know. If it had been you . . .' I crush my hand to my mouth, horrified at my slip. That's Lucy, putting stupid ideas in my head. 'I almost told him so many times,' I stutter, my face burning up. 'But I was scared of not being who Rex thought I was.'

272

Jake holds his hands out in front of the fire, warming them like slices of toast.

'And it all happened so quickly, the wedding, everything. The days just rushed past and I . . . I just never got round to telling him, and the longer I hadn't told him the more difficult it *was* to tell him.' I take a large gulp of wine. 'When I met Rex I was so miserable, Jake. I felt ugly, fat, unwanted, blighted by what had happened with Hector.' Jake shakes his head. 'Rex changed all of that. I couldn't bear the thought of losing him. Of going back to that.'

'Right.'

'I'm not condoning what I did. I'm really not. But I knew Rex wouldn't want me if he knew. He was so moralistic, so black and white, so repressed Catholic about it all.'

Jake opens his mouth to say something then seems to think better of it.

'He used to say I was this . . .' I laugh hollowly, gulp back more wine. '. . . this free-spirited, pure woman. That's why I couldn't risk it.'

'This doesn't sound like an honest marriage to me,' Jake says simply, staring gloomily into the fire.

'We were in this bubble of happiness. I didn't want to pop it.'

We are silent for a moment. Then he glances over to me, smiles a small smile. 'Nutter.'

My eyes fill with tears. I can't bear the idea of losing Jake's respect. 'You think I'm despicable?'

'I think you have fucking awful taste in men. Hector sounds like a total pillock.' Crouching down, he leans forward to stoke the fire, the musculature of his back visible

273

through his sweater. I recollect the feel of it beneath my fingertips and yearn to touch it.

It has been five days since we kissed. Outwardly at least, the awkwardness between us has gone, helped by the fact that Fran is still away, so we don't have to face up to what we've done. In its place we have cultured a watchful civility, only undercut by the jolts of electricity that happen when we accidently brush against each other in the narrow hall, or when I turn around and find him looking at me.

'You still look cold.' Jake pulls the reindeer skin hide off the back of the sofa and flaps it out on the floor next to the fire. 'Here.'

I move from sofa to hide, relishing the fire's intense lick of heat. I pull my knees towards me. 'What a week.'

'You can say that again.'

I sink my chin to my knees, studying him, noticing the way that the stress of the last few months has hollowed his cheekbones, shaved off his round-cheeked boyishness. He looks lived-in, more grown-up handsome. Older. Wiser. I catch myself looking at him. Lucy's fault. I wish she hadn't said that stuff.

'What are you thinking?' he eyes me curiously.

'You believe Mandy, don't you?' I say, because I can't tell him what I'm really thinking, and Mandy is still a subject at the forefront of my mind.

He sighs. 'I'm willing to withhold judgement until we know for sure.' He takes his glasses off, rubs them on his tattered denim shirt.

'Ever the rationalist.'

'Well, I think it sensible considering the allegations.'

'Do you really believe Rex could have had a secret like that and not told anyone, Jake? Surely he would have told your mum? You? It doesn't make sense.'

'He was able to keep a secret. I'll say that about my brother. Even as a boy he told lies all the time.' He shrugs. 'Stupid pointless lies.'

'About what?' I too learnt to tell lies. A mistress always does.

'Oh, you know, he'd come top of the class in spelling again or he'd been chosen for the county cricket team but turned it down. Even when Mum realised it was bullshit, she thought it was cute. She indulged him.'

I think about this for a moment. 'Was I a secret?'

He pushes his hair off his face. It is golden in the firelight, longer, wilder, in need of a haircut. I like it like this. 'No, you were never a secret. The opposite. He told me and Mum about you the day after you'd met, that he'd met someone he really liked. And he introduced us to you pretty quickly after that.'

'What did you think of me when you first met me?'

'Ah.' He cracks his big smile. 'Young. Beautiful. Dirty laugh. Mad red hair.'

'Lightweight?' I lower my head to my knees, trying to disguise the blush of pleasure burning across my cheeks. Am I flirting? I mustn't flirt. 'I worried you and your mum thought I was too lightweight for him.'

'No. Not lightweight. Chirpy. Fun. Unspoiled.'

I scoff loudly. 'Ironic.'

'You made him happy, Gina.'

I fiddle with the edge of the hide, rolling it back and forth in my fingers. 'It wasn't enough though, was it? I didn't make him happy enough.'

'I don't think Rex is capable of being happier than you made him,' he says simply.

'Jake?'

'Yes, Gina,' he says, in the manner of an adult answering the millionth question from a curious child.

'I know you love Rex. But do you like him?'

He looks surprised by the question. 'Like? Don't know about that. He could . . . can be a selfish little shit.'

'Sometimes I feel I'm the only person on the planet he didn't piss off in some way. It's like the person I know is not the same person everyone else knows.' Jake's silence feels damning. 'The funny thing is, until he disappeared, I thought everyone saw Rex as I saw Rex.'

'We're different with different people, aren't we?' he says diplomatically. 'Some people bring out our better selves.'

'You bring out my better self,' I blurt without thinking, because it's true and sometimes the truth will out.

He laughs, frowns. '*Me?*'

'Well, yes. I don't feel I have anything to hide with you. I'm just me. And that makes me feel . . .' I hesitate, search for the word, surprised by my own wine-loosened tongue. '. . . better. I can't really explain it. More at ease. Kind of grounded.'

I'm not sure if his eyes fill with tears or if it's the smoke from the fire, but he gets up quickly, keeping his face averted, and fiddles with his stereo until music – Mumford & Sons – fills the room.

'Jake, you have been such a wonderful . . .' I search for the right word and my brain blanks. The guitars kick in. '. . . friend.'

He stabs the fire hard, showering sparks: like the bonfire night sky the evening my waters broke and everything in my life back-flipped. I notice his arms, covered with curled golden hairs, the width of his chest, his big head housing that wonderful brain. And I have to fight the urge to crawl towards him, curl my body around his and just lie there, sealed in by his skin, cradled within the cave of his ribs like a child. He catches me staring. I look away, aware that he is now watching me intently. And I find that I don't mind being watched by him, that there is something nice about being the object of his steady gaze. 'Jake?'

'Yes?' His eyes do not leave my face.

'Sometimes I talk to Rex.' I put it out there, my peculiar little secret, and wait for his reaction. For once I don't feel exposed by it. 'I talk to him all the time. In my head. Is that weird?'

'Yeah.'

'Oh.'

He shrugs. 'But I do it too.'

Something lifts from my shoulders. 'You do? *Really?*'

'I tell him to come home and grow some fucking balls.'

'I'm glad it's not just me. Sometimes I feel like I might be losing it.'

'I'll tell you when you finally lose it, Gina Adler.'

I lean closer to him then, as if it's his warmth that has made me realise I am cold. And I don't know whether it's the music or the fire or the snow falling outside or the fact that

I've just told him something that I could never tell you, but I wish that this evening could go on forever.

'Stay here, Gina,' he says with sudden intensity. 'Don't shoot off to Derbyshire as soon as Hope's out of hospital. Stay with me.'

'I can't. I need to go before . . .' I stop. Before what? Before my feelings get any more confusing? Lucy can't be right. 'I need to be with my family, that's all.'

His face falls. 'Sure.'

I take his hand, bring it up to my cheek, warm and solid and infinitely comforting. I close my eyes and fight the urge to kiss it, to slip his fingers into my mouth. My body starts to rush with blood and wine and fire.

'So Fran comes back tomorrow,' he says coolly. 'We go back to how we were?'

'Yes, yes we do, Jake.' I drop his hand.

'I'm not sure I can do that, Gina.'

'We have to.'

He lets the moment stretch almost to breaking point. 'Do we?'

'Yes.' I close my eyes. Lucy's words wheel around my head again. 'Yes we do.'

'This is so fucked up.'

'Don't.'

He strokes the contour of my cheek very slowly with the back of his hand. 'Do you know the worst thing?'

'Jake, please don't. Let's not go there.'

'I am scared of Rex coming home now.'

'Jake, please.'

'I don't want my brother to come back. And I hate myself

278

for it.' He shakes his head despairingly. 'Now you're going to hate me for saying it. I've fucked up again.'

'Oh, Jake.' I take his head with both hands and press it to my breastbone, his breath warm against my skin. 'Don't you see? I could never ever hate you. That's exactly why I can't stay.'

'Do you remember that time in my mother's garden? You were on the swing . . .'

'I remember.' The low autumn sun. My hands on the cool ropes. Jake scuffing his foot into the fallen crunchy leaves.

'I had this weird feeling about you.'

I hold my breath very tight.

'I thought you were so beautiful, Gina. I didn't know where to look.'

'Shh.'

'Sorry. I'm sorry.'

'Jake, shall we dance?'

'*What?*' He looks at me as if I've gone mad.

'Dance. Can we dance before everything goes back to how it was? That's all I want, one dance with you.'

He pulls me up, slips his arms around my waist, presses me against his chest. 'You're a sucker for punishment, I see.'

Forty-four

Shoulders thrown back, neck long, Clarice takes small balletic steps into the ward as if it were a ballroom floor. She's wearing a scarlet fitted coat. Patent beige pumps. Hair swept up in a chignon. There is a rustle of attention as magazines are put down on laps and nurses pause in their duties: she is one of those women, even in her late sixties. I try to shove my nipple back into the bra. You once told me your mother never breastfed you because she didn't want to ruin her breasts. I don't want her to see mine.

'Oh, really, please don't stop what you're doing.' Clarice looks down at my breast warily, keeping a safe distance. My own mum has an annoying habit of poking it with her finger, force-feeding the nipple into Hope's mouth. 'Little babies must eat.'

'I was just giving up anyway.' I hide the offending breast under a white muslin square. 'She's still not nursing. All a bit hopeless, I'm afraid.'

'The bottle is better.' She smiles, brushes snow off the shoulders of her coat. 'Try a bottle, Gina. Easier. Keeps baby's belly full.'

'She still needs to suck from a bottle, that's the thing. I can't take her home until she can suck, otherwise she's stuck with those horrible nostril tubes. Please, Clarice, do sit down.'

Thinner than ever, she perches birdlike on the edge of the chair, as if trying to avoid touching too much of its surface area. She gazes down at Hope, her blue-powdered eyelids crinkling with a small smile. At that moment I can see Clarice looking down at you as a baby, and how she must have adored you over the years, as a boy, muddy from football, as a teenager, plotting your travels with pins on the map on your bedroom wall. She's still waiting to see you as a father, the final bit of the circle. I guess all mothers, even the Clarices of the world, want that.

'I hope you don't mind me popping by unannounced like this.'

'Not at all!' I say with possibly too much gusto.

'I was having lunch with Jake.' At the mention of his name my face burns up. 'He said you were here. I wanted to come and tell you in person that we've just had a big donation to the Find Rex fund.'

'That's wonderful!'

'I thought we could use it to have . . . one last roll of the dice and offer a substantial reward for information leading to his whereabouts. What do you think?'

'Brilliant, let's do it.' Hope's tiny hands snatch at the air. If I could chose between her having a father and me having a husband, I would let her take my place every time, I realise. I'd lose you so she could have you. 'Thanks, Clarice,' I say, smiling up at her.

'Oh, it is not me you have to thank.' Her mouth twitches. 'Actually, Gina, I feel ashamed of myself for not visiting more.'

'Oh, you don't need to apologise, Clarice!'

'The baby is a reminder that Rex is gone, you see.'

'I know, I know. Clarice, it's quite alright, honestly.'

She worries the little black beads at her throat. 'I'm afraid that I've found Hope's fragility frightening, the idea that I could have lost her too . . .'

'We're not going to lose her, Clarice. We're not going to lose her, I promise.'

Her lips twitch again and I think she's going to cry. Instead, she smiles. And for all its tension it is a warm smile, full of tooth and gum. She's one of those people, so cool, that when she reveals a bit of sunshine you want to bask in it. 'Yes, Jake has made me see sense.' She looks faintly embarrassed by her own humility. 'I hope you forgive me.'

'There's nothing to forgive! Oh, Clarice, it's been the most terrible time for you, for everyone. And with Mandy's . . . claim. It's too much for you to take in.'

Her lips tighten and a starburst of lines spread around her lipsticked mouth. 'Yes. And that.'

'Will you meet her, Clarice?'

'Perhaps.' She glances at me, offers a weak smile. 'You're not convinced, I see?'

'Rex wouldn't have done that,' I say defiantly.

Worryingly, she doesn't immediately agree with me. 'If this is true, this . . . this business with the boy,' Clarice sighs, sounding exhausted by the subject, 'well, all I can say is that I didn't bring Rex up to be a coward, Gina. I brought him up to be a decent human being. I am not impressed. Not impressed at all.'

'We haven't heard his side of the story. There would have been a reason, Clarice. If it were true. Which it's not.' I'm aware of the desperation in my voice now.

'There is never a reason to behave like that to a woman. It is not just naughty. All men are naughty! They have their brains in their trousers, we women must accept that. But not telling your own mother about her grandchild.' She shakes her head in disgust. '*That* is unforgivable.'

For the first time I get a sense of your mother's loyalty wavering and it scares me. If your own mother won't believe in you, who will? 'I don't understand why you'd believe Mandy, Clarice.'

Clarice stiffens. 'I know my son.'

I swallow hard. 'And I don't?'

She won't meet my eye. 'He did not always tell the truth, Gina.'

I hold Hope very tightly. Lies, Jake had said, little pointless lies.

'Gina, Rex is a wonderful son. I love him very, very much.' Her voice cracks and her hand flies to her throat again. 'Who could not love a man like Rex? So full of life. So intelligent. Such a big heart. But he is complicated, I'm afraid. Just like his father. The best men always are.'

My breath catches in my throat. I don't want to say anything in case it stops this rare free flow of Clarice's thoughts.

'I am beginning to wonder, did he leave us like his father left him?' She presses her temples with her fingers as if trying to rid herself of an onslaught of memories.

'His father died in an accident, Clarice. That's not the same as leaving,' I point out gently.

'*Mais oui*, he slipped!' Clarice releases a shrill parrot squawk laugh. The nurses look over curiously. 'He slipped.'

My heart starts to slam. 'He didn't slip?'

'We will never know if he slipped off that mountain, Gina.'

'Rex said he died heroically, doing the sport he loved.'

'He wore no ropes. They found him with no ropes.' She blots a tear in the corner of her eye. 'And he was strange, strange before he left, Gina.'

'Strange?'

'Distant. In one of his dark, strange moods, you know.'

I nod like I do know, although I don't. You never mentioned your father's dark moods. You portrayed him as a breezy swashbuckling bear of a man.

'I had a bad feeling about the trip because he was so low at the time. Now maybe they'd give him pills or something, I don't know. It was different then. Ronald was so macho, so bloody English, the idea of going to a doctor because he felt . . . sad. No, he just couldn't do it. And he liked being like that, I think.' She smiles to herself. Clearly, she liked it too. 'The other times – when he wasn't down – he was so full of life. Kind. Funny. He could make people laugh! Everyone adored him. He wasn't scared of anything, nothing at all. What's the word? Indomitable.'

Fear balls in my stomach: like father, like son?

'I never told Rex, or Jake, about . . . my doubts,' Clarice adds quickly. 'I wanted to protect them, Gina. I wanted to keep his memory intact. He was a good man.' Clarice touches

284

Hope's cheek gently. I have to fight the urge to pull Hope away because it feels as if history might reach out with grey wrinkled hands and contaminate her innocence. 'All the years I've done my best to ensure that Rex remembers his father as a hero, an adventurer. I thought that would be good for him.' She stares down at Hope wistfully. 'I'm not sure if I pulled it off. That is the problem.'

What a confusing, complicated childhood. Oh, you poor thing, Rex.

'It is my fault,' she says without self-pity.

'This is not your fault,' I say, feeling a wave of compassion towards this glamorous, fragile lady sitting next to me. 'None of it is your fault, Clarice.'

'I'm afraid it is always the mother's fault.' She smiles, stands up abruptly. 'Now I must get my train or my dog will starve. Take care, Gina, little Hope. *Au revoir.*' She kisses me on the cheek, leaving me reeling as her pumps click away down the lino corridor. I'm so stunned by what she's just said about your father's accident that it takes a moment for it to register that Hope is sucking.

Forty-five

'Hope's breastfeeding! They're going to discharge her,' I scream excitedly into my phone, kicking up the snow with my red wellies. 'On Monday! We'll be coming to Derbyshire next week, Dawn. Can you bloody believe it?'

'Oh no. Next week? Oh, sis. We have a problem.'

'A problem?' I repeat, unable to comprehend how anything could be a problem today. I could dance down the street.

'Danny has chickenpox. No, I'm not flipping joking. The worst possible timing, I know, I know. Tom will get it for sure, so we'll have to wait for them both to get to the non-infectious stage before you and Hope can come and stay. You can't possibly risk the baby getting it, what with her being so little. Sis, I am so sorry. The law of sod in action.'

I sniff back the tears. 'I was looking forward to coming home in time for Christmas.'

'Home? You know I think that's the first time you've called Derbyshire home in years,' marvels Dawn.

'Having Hope . . . it's made me miss Derbyshire. It's funny, I can't really explain it.' I also can't explain that confiding in Jake about the affair with Hector has taken all the power out it. Derbyshire is no longer the place where I cowered at the side of the road in the darkness. It is, despite everything, just home, a lovely, ordinary home. Not glamorous. Not perfect. Not fucked up. God, I'm grateful for it. It's snowing. And it's almost Christmas. I crave my mother's burned mince pies. I want to see Dad in a paper cracker crown bouncing Hope on his knee.

'Gina, I think I understand, probably more than you think I do. I'm not a total bumpkin you know.'

'I don't think that.'

Dawn laughs. 'You so do.'

I feel a shiver of shame. Because the truth is I did think that, once, in a different lifetime, when I was cocky with luck and love. I don't now.

'Do you not think there was a part of me that would have loved to have gone to London and had your life, Gina?'

'No way? You wanted to come to London?'

Dawn pauses. 'Well, yeah. Yeah, I did actually.'

'Blimey, Dawn.' I thought I was the only one who sat at bus stops where buses came once an hour and dreamed of the big city. 'Why didn't you then?'

'Oh, I'm too fat for London, sis.'

'Don't be ridiculous!'

'And I don't have your talents. What would I have done? Arrived at King's Cross waving a hairdressing diploma above my head? Come on.'

'Absolutely. London always needs hairdressers.'

'I hated hairdressing, as you know, all those smelly scalps and stinky hair dyes. Besides, I had Gareth and . . .' She pauses. 'The folks are getting older you know, Gina. They need someone around. Someone looking out for them.'

'Older? I always think of them frozen in time somewhere around 1978. Eating cottage pie and peas.'

'They're pushing seventy.'

'I'm sorry, Dawn,' I say, starting to cry quietly, overcome. And not just by the image of my parents eating cottage pie.

'What for?'

'For being so crap these last couple of years, so wrapped up in myself.'

'Well you did go missing for a while. But the old Gina is back now.'

'I'm not . . . not sure I am that person, not the sister you think I am,' I stutter tearfully, thinking of Hector and the abortion and all the things I never had the balls to tell Dawn.

'Don't be so bloody melodramatic. Look, I don't care what you've done, what secrets you keep, sis. Chances are I guessed them long ago anyway. Or I've done far worse and not told *you*. Fancy that, eh? The double life of Dawn Richards!'

I laugh through my tears.

'I hate to inform you but you've barely changed since you were six, Gina. You're just Our Gina. We wouldn't have you any other way. And right now you need to sort out what you're going to do next. Now,' she says, getting into her bossy stride. 'The logical thing would be to go and stay with Mum and Dad. It'll be a bit of a squeeze. Mum will drive you nuts and Dad will probably drop the baby, but it won't be that bad. Oh . . . Oh no! Christ almighty. Danny has just vommed on the rug. Got to go! Call you back later.'

I push open Jake's front door, walk straight into a mound of bags in the hall: Fran's back! Oh God. Oh God. Will I be able to carry this off?

'Hi,' Fran says, turning to face me in the kitchen. Her eyes are red and puffy, clearly she's been crying. I feel a shudder of guilt so visceral it's as if someone's emptied a tray of ice cubes down my back. I glance at Jake. He looks away. Fearing the worst, I start to gabble inanely into the awkwardness. 'You're lucky to be able to land. You know how this country comes to a jolting stop whenever a flake of snow falls.'

'Just made it actually, Heathrow's cancelled loads of flights. How's Hope?'

'She will be released on Monday,' I grin despite everything. Nothing will crush me today. My baby is coming home.

'That's great,' says Fran with genuine feeling. 'About time she got out of that hellhole.'

'Dawn's twins have got chickenpox so I'm going to go straight to my parents' house until they're better.'

'Shit,' says Jake.

'Where do your folks live again?' Fran asks quietly, looking like she's struggling to sound normal. 'Scotland, isn't it?'

'Derbyshire.'

'It'll look lovely in this snow.'

'It will.' We both smile determinedly, trying to pretend that she has not been crying, that I haven't noticed, that everything is normal. 'Well, I'm just going to have a bath, you know what the hospital is like . . .' I start to walk out of the room, trying not to sprint.

'Wait a minute,' calls Fran sharply.

Something about her tone makes me freeze.

'Fran,' Jake mumbles. 'Not now.'

'Why not now, Jake? Are you hoping to hide it from her?'

Oh no, oh no. I swallow hard. Does she know? How has she found out?

'Gina, you may have noticed the bags in the hall.' Fran's voice quavers. 'I'm moving out.'

'But you . . . you've just got back,' I say stupidly, glancing at Jake. He shields his eyes with his hand, like a little boy who is trying to pretend it's not happening. Oh, Jake. What have we done?

'Sometimes you see things at a distance that you don't see when it's staring you in the face, Gina.'

She knows. She knows. 'I'm sorry, I'm so sorry, Fran.'

'Gina,' Jake says quickly. 'You don't need to listen to this. Go and have your bath. This is between Fran and me.'

'I will go today, Fran,' I blurt, mortified with self-loathing. 'I will find somewhere else. The last thing in the world I wanted was to come between you two. I . . . I . . .'

'Gina, please. Have your bath,' says Jake more desperately now.

'Hang on a minute.' Fran narrows her eyes, looking from me to Jake and back again. 'Why do you think this is about you, Gina? Am I missing something here?'

Fuck. Have I critically misread the situation and dumped us in it? I start to back very slowly out of the door.

'Gina? *Everything* is about Gina!' she shouts at Jake. 'Gina and your dead fucking brother. Yes! You can both look at me like that. Someone has to say it. He's dead, dead as a fucking dodo, guys, and the sooner you both accept it

290

and move on, the happier everyone will be. For months – months! – this . . . *thing* has taken over our lives! How can we have a normal life, Jake? Me and you? How can we move forward with Rex hanging over us? It's like a curse. I feel jinxed by your selfish arsehole of a brother.'

I reach the stairs, start clambering up them two at a time. The truth hits me hard: we have come between them, Rex. You and I. Together we have created a sinkhole, pulling everyone down with us.

'Run! Go on, run from the truth! You know what, Gina?' Fran yells after me. 'I don't think you're the only one who has lost their man around here. We've got more in common than you might think.'

Forty-six

I tread the snowy streets of Harlesden for two hours before finally answering Jake's call. He reassures me that I haven't totally destroyed his life and points out that there is only so long you can nurse a coffee in Starbucks without looking like a weirdo. When I get back, Fran and her bags have gone. Jake looks totally gutted.

Over the weekend our roles reverse: I want to help him as he has helped me. When I'm not with Hope, trying to fatten her up in hospital for her departure, I am trying to pep up Jake's spirits. I'm not very successful. He is clearly flattened by Fran's departure, his face pale, strained and unshaven. It is hard to believe that we once danced in each other's arms in the living room. That he carried me out of the snowy garden. Lucy had it all wrong after all. He is not in love with me. This is a broken-hearted man.

On Saturday night I decide to take matters into my own hands. I close the door to my attic bedroom, steel myself, pick up the phone and call Fran. I'm surprised when she picks up. 'Fran, it's Gina.'

'Hi,' she says coolly.

'Are you OK?'

She snorts as if it is a ridiculous question to ask, which I suppose it is.

'He's wretched, Fran. He loves you so much. I'm going on Monday and you'll have the space to get everything back together, back as it was before Rex . . .'

'Stop, Gina, please. It can never go back to how it was.' I hear voices in the background. I wonder where she is. Probably sobbing on a girlfriend's sofa, while I'm here, cuckoo in her nest. 'It's broken.'

'You can put it back together, really you can.'

'What would you know, Gina?' she asks scornfully.

'Well, if Rex walked through the door I wouldn't consider the relationship broken. I'd pick it up, stick it all back together.'

She laughs hollowly. 'And that is why men marry women like you, Gina.'

I don't quite know what to say, unsure if she's insulting me or paying me a compliment.

'I'll tell you one thing, though. Rex is not about to walk through the fucking door, Gina. That new reward is a total waste of time.'

'I'm not talking about him. I am talking about you and Jake,' I reply, refusing to rise to her.

'But can't you see it's all connected? Holy crap, you can't, can you? You can't see what's under your nose.'

'Sorry, Fran, I don't . . .' The conversation is not going quite to plan. I begin to regret making the call. 'Look, I wanted to tell you how much Jake missed you, in case, well, in case it made a difference. That's all.'

293

'Sweet thought, thanks.' Her voice drips with sarcasm.

'Oh, you should see him, Fran. He's like a lost soul. You must remember that all the stuff with Rex has hung over him like a cloud, and it's my fault for letting him get so involved. And now there's Mandy . . .' I stop. I can hear a voice clearly in the background. And it's a man's. Yes, definitely a man's. Who is it?

'Oh, just go back to Wales, Gina, and get on with your life, for God's sake.'

Something flips in me then. 'I'm not from fucking Wales, OK? Or Yorkshire. Or Scotland. I'm from *Derbyshire*.'

'OK, keep your bouff on. One minute . . .' Fran speaks to the man in the background with a suppressed giggle. 'Look, Gina, it's not a great time to talk, I've really got to go.'

Forty-seven

Monday, the weather has worsened. My parents and sister are snowed in. The railways are up the spout. Cars and lorries have spent the night stuck on the M1, people sleeping in their vehicles, huddled beneath blankets. The motorway is now closed. The roof of a Scottish scout hut collapsed under the weight of the snow, killing a caretaker. Three people have died trying to rescue their dogs from frozen lakes. The Tube is running a limited service, despite being underground. Outside, with wind chill, it is minus fifteen. It feels like your ears are about to drop off. The coldest winter in decades, the country has frozen to a standstill.

'Ready, baby?' Lucy tugs the pink bobble hat that Mum knitted further down Hope's apple head. 'I think we're going to need another blanket. That doesn't look warm enough. Where's the one Femi bought?'

I dig into Hope's hospital bag and pull out a crocheted blanket.

'One more, I think we need one more.'

'Lucy, we need to be careful not to overheat her. It's easy to overheat babies apparently.' I pull the hat up from her nose, anxious that it might block her breathing.

We frown at Hope, puzzling over where the invisible line between overheating and hypothermia might lie. I wish with a sharp pang that Mum or Dawn could have got here before the snow set in. They'd know what to do. But they are still shovelling their way out of their houses. Jake is interviewing a film director I've never heard of and can't be here either. It's just me and Lucy: two women less suited to look after a premature baby in the coldest winter for decades would be hard to find.

Brenda appears, smiling. 'Last bit of paperwork. Finito.' She hands me the final signed form that we've been hanging around for. 'About time this one went home, eh?'

'Is she going to overheat, Brenda?'

'No, it's Arctic out there. Just make sure you unwrap her when you get back home. And keep her indoors after that, until this bad spell's over. She's still pretty new.'

Lucy and I stare helplessly down at this newly minted human being. I fight the urge to cling to Brenda's nurse uniform. 'I can't really thank you enough, Brenda.'

Brenda laughs. 'Glad to be of service. Off you go then. What are you waiting for? Out of here, all of you! I declare this baby fully baked.' She rubs my arm warmly but briskly. I guess she's done this goodbye hundreds of times. 'All the luck in the world, love,' she says and walks smartly over to console a sobbing new mother of a baby born seven weeks early.

I walk carefully up Jake's path, terrified of swinging the car seat too hard – shaken baby syndrome? – or skidding on the ice and catapulting her over next door's box hedge. Hazards! Hazards everywhere! I try to work out how to use my door keys while still holding the car seat and can't. Lucy takes it from my fumbling fingers. As soon as the door is unlocked I snatch Hope back because I want to be the one carrying her over the threshold.

The house is as hot as the hospital: Jake has thoughtfully banged the heating up. I rest the car seat down in the living room, and put my hand in front of Hope's mouth to check her breathing, amazed that she's survived the journey. I attempt to undo the seat buckle and can't. This wakes her up. She starts to bawl. Something in my body flares red at the sound, as if it's connected in some way to my central nervous system. My breasts tingle. The seat buckle is impossible.

'How can someone so little make so much noise?' marvels Lucy.

'Ow!' I finally unclasp the buckle, nicking my finger in the process. Hope screams louder as if it's her finger I've nicked, not mine.

'I'll make a cup of tea,' Lucy says, disappearing. 'Oh, look, Gina, come here! Check this out,' she calls from the kitchen.

On the kitchen table is a bunch of pink roses, a plate of pink macaroons, a bottle of pink champagne, two glasses, and a note from Jake: 'Welcome home, girls.'

'God, he's so sweet,' Lucy sighs.

Hope starts to nose butt me.

'Look, she's trying to eat your neck!'

'Just give me a second, Hope, I'll feed you.'

Hope will not give me a second. Hope wants feeding now.

Noise explodes out of her lungs. Nurse! I want to shout. Brenda! But there is no nurse, no Brenda, no one who knows what they're doing. Panicking as the cry gets more urgent, I grapple for my boob, tugging the damn thing towards my arching baby, twisting it agonisingly into her mouth. Hope splutters and cries, spits out the nipple. I shove it back in, she loses it again, wails louder. We do this four times until she's finally latched on and feeding properly.

'Phew.' Lucy looks traumatised now. 'That was loud.'

Moments after the feed comes a splattering yellow poo. 'Oh God,' I say, as if I've never seen one before. 'Oh God.' My brain goes blank. What do I do? Flustered, sweating, I empty the hospital bag on the kitchen floor. The nappies are squashed flat at the bottom. Nappy between my teeth, I lay her out and start to peel off her poo-covered babygro.

'How come she's got poo up her neck? How did it get there?' wonders Lucy, stepping backwards.

Hope slams a foot hard into the dirty nappy, twists over and possets her last precious feed all over the kitchen floor.

'Carnage!' Lucy laughs. 'If Fran hadn't left last week, she'd be leaving now.'

'Just help me, will you?' Hope starts to cry, really cry this time, as if the last stereophonic screech was just a warm-up for this. 'It's OK, Hope. Shh, shh. It's OK, one more minute. Urgh. Shh. Oh no, not that foot too. Wipes, Lucy! Wipes! No, not kitchen roll, wipes for fuck's sake. Pass the nappy bag, yes, yes, that thing. Oh my God, there's more coming!' I feel a flood of pathetic tears wash over my face, splash down on to Hope's filthy babygro. 'Oh look at her. Oh no.'

'Hey, stop, Gina. Just stop. Take a deep breath. It's O-K.'

'I . . . I . . . just don't think I can do this on my own. I can't do this.'

'Gina,' says Lucy sternly. 'You were not beaten when your husband went missing. You were not beaten when you found out you were pregnant. After all that, Gina Adler, are you telling me you are to be beaten by a *poo*?'

Forty-eight

I wake with a start, terrified I've smothered Hope. My fingers search beneath her nose. Yes, she is breathing. Thank God. Thank God. This keeps happening, me feeding her in the early hours, falling asleep as I do so, crushing her with my swollen monster breasts. It's surely only a matter of time before I kill her. Why didn't anyone tell me that breastfeeding was so dangerous?

The alarm clock beside my bed says it's three am. Tiredness gnaws like a rat. It's making my eyes go funny. I've started to see you in the shadows pooling under the eaves, pixelated, ragged, a pirate emerging from a storm. I'm not sure if it's my brain playing hallucinogenic tricks or if an essence of you has somehow managed to defy the laws of physics and find your way back to me. I think of the movie *Cast Away*, and all those stories of men who are lost at sea, presumed dead. When they do return home they find their wives have married someone else.

Hope nuzzles me, starts to feed. As she feeds, something drains from me, milk, energy, sadness, all at once. Tracing the whorls of Hope's ears with my fingers, I search for you in the contours of her face. I'm still waiting for your dark hair to sprout on her head and her eyes to darken to walnut brown. But she's still bald as an egg, her skin pearl-fair, her eyes the grey of a beach pebble. Oh, she is so very beautiful. She's so beautiful it scares me. Now that I have her, I'm terrified of losing her.

I hear Jake's footsteps coming up the stairs. 'Gina?'

I pull the muslin over Hope's head to hide my sore red nipple.

'I saw your light on.' Jake, wearing his grey flannel dressing gown, sits down on the edge of the bed. 'Couldn't sleep. Sorry. I guess insomnia must sound like a luxury to you now.' He looks up at the skylight above the bed. It is covered in a thick puff of snow. 'Still snowing, huh?'

'It feels like it'll never stop.'

Jake looks down at Hope and smiles. Since she's joined us in Harlesden, his glum mood has shifted. She's had an extraordinary effect on him. Baby Prozac. 'Little buddha.'

Hope twitches her toes in response to his voice.

'Yeah, right. I'm calling her Lungs. Dad says I was a screamer. He says it's karma.'

'My dad always says I was an easy baby. You know, came out into the world at the right angle to the universe.'

'Now you're just trying to make me feel better.'

'Yeah, yeah.' He dips his head, coos at Hope.

'You're lucky to have a dad to tell you this stuff. I'm not sure Rex had that.'

He sits up, frowning. 'No, he didn't have that after Ronald died. Tough, really tough.'

I follow the satisfying snub of Hope's nose with my little

finger, thinking about what Clarice told me about your father. In this strange late hour any conversation seems possible. 'Didn't Rex see your dad as his dad at all?'

'Christ, no. It took a long time for Rex to accept him as a stepdad and then Mum and Dad split up.' He winces apologetically. 'Not exactly The Waltons, I'm afraid.'

'Clarice told me that Ronald suffered from depression,' I say, testing the water, wanting Jake's take on the family. 'At least that's what I thought she was saying.'

'Bipolar, yeah,' says Jake casually, cupping Hope's foot. 'I suspect that would be the modern diagnosis.'

'Bipolar? That's quite extreme.'

'Manic depression is the other term for it. But he was never diagnosed. I could be wrong.'

'That's what your mum thinks?'

'I have no idea what Mum really thinks about it all. She is very . . . private, I guess. That period of her life, after Ronald died, was not the happiest. She doesn't like discussing it.' He smiles resignedly. 'As a family, we all skirt around the subject like a pothole in the road, functional lot that we are.'

I try to imagine my own family's response. What would they do? Talk about it incessantly. Dawn would probably use it as a conversation opener at one of her coffee mornings.

'And then to die in a terrible accident,' I say, careful not to give anything away. 'Such bad luck.'

'Well, that's one theory.' In the gloom, his eyes are bright, watching me closely. 'Gina, there is some doubt over whether what happened to Rex's dad was an accident.'

I exhale with relief. 'Your mum said as much to me the other day.'

'She didn't? Well, there's a turn-up for the books, Mother actually being open about stuff for once. You should feel honoured.'

'I'm so relieved you've mentioned it now. She said she hadn't told you or Rex. I didn't feel I could say anything.'

'Oh, I worked it out for myself years ago, overhearing conversations between Mum and her girlfriends late at night. Telephone calls. That sort of thing.' He shrugs. 'Hey, it was the seventies.'

'Did Rex guess too?'

'He must have done. But we never talked about it. It was off limits. He was competitive about fathers, wanted his to be better than mine. He couldn't be open about it, I guess he got that from Mum.' He is silent for a while, reaches for Hope's hand. She grasps his little finger. 'He chose to see it as an accident, I think. You have to make a choice in the end, don't you? You have to decide what memories you want to be left with.'

For some reason this kills me.

'Hey, don't cry. I've made you cry, I'm so sorry.'

'It's not you, it's just sad.' There I am getting pissed off with my family because they talk too loudly and eat too many cheap biscuits and phone all the time. 'It makes me miss my family terribly for some reason.'

'Not dug themselves out yet?'

'No. It's like the deep freeze up there.' I look up at the skylight. Flakes of snow are falling harder again. 'I'm sorry about this, Jake. You must think you'll never get rid of me.'

'I don't want to get rid of you.'

We gaze at Hope in silence. I like this, the way that Hope

303

removes any reason for a conversation. We can just watch her for hours. It's like sitting in front of a flickering fire.

'Are you alright, Gina?' he asks eventually, looking at me like I'm not. 'You've seemed pretty low and tearful since you came out of hospital.'

'Yeah, yeah, just trippy tired, I think.' The moment I say this I start to cry again. I brush the tears away. 'Hormones,' I joke weakly.

'What's the matter, Gina? Apart from the obvious.' Jake has this ability to make me feel like the only person in the world that matters sometimes. 'Tell me.'

'I don't know. I'm so thrilled to have Hope out of the hospital. I love her so much. I should be happy. Maybe I just miss Mum, I don't know.' I try to smile bravely. 'As soon as the weather eases a bit, Mum will be here. I'll be fine. Don't worry about me.'

'Well, I do. Lucy is worried, too.'

'You've been talking to Lucy?' Something in me tightens. Lucy with her silly romantic theories. God, I hope she hasn't said anything.

'Only as she was leaving the house yesterday. I don't have a hotline.'

'My mother would feel left out if you did. She'd insist on a conference call.' I force the joke, trying to prove to myself that I can do this on my own, that it isn't beyond me, that I don't feel totally overwhelmed.

'I'm sure it's natural to feel up and down,' he suggests gently.

'I just feel so . . . so empty.'

'Hey, Gina, it's alright.' His eyes are so tender they set me off again. 'I'm no shrink but I should imagine it's no surprise if other feelings kind of catch up with you now. You've held it together so well up until now.'

I look away from him, into the shadows of the eaves. For a moment I swear I see you again, a flash of your black eyes. Watching me. Watching Jake. Waiting for us to slip up again. Did Jake and I really dance in the living room? Did we *kiss?*

'You do know that you are a wonderful mother, don't you?'

'Hardly.'

'You are. You're brilliant. I don't know how you do it.'

'She's not got a father. We're skint. I'm a mess. I . . . I can't even breastfeed properly. I'm so tired I worry that I'm going to forget her or something. Leave her behind somewhere like an umbrella. Or she'll get meningitis and just . . . just die.'

'Right.' Jake's jaw sets determinedly. 'Listen, I've got a proposal. Scrap that, it's not a proposal. It's a plan.'

'A plan?' I slump back against my pillows. It hits me that Jake is nothing like the bumbling boyish man I met in your mother's garden that time, nor the bewildered younger brother in the cabin in Tarifa. 'A plan sounds kind of exhausting.'

'I'm due holiday.'

'For God's sake take it. Go someplace hot. I would if I were you.'

'No, I am going to stay home and help you.'

Somewhere in the befuddlement of my head, relief flickers like fireworks in a cold, black sky.

'I'm aware that there's a strong chance I'll be just another extra child under your feet, but I will do my best to be of practical use. What do you say?'

'Um . . .' I hesitate. I'm wearing a polycotton nursing nightie. I have baby sick in my hair. I see my husband in the shadows beneath the eaves. It is safe now. 'I'd love that, Jake. I really would.'

'Brilliant.' He grins widely.

'There is a small possibility it may not feel like a holiday, Jake.'

'Come on, how hard can it be?'

Forty-nine

It's five thirty am. Having exhausted all other tactics – musical teddy, iPhone apps, lullabies – Jake has been jiggling Hope along the hallway in her pram on and off for the last two hours. She is still screaming. I'm close to it myself. 'Now, Hope, do we think it's still too cold for a walk outside?' Jake asks calmly.

'It's minus fifteen and pitch black,' I point out.

'Sensible point. Shh, Hope. Shh.'

Hope turns up the volume. Jake bends down into the pram then darts backwards. 'Oh.'

My heart sinks. 'Not another one.'

He picks her up, revealing the back of her pink babygro, damp and brown. 'The eagle has landed.'

I groan and pull myself off the armchair.

'Sit down. I'll do it.'

Too tired to argue, I slump back into the chair, watching Jake scrabble through the poppy-print nappy bag. It's like a military bomb diffuser's bag in its complexity. It's got too many pockets. Neither of us can ever find the right bits. Hope makes the nappy change as difficult as possible, thumping her heels, arching her back, roaring with indignation. Jake emerges from the exercise splattered and sweating, his glasses misted up. The noise is intolerable.

'I'll feed her.'

'I thought we were going to try and space her feeds?'

'Screw that. I can't listen to this any more. Hand her over.'

'Let me look up the troubleshooting feed bit in the baby manual.' He scratches his head, looks around the room dead-eyed with exhaustion. 'Where is the manual?'

'For fuck's sake, forget the bloody manual, Jake! Just hand her over.'

Jake carries her at arm's length towards me like a grenade. I unbutton my nightie, no longer caring if he sees my enormous ugly tits. She feeds. Silence. Blissful silence. Jake collapses into an armchair. 'Now, what I was saying about me being the baby whisperer . . .'

I manage a laugh.

'If I had breasts it would be a damn sight easier.' He pushes his glasses up his nose. 'Sorry, I'm not being a huge help, am I? The cat is better at this than me.'

'Jake, it's just a relief not to be listening to the screaming alone. But perhaps we should try using a bottle, too? It's best to get her on it early, that's what Dawn says. Otherwise she'll never accept it and I'll have to breastfeed her until she goes to university.'

'Better get on to it then.' He looks at his watch. 'It's almost proper morning now.' With the arthritic sigh of a suddenly aged man, he rises from the chair. 'After you've finished feeding her I'm ordering you back to bed.'

'I can't go back to bed. She'll howl like a rabid banshee if I leave her.'

He shrugs. 'I've sat through worse at Cannes.'

I'll never sleep, I think, as I reluctantly close my door to try to shut out the sound of Hope's wails from downstairs.

I wake up almost three hours later.

My clock says it's eight thirty in the morning, although the room is dark. It takes me a moment to realise that the skylight is completely covered in snow, blocking out all the daylight. It takes another moment to realise that I cannot hear Hope.

'Jake?' I clamber out of bed, panicking.

No answer. Prodded by fear, I bound down the stairs. 'Jake?'

They are in the living room. Jake is lying on the reindeer hide in front of the glowing embers of an expiring fire, glasses askew, snoring loudly, his arms wrapped around Hope who is fast asleep on his chest, gripping his ribs like a baby monkey. I stand there for a moment, not wanting to wake either of them.

'Jake?' I whisper, kneeling down and peeling his arms off Hope.

'Huh?' He opens his eyes, squints to focus, immediately drops back to sleep.

Hope stares up at me with those large, round eyes that can see into my soul. I take her upstairs, leaving Jake snoring on the rug. For once it is a quiet, restful feed.

Over the next twenty-four hours we discover that lying on Jake's chest is a failsafe means of calming Hope down from her more operatic rages. If she's not hungry, if she's not got a dirty nappy, the thing that is bothering her – and I still don't have the foggiest what it is – seems to be eased by lying on his chest. My chest doesn't have quite the same effect because she starts rooting for milk. She especially likes it when Jake hums, or, as I find out again later that day, snores. While just the sight of me holding a bottle sends her into a wild rage, he manages to coax her to take it; I become friends with the expressing machine again.

The lead story on the news remains the weather: 'Country in gridlock'; 'Worse to come'; 'Britain's worst winter in 150 years!'; 'Grit runs out!' We are all advised to only make essential journeys. The health visitor cancels her appointment twice. Jake has to hack icicles off the windows and shovel snow from the front path like a pioneer homesteader so that he can get out and buy supplies. The city's sharp edges are blunted. Sometimes the snow comes so thick you can't see more than a couple of feet ahead. London is in lockdown. Businesses and commuters are despairing. But I love it. I love being cut off, suspended in our own irregular twilight world, just me, Jake and Hope. We have firewood, food and a stockpile of nappies. Everything we need. In this swirling white blur, the past fades, burnt away by the urgent, noisy demands of a baby. Days are broken down into dozens of small events: a burp, a nappy change, a tiny fist gripping my finger, Hope snoring on Jake's chest. There's little time to think. And not once during this period do I see you watching us from the shadows beneath the eaves. For now at least, you leave us alone.

Fifty

'So Jake's taken paternity leave, has he?' Lucy presses the warm mug of tea against her cheek and grins.

'No, Lucy,' I reply wearily. 'He's taken something called a holiday.'

'A holiday!' hoots Femi, sitting cross-legged on the rug in front of the fire, clicking open pistachios with her teeth. 'That's how you sold it to him, is it? Like your style, girl.'

'I have to say that he's proving rather paternal for someone who once claimed to have *no* interest in having children,' adds Lucy wryly.

I feel the heat rise in my face: secretly I've been thinking the same thing.

'Oh, bless him.' Femi roots around the bowl for an unshelled nut. 'Every mother could do with a Jake in their life. We need to clone him.'

'Well, I have to admit he has been handy.' This has to be the year's biggest understatement. 'He's an expert burper. Good at calming her down.'

'Nappies?' asks Femi. 'Test of a real man.'

'Come on, Hope's most apocalyptic nappy must be a walk

in the park compared to living with Fran.' Lucy bends down and rubs Hope's nose with her own. 'I am hopelessly in love with you, Hope,' she croons, and Hope makes a happy clucking noise at the back of her throat. Part of me wishes Hope would scream at Lucy like she does me, just to demonstrate what she's like at three in the morning.

'Miss chill pill, eh?' says Femi, looking over and smiling at Hope.

'She's normally quite highly strung. I worry I've given birth to my sister.'

At the sound of my voice Hope swivels her head to look for me. Our eyes lock. Hit by an overwhelming urge to retrieve Hope from Lucy's knee – it's silly but I get jealous when other people hold her – I swoop her away, squish her against my shoulder and inhale her head. I've always found the smell of other people's babies too sweet and cloying, but I could sniff Hope forever.

'A natural.'

I laugh. 'Hardly.'

'You are!'

'You do look knackered, though,' observes Lucy. 'The badge of the new mother.'

I can't help feeling annoyed. 'Lucy, she never sleeps for more than two hours. You spend longer than that having your highlights done.'

Hope lets out a little squeal. She screws up her face tight and pink so that she looks a like an ancient alcoholic Tory MP.

'Oh, she's got wind,' says Femi. How the hell does she know that? 'I'd try putting her on her tummy. Always used to do the trick with mine.'

I flip her over, pat her back. The manoeuver is successful.

Femi smooths the baby blanket over Hope's back. 'Baby, it's cold out there.'

'I don't remember any cold like it, do you?' Lucy says. 'As we now appear to be living in Alaska, I've ordered myself a new fake fur coat. Trapped it myself on ASOS.'

A fake fur coat. How lovely. How alien. I wonder at the shiny sheaves of Lucy's hair and Femi's painted red nails. Having resigned myself to looking like an AC/DC roadie, their grooming strikes me as nothing short of miraculous.

'I heard about the reward. No news I take it?' says Femi, in the hushed reverential voice that people now use when they bring you up in conversation. Like they're talking about a dead person.

I shake my head. 'Not yet.' The doorbell rings. 'Excuse me a sec.'

I open the door, expecting Jake's Amazon delivery that was due this morning.

Mandy. Bold as you like, standing on the doorstep in a long sheepskin jacket.

'Oh my God.' I'd tried so hard to push her to the back of my mind. 'What are you doing here?'

'I wanted to pay you a visit.' There is hesitancy in her smile, as if she's half expecting me to shut the door in her face. She opens one side of her coat. My astonished gaze drops to the dark, curly-haired boy standing beside her. 'Gina, this is Ryan. Say hello to Gina, Ryan.'

Ryan stares back at me, his dark eyes meeting mine shyly. 'Hello,' he says. Gosh, that dimple.

'Go on, Ry,' Mandy whispers. Ryan offers me a small bunch of snow-white flowers.

'Thank you,' I say stiffly, taking them from his hands. 'They're lovely.'

'Everything OK?' Lucy calls from the sitting room. I don't reply. Ryan shivers.

'It's freezing, you better come in,' I say, taking pity on the poor boy that Mandy has dragged up here as some kind of manipulative bargaining tool.

In the living room I have to introduce them all. 'Femi and Lucy, Mandy, Ryan.'

Lucy's eyes saucer.

'Nice to meet you,' says Femi cheerily, not realising Mandy's significance. She winks at Ryan. 'Now you have got a nose the colour of a blueberry, young man. Why don't you come and sit next to the fire?' Ryan squats down, takes some football cards out of his pocket and starts to shuffle them. I notice the sprig of exuberant dark hair that stands up at the back of his head like something from a Tintin book. Tiny ears that sit close to his skull. A streak of blue felt tip pen on his cheek.

Oh, that dimple.

'I went to the hospital. They told me Hope had been discharged,' says Mandy quietly. I notice the deep blue hollows beneath her eyes. The cheery confidence has gone. I almost feel sorry for her until I remember what she said.

'Let's put the kettle on. Come on, Femi,' Lucy says, regaining her composure. She steers a bemused Femi out of the living room.

'She's so much bigger.' Mandy drops her black handbag

314

to the floor and reaches for Hope's thigh. I instinctively pull Hope away. Hurt flickers across Mandy's face. 'I'm sorry just to turn up like this, Gina. I didn't think I'd get an invite, so thought I'd chance it.'

'Impressive in this weather.' My voice sounds cold and sardonic, not at all like me. A little bit of me is ashamed of speaking to her like this, despite everything. I remember how much I liked her when we first met.

'A bit of snow never slowed us down, did it, Ryan?'

Ryan grins. That grin. Or is my mind playing tricks?

'Here, Ryan, come and have a look at the baba.'

Ryan gets up and dutifully walks over. He smiles at the baby without a huge deal of interest before turning his attention back to his football cards.

Femi pops her head around the door, her eyes bright and darting. Clearly, Lucy has told her about Mandy. 'Got any biscuits, Gee?' She can't keep her eyes off Ryan now.

'Cupboard above the cooker.'

She winks at Ryan. 'Do you want to help me hunt them down?'

Mandy nods at Ryan who follows Femi out of the room.

'You still don't believe me?' Mandy says once they've gone.

'I don't have any room in my head for anything else, not right now. I don't even want to think about it,' I lie. Obviously I've been thinking of little else.

'The early days are the hardest, I remember that. And God knows, you've had it a damn sight harder than most, Gina.'

'This makes it harder. You make it harder, Mandy. Can't you see that?'

315

She flinches like I've slapped her. 'I'll leave.' She picks up her bag. 'Ryan,' she calls around the door. 'Sorry, love, but we've got to go.'

Ryan appears at the door, his face crumpling. 'But I want to stay here and eat biscuits.'

She reaches for his little hand. 'I'll buy some in a shop. Come on.'

'Can I have Hobnobs?' Ryan asks Mandy as they walk towards the front door. 'The chocolatey ones? Please, you said.'

'Wait!' I call after them.

Mandy turns to look at me warily, her eyes glistening.

'It's OK,' I stutter. 'I . . . I have Hobnobs.'

Fifty-one

It happens slowly at first. The ice creaks and cracks. The icicle knife-points drip and blunt. The streets turn from virginal white to a dirty slush yellow. The melt exposes dog mess and rubbish, the city's grimy skin. The snow gone, life threatens to pick up where it left off. Jake returns to work. He phones at lunchtime to tell me that the anonymous donor who made the £10,000 contribution to the Find Rex fund is Hector Grimes. As I put the phone down, stunned, Mum arrives carrying three battered tins of cake. 'A slice of your favourite lemon drizzle, love?' She plants a sloppy wet kiss on my cheek.

With my mum around, something inside gives up. I stop trying to be brave. I stop trying to understand things. I want her in touching distance all the time, like a small child. Mum senses this and sits wedged up against me on the sofa, one hand cupping mine, watching over me as I try to eat, worried by my uncharacteristic lack of interest in cake. Later that afternoon she has a bath because Hope has vomited down the neckline of her blouse. Without her in the room dread races towards me like a giant wall of black water.

Panicky, heart racing, I strap Hope into the bouncer, pace the kitchen, looking around for things to do – there is so much to do, nothing at all that will make any difference – and decide to sterilise her dummies, boiling them in the saucepan. They bob up and down in the water. I nudge the teats beneath the surface with a fork. Something red grabs my attention: on the shelf next to the cooker, the stack of Match Attax cards Ryan left behind. I flick through the loved, battered cards of a sweet little boy, and sink hopelessly to the floor.

You failed Ryan. You failed Mandy. Moral, upright Rex Adler. The very worst kind of coward. Did you really think you'd get away with it? You must have known there was a high chance that Mandy would out you. It was a high-risk strategy. But you always did like gambling, didn't you?

I press Ryan's cards against my face and everything I've tried so hard to hold together for so long starts to unspool, the way a knitted blanket can unravel from one pulled stitch. Memories fly out of my brain like bats from a cave – Jake's mouth slightly open, the second before I kissed it, the pot of Carmex with your fingerprint in the gunk, Hector telling me he's getting divorced, Ryan's dimple – and dive-bomb towards me. I cannot get my breath. I cannot breathe. You lied to me. You stole my marriage. You stole our past. And as the ceiling sinks and the walls wobble and compress, all I know is that you found me that day on the Heath – a mugged, silly, hurt thing, yearning for my own happy ending – and you turned me into this.

* * *

I'm not sure how much time has passed, only that it's dark now. I am on the sofa, the edges of a duvet tucked in tight. Mum's face hovers above me, round and grey like a moon. She says she found me curled into a ball on the kitchen floor. The saucepan had boiled dry and was starting to smoke. Hope was screaming in the bouncer. She says that I am not well, not at all well. She brings Hope for a feed, takes her away again afterwards. She makes cups of tea that I can't drink, offers cake that I can't eat. My mind drifts, no longer caring if it slips beneath the surface, the fight all gone. I am aware that something bad has happened, that something has broken, but I have no idea what.

I hear Jake and my mother's hushed voices in the hall, footsteps on the wooden floor, someone coming closer. Jake kneels next to me, presses Hope's butter-soft cheek against mine. We are like that for a long time, me, Jake and Hope, Mum shuffling anxiously in the background, a blot of blood red in her burgundy cardigan. I am aware of being lifted, losing the press of the rough upholstery fabric. For a moment I am back in the snowy garden. Hector has just left and Jake is carrying me to the fire. Then I am in Jake's double bed in his bedroom. I drift back off, only to awake with a start in the pitch black, the curl of your hairy calf against my bare sole. I reach out to you. My hand meets something soft and warm.

'You OK, love?'

The soft, warm thing is Mum's nightie. Startled, I pull my hand away. 'What are you doing here?'

'You need a bit of TLC, that's all. I thought I'd sleep in here tonight.'

319

I think of the smoking pan. It makes me feel sick. 'Where's Hope?'

'In the Moses basket, down there.'

I reach out for her, feel the reassuring rush of her breath through my fingers.

'I am sorry, Mum.' My voice is a hoarse whisper.

'Don't be daft. It's my fault. I should have got here sooner. You go back to sleep, love. You need to rest.'

'Rex lied.'

'Sorry, love?'

'It was all a sham, Mum. He lied. By not telling the truth he lied.'

'Shh. Sleep now.'

There is a pattern of red dots on the inside of my lids, like the imprint of a thousand screaming light bulbs. My heart starts to drum again. I am certain that I won't sleep. And I don't.

The sun comes up drearily. Condensation pours down the windows. Mum is snoring, her face in sleep old and babyish at the same time. I try to get out of bed but my knees buckle like someone's knocked out my knee joints with a mallet. Oh God, what's happening?

No one knows. Not even the doctor, who makes a house call and prescribes anti-depressants. I gulp them down, hungry for anything that might make me normal again. I still don't feel normal. I feel weird. But I do sleep.

Then, one morning, it happens. Just as I've imagined a thousand times. Footsteps on the pavement beneath the window. A cough, a pause, another footstep. It is a footstep I'd recognise anywhere. Trembling, summoning all my

320

energy, I pull myself up off the bed with a groan and slide along the bedroom wall. The stairs are miles away, almost insurmountable. I can see your unmistakable shape through the mottled glass of the front door now, short, tense and wiry. I stumble downwards, two stairs at a time. 'Rex.' I open the front door, lurch into your arms. 'Where have you been?'

Fifty-two

Mandy

Mandy glanced at her watch. Late. Where the hell was she? She scanned the crowded Soho café where people were hunched over vats of coffee, tapping out messages on their phones on chunky wooden tables. It was a bloody silly place to meet, she'd thought so at the time but hadn't dared say anything, not wanting to risk her cancelling. Fran's curiosity had reeled her in, as Mandy had hoped it would, but she still half expected her to be a no show. She ordered a cup of tea and waited.

Twenty minutes later, a blonde walked in wearing a fitted cobalt-blue dress, the kind of dress that Mandy would only ever dare wear to a cocktail party, never at eleven am on a weekday morning. The woman looked around the café, clearly searching for somebody. It must be her. Mandy waved.

'Francesca.' The woman introduced herself. 'Nice to meet you.' Her handshake was brisk and firm. 'The usual,' she smiled to the hovering waiter, pulling out a wooden stool and sitting down, one skinny leg draped over the other, her acid-yellow heel dangling. A latte arrived seconds later. 'I'm afraid I haven't got long,' she said with a small, hard smile.

'Oh, it won't take long. Thank you for agreeing to meet me.'

'Well, you said it was vitally important,' Fran said, eyeing Mandy curiously. 'However, as I mentioned on the phone, Jake and I are no longer together. So I'm not sure there's anything I'm going to be able to help you with, I'm afraid.'

'Oh, I think you can. It's about my boy.'

Francesca's eyes widened. She shifted on the seat.

'His name is Ryan.'

'Right,' she said, uncomfortable now.

'I'll cut to the chase, Rex is his father.'

Fran's features constricted minutely. But she did not look shocked. 'As I said, I no longer have a connection to that family. At the risk of sounding heartless, Mandy, I've had about as much of Rex's business as I can stomach.'

'Rex knew he was the father. He once told me that the only person he'd ever confided in about Ryan was a woman called Francesca,' Mandy said, watching her reaction carefully. 'I never knew who that was until Gina told me that you, Fran, had just split up with Jake. I remembered the name and it all fell into place.'

Fran paled. 'Clearly, you're mistaken.'

'You are that Francesca. The one who works in mobile phones.'

'I have absolutely no idea what you are talking about.' She held her handbag tight to her shoulder, preparing to leave.

'Rex told me that you knew, you knew about Ryan.'

Fran stood up. 'I think I've heard enough. I'm a busy woman.'

'Why didn't you speak out?'

'I don't want to be involved, OK?' She glanced about her furtively, as if checking no one was listening in to the conversation. 'Not then. Certainly not now.'

Rage made Mandy bolder. 'But a child is in the picture here, Francesca. Two children now. And a vulnerable wife. She has a right to know the truth, don't you think?'

'Holy crap, get a DNA test.'

'It wouldn't have been necessary if you'd done the right thing.' Mandy wanted to deck her.

'There is absolutely nothing I can do to help you out of this predicament, one entirely of your own making,' Fran replied curtly.

'You were sleeping with him, weren't you?'

She looked visibly shaken, her mouth slackening.

'I know you were.' She didn't know. She had a hunch. And from the look on Fran's face she was damn well right.

Fran sat back down on the stool, pressed her fingertips into the bridge of her nose. 'It was before he met Gina,' she said, collecting herself. 'When he met Gina everything changed. It ended.'

'But you were with Jake at the time. His *brother*!'

'Look, we were very discreet. As soon as the damn affair finished we gave each other a wide, wide berth. We avoided duplicitous, hypocritical family get-togethers as much as possible. He kept Jake at arm's length,' she said as if this made it all OK. 'I didn't get chummy with Gina. We tried to behave with some dignity.'

324

'Dignity! If you call that—'

'You're playing with fire, Mandy.' Fran's eyes flashed dangerously. 'Believe me, you're out of your depth here. This can't come out, do you understand? It may save you the small hassle of going to get your son's DNA tested but it will destroy that family, totally fucking obliterate it. Think how much they've been through. Is that what you really want?'

Mandy thought of Ryan, her wonderful boy, whose existence and paternity had been denied for so long. And all this time, this woman had been colluding in it. The bitch. She hated her with a passion. 'It's not what I want.'

'Is it money you need? I am more than happy to pay for the DNA test so you can get it fast tracked, today, if needs be.' Fran reached into her bag for her phone with fumbling fingers. 'I will get my secretary to sort it out.'

'I don't want your money.' Mandy fixed her with a nail-hard stare. 'I want to know why you didn't tell. For my own peace of mind, I need to know.'

'He told me that if I ever told anyone about Ryan, he'd tell Jake about me, me and him, OK? That is why.'

'So you lied . . .'

'I didn't lie. I just didn't tell. I had no choice.'

'Surely Rex disappearing was your cue? Fucking hell. *Surely?*'

'It would have opened up a can of worms. Imagine the questions, Mandy! How did I know? Why hadn't I said anything before? No, it would have been a disaster.' Fran shook her head defiantly. 'I'm sorry but this is not my fucking mess, OK? It's yours. Don't make your problem my problem.'

'How can you look Gina in the eye?'

'Easily. I'm hurt, too. But I have to hide all my feelings away, pretend I was never involved with Rex, never loved him, like a bloody mistress at a funeral.' She actually sounded sorry for herself. 'It's been hard.'

'*Hard*? I tell you what hard means. Hard means bringing up a baby on your own, not knowing if you can afford the month's rent, not knowing if the father of that child will ever want to be involved, not knowing if anyone will ever believe you. *That* is hard.'

'OK, OK, point taken.' Fran squirmed. 'But this is nothing to do with me now. I was in love with Rex. It was a mad passing affair. It's over, long over. It was a different life, OK?' Fran stood up and started to weave her way out of the crowded café.

'Well, believe me, your lives have just collided!' Mandy bellowed after her. A sea of heads looked up from their phones at once.

Fifty-three

You are falling against a cerulean blue sky, arms outstretched, legs pinned together. Like a diver. Like Superman. Falling, falling, through the blue, the clouds, skimming glass stars. Just as you are about to hit the ground, I wake with a start, covered in sweat.

'Gina? You OK, love?' Mum is sitting beside me. She wipes my forehead with a tissue. 'It must be too hot in here. Or is your leg giving you gyp?'

I become aware of a throbbing ache on my kneecap.

'That's quite a bruise.' Mum picks up a corner of the duvet and inspects my knee. 'You gave your dad a right old shocker, falling out of the front door like that.'

'I thought it was Rex. I was sure it was Rex.'

'You just got muddled, love. Nothing to worry about,' says Mum, as if reassuring herself. 'Nothing to worry about at all.'

'I heard his cough. I heard his footstep. I *saw* him through the door, Mum.'

She tucks a strand of hair behind my ear. 'It's that

imagination of yours playing tricks, I'm afraid. You've been chatting away to him in your sleep, too.'

'I have?'

Mum frowns, averts her eyes. 'Yes, love.'

'What have I been saying?' She is silent. 'Mum?'

'It was about him not answering you or something. It was making you quite . . . agitated.'

'I don't remember.'

'Now, here's your pill. A glass of water. Come on, Gina. You must take it.'

Reluctantly, I swallow the pill and soon my eyes start to close again. Later, I am aware that Dawn is sitting beside me, regaling me with stories about our childhood. Dad next, telling me that he's going to make Hope a rocking horse soon as we get back to Derbyshire. When I'm better. Lucy too, I think. Femi's laugh. Mandy? I think it's Mandy but I'm not sure. And Jake. I know it is Jake because I recognise the weight of his hand on my upper back. The timbre of his voice soothes me.

One day Clarice comes, and the sharp, lemon essence of her reaches into the fug of my brain and wakes me up. I do not want her to see me like this, Clarice of all people. She pulls up a chair next to the bed. I pretend to sleep. 'Can you hear me, *ma cherie*?' It's the first time she's ever called me *cherie*. 'I'm so very sorry you're like this.' She is silent for a while. My blood whooshes in my eardrums. I feel her watching me. 'It is not your fault that Rex is missing. You mustn't ever think it is your fault. There was always a part of Rex missing, you see. Even when he was a little boy. I worried that he'd try and fill that emptiness with work, money . . .

328

whatever.' Her voices breaks. 'No one could fill it, not even you, Gina.'

I feel the tears prick. They start to make my eyes itch. It's getting harder to feign sleep.

'When I was young, after Rex's Dad died, I curled up into a little ball, too. I wanted the world to stop. Just like you do.' I feel the lightest of feather touches on my arm. 'I just wanted you to know that I understand. That you'll be OK again. I will help you get better, I promise from the bottom of my heart. You are my daughter now, Gina.'

Slowly I open my eyes. And I see Clarice properly for the first time.

Fifty-four

'Little Star of Bethlehem'. Coming from the street below. Blearily, I swing my legs over the side of the bed and plant my feet on the rug. It feels strange supporting my own weight so I lean forward and rest my elbows on the cool window ledge. In the street below is a huddle of people in brightly coloured bobble hats holding sheets of paper. Singing.

'My God, you're up!' Mum is at the bedroom door, a wondrous smile spreading slowly across her face, as if I've been resurrected. 'Oh, love. Come here.' She hugs me for ages.

'Is it Christmas?'

'Soon, soon.' She rubs my arms. 'Oh, it's so good to see you standing. You've no idea.'

'How can it be Christmas? I don't understand. Where's the time gone?'

'You've not been very well, love. Here, sit down.'

'It's those pills. They make me fuggy. I can't think straight.' I clutch her hand, scared again. 'You've been here all this time?'

'There's been a right merry rotation of us, but I've been here all the time, yes. Are you hungry?'

'Starving.'

She beams, delighted. 'I'll tell Ted to put the cottage pie in the microwave.'

'Dad?'

'He's downstairs. I'll be back in one sec.' I hear her clatter down the stairs, the murmuring of voices below. She returns, bright eyed, grinning, a few moments later, holding a hairbrush. 'I've been itching to brush it. Can I?'

I lean against her knees, losing myself to the rhythm of the hairbrush, its tug and pull through the tangles. 'What happened, Mum? What happened to me?'

'It got too much. That's all, love. You were totally exhausted and I think . . . well, I think it all hit home. Finally.' She gives me a powdery kiss on the cheek that smells slightly of biscuits. 'You needed a bit of looking after, that's all.'

I whip around to face her, my red hair a blaze of static. 'I can't live like this.'

'No, love.' She strokes my cheek with the back of her hand. 'You can't.'

It feels like years since I've seen the kitchen, not days. Dad and Jake don't notice me immediately. They are joking about football managers, Dad opening a tube of Pringles with his teeth. Jake has Hope over his shoulder, dribbling milk on to his blue denim shirt.

'Gina!' A moment of slack-jawed amazement when they do see me. 'Now that's more like it,' grins Dad, pulling a chair back for me. 'Mum's done her famous cottage pie. You've picked the right evening to emerge.' I wonder if they've been instructed not to mention my mental state.

Jake's eyes are full of light. I smile shyly back at him. 'Do you want Hope?' he whispers.

I reach out for her, my beautiful baby. She grips Jake's shirt with her little wet fists as I pull her away and keeps her eyes fixed on him as I hold her tight. She feels heavier than I expect and fine black hair feathers at the nape of her neck.

Mum shakes a rattle in Hope's face. 'Mr Rattle?'

'Jake here has been invaded by Mothercare's finest, haven't you, Jake?' says Dad, cheerily. 'Mothercare and Mother, I should add.'

'Enjoyed the invasion, Ted,' says Jake dryly, as if they've been friends for years. 'Just not your red socks in my white wash.'

'I thought pink shirts were all the rage down south, son?'

'I promise to pick up some new white shirts next time I'm in town, somewhere nice. Next?' Mum waggles the rattle again.

'You've paid for the shirts ten times over by all your cooking,' says Jake.

'Is he always this smarmy?' Dad asks me, giving Jake a fake punch to the arm.

The hall phone starts to ring.

'That'll be that Rupert Murdoch on the line for you again,' quips Dad.

Jake laughs, walks to the phone in the hall. He has a nappy sticking out the back pocket of his jeans like a white padded wallet.

'Just seeing you sitting there is making me the happiest dad in the world, love,' Dad says.

'You're doing brilliantly, Gina. Just brilliantly.' Mum squeezes my hand.

'Has Hope been OK?'

'Your milk's been in fine,' Mum replies, as if this is all that matters.

'Princess Hope, I call her. She's in charge this one. Just you wait.' Dad reaches for his glass of beer. 'What goes around, comes around. As I say, karma, Gina.' He raises his glass. 'Karma.'

'Oh stop it, Teddy. She's not well enough for your teasing.'

'Where's Dawn?'

'Back home, getting everything ready for you. The twins are better now.'

I feel a spike of panic.

'But only when you're ready, love,' Mum says quickly, looking worried by my expression. 'There's no rush. We're quite happy here, aren't we, Ted?'

'As a sandboy. I don't care where I am for Christmas as long as I've got a proper feed.'

'Sue Pratt said she'd send us one of her turkeys.'

Dad raises his glass. 'You can take a woman out of Derbyshire, but you can't—' He stops.

Jake is standing in the doorway. His face is pale green.

Dad stands up. 'You alright, son?'

'It's Rex.'

'Oh.' Mum covers her mouth. 'Oh no. Not today.'

Dad puts an arm around my shoulder and holds me very tight.

I feel icy cold. 'Jake, what is it?'

Dad holds me tighter. In that moment everything is

suspended, the space between a plane's engines stalling and it plunging to earth.

'They've found him, Gina.'

'Is he . . . ?' Deep down I already know.

Jake closes his eyes. 'I'm so sorry.'

Fifty-five

Mandy

The group of Moroccan boys tightened their circle around Ryan and his cheap handheld game. There was a ripple of giggles, a prodding of little fingers. Ryan handed the game to the boy next to him. He looked at home here, nut brown and happy. But Mandy was still in a state of shock. The blasting heat, just the whole bloody scale of the place, she wasn't prepared for it. Like most things that had come into her life recently, it was nothing like she expected.

Mandy had to prep her eyes on the lowlands where grumpy camels grazed on scrubby grasses, past the line of small, wizened trees, before she took in the dizzying peaks. She'd never seen anything like it. It took her breath away. The Atlas mountains soared up, huge terrifying slabs of rock. She could almost see Rex, a wiry silhouette scrambling up to the peak, framed by the bright blue sky. But it wasn't that peak. This wasn't where it happened. It would take a tough two-day trek to get to the gorge where Rex was found, a journey that would be too much for Ryan, and for her own bunions come to that. Anyway, she wasn't sure she wanted to see the exact spot where they found him, the horrible rocks on to which he'd smashed.

Mark had pointed out that it was always going to be a long shot, tracing Rex's last footsteps. And sure enough, although they'd tried they'd got nowhere. Few seemed to remember Rex from the photos. This might have had something to do with the fact that he looked nothing like the photos when they found him: long-haired, straggle-bearded, wearing dirty clothing and old walking shoes. The Rex in her photos was a successful man in an expensive suit, a cleanly shaven successful fortysomething, not someone who would have fallen off anything. Besides, there were numerous villages – all smelling intoxicatingly of cinnamon, mint and trash – that he could have passed through before going up into the mountains, many places he could have camped without drawing attention to himself. The mountains were full of intrepid trekkers, lost Western souls trying to find meaning in the heat and dust of north Africa.

No, she'd have to return with other things, mementoes. She loved a memento. Spotting a neat, pleasingly round red rock, Mandy bent down, picked it up and dropped it into the tapestry carpet bag she'd just bought off a particularly persuasive bag seller. The rock would go into the metal box with all the other things she'd collected for Ryan, the box that could finally be brought down from the attic into the open, explored and admired, no longer a shameful secret hidden away. One day Ryan would want to see all this, she was sure of it: the rock, the photographs, the DNA certificate. He could lay them all out on the floor like pieces of an incomplete jigsaw.

What should she tell him? That was the question that had woken her every morning, watching that fat red sun rise behind the dark wooden fretwork of the riad window. In her heart she knew it could only ever be the facts, however difficult. Yes, she'd tell him the facts and he'd have to fill in the gaps and choose his story; perhaps choose – or reject – his own father. As he never knew Rex, Ryan could do that.

There were good things to come out of the whole sorry mess. Ryan had a trust fund to help him along in life – it's what Rex would have wanted, Gina had insisted – a baby sister, a French Nana who'd opened her arms to him in a way she'd never dreamed possible, as well as that lovely rabble of a family up in Derbyshire. 'Our Ryan,' they called him.

She was glad she'd kept her mouth shut about that sordid business between Fran and Rex. How would that have helped anyone? As Mark said, there was a time for speaking out and a time for keeping the barn door shut. Rex's secret would die with him. Fran could keep her dignity.

So these were the facts: a British man had set out alone, badly prepared, in the Atlas mountains. He had evidently slipped and lost his footing on the edge of a famously perilous gorge. Accidents like that happened all the time. Explainable.

What was a damn sight harder to explain was the fact that when a walker found Rex's body it was still warm.

In the shocking, terrible aftermath, they'd all tried so hard to find out what happened, what Rex had done, where he had been all those months. They'd got nowhere, discovering only a weak trail around budget boarding houses in Marrakesh. In her opinion, Rex had suffered some kind of breakdown; the thing that had been slowly breaking in him all those years had finally broken. Whatever the truth, she was glad that the family had taken the joint decision to stop puzzling over it and allow their memories of Rex to rest in peace.

'Mum, can I go see the camels? Over there.' Ryan pointed to the camels in the scrubby distance. A little boy with vivid green eyes and black hair stood next to him, arm around his shoulders, as if they were lifelong friends. 'Please.'

'Ryan, I really don't think . . .'

Mark's arms slid around her waist from behind. 'Let him go,' he whispered into her ear. 'He'll be fine.'

She hesitated. Ryan gazed up at her hopefully. 'Oh, go on then, go and enjoy yourself.' With a kick of dust, her little boy was gone.

Fifty-six

Sixteen months later

Syrupy sunshine pours through the trees to the damp graveyard floor. I am relieved all over again that Rex is back home in Kent, a few feet from his father, not lying undiscovered in some scorched ravine miles from home.

It's been a while since I visited, brought twine-tied bunches of pink Sweet Williams. But I've had to cling on for dear life in the year and a half since they found Rex's body. Since the line went dead. That's been the hardest thing. If I try to speak to him now, my words echo back at me. At first the loneliness of it was unbearable. It's taken me this long to realise that the very thing I feared most was the thing that liberated me. The day Rex was discovered dead was the day I started to come up for air, slowly, slowly, like a diver ascending the deepest, blackest ocean trying not to get the bends.

Somehow in losing Rex, I found myself. And I've never felt more intensely alive than I do now. Never more blessed.

I trace my fingers over his name carved into the cool granite. 'Beloved husband, father, brother, son, adventurer.'

All true. Whatever anyone says, I will not go back to the past and edit it in the light of what has happened. It would be like cutting bits out of old photographs. I will preserve Rex as the runner on Hampstead Heath who mugged my mugger. The man who held my hand as we ran down the Strand in the pouring rain, laughing hysterically, berserk with happiness. The man who showed me how to build a bonfire on a beach, made me love my freckles. After all, he was my Rex Adler, not Mandy's or Jake's or Clarice's. We are all different selves with different people, like Jake once said. I still believe I got the best one, even if it could not be sustained.

'Sorry to interrupt.' Jake emerges from the trees. Hope is on his hip, trying to yank off his glasses.

I smile at the sight of them. 'That wasn't a long walk.'

'Timed to perfection. Wipes?'

'In the nappy bag.'

'You had the nappy bag.'

'I didn't.'

'You did.'

'In the car?'

'Bollocks. We could improvise? I have tissues.' Jake's eyes alight on the gravestone. 'And a handy flat surface . . .'

'No!'

'Joking. I'll meet you back at the car.' He picks up Hope's hand, flaps it to a make a wave. 'Say bye bye, Mama.'

'Da-da-da.' She rolls her favourite word around her mouth and lunges for Jake's glasses, squealing with triumph, wheeling them around her head.

'Wait a minute. I'll come with you.'

'You don't need to come. I don't mind.' He grabs his glasses, shoves them back on his nose.

'I need to eat.'

Jake offers his hand and pulls up my great heft until I am in kissing distance. 'When the lady is hungry, the lady must eat.'

I am far bigger and hungrier than I was in my last pregnancy. 'Eating cake for three now, sis,' as Dawn loves to remind me. 'Told you so. Resistance is futile.'

We follow the path toward the woods. A small white butterfly flutters up from the ground. Hope points to it, laughs. And as it disappears into the thick green undergrowth, I whisper, 'Goodbye, Rex,' beneath my breath, just in case there's the tiniest chance he can still hear me after all.